What a Shame

What a Shame

Abigail Bergstrom

HODDER &
STOUGHTON

First published in Great Britain in 2022 by Hodder & Stoughton
An Hachette UK company

1

Quote from *The Ayahuasca's Tests Pilots Handbook* (p.209) © Chris Kilham,
first published by North Atlantic Books in 2014

A CIP catalogue record for this title is
available from the British Library

Hardback ISBN 978 1 529 36707 2
Trade Paperback ISBN 978 1 529 36701 0
eBook ISBN 978 1 529 36704 1

Typeset in Plantin Light by Palimpsest Book Production Limited,
Falkirk, Stirlingshire

Printed and bound in Great Britain by Clays Ltd, Elcograf S.p.A.

Hodder & Stoughton policy is to use papers that are natural, renewable
and recyclable products and made from wood grown in sustainable
forests. The logging and manufacturing processes are expected to
conform to the environmental regulations of the country of origin.

Hodder & Stoughton Ltd
Carmelite House
50 Victoria Embankment
London EC4Y 0DZ

www.hodder.co.uk

For all those brave warrior souls who have brought their shame out into the light.

There is a pain – so utter –
It swallows substance up –
Then covers the Abyss with Trance –
So Memory can step
Around – across – upon it –
As one within a Swoon –
Goes safely – where an open eye –
Would drop Him – Bone by Bone.

–Emily Dickinson

Curses are like processions.
They return to the place from which they came.

–Giovanni Ruffini

Prologue

At first there was drama and morbid excitement – all the morose trimmings that come with the early stages of mourning and grief. People came over. They brought pre-cooked food, wrapped and marinating in flavours, flowers from the fancy florist and other small appropriate gifts. They wore black – respectfully – to both of your funerals: dark, smart clothing on a grey day to a brutalist crematorium, and dark, sullen moods to a flat we once shared where remnants of your dead skin were still in the carpet. Now that you're both gone I'm struggling to decipher which thread of grief belongs to each of you. It's a wiry tangled mass in my chest, like those metal scourers you use to scrub stubborn pans. Each coarse steel strand is more tightly coiled than the last, and when amassed tightly in your hand it's soft to touch. Only when a single strand frays loose is it sharp and painful; I think that's why it's easier to keep you both matted together.

After your illusive departure, my friends pretended they didn't have plans for the weeks that followed. They came over with wine. People fussed over me, and when I sat down at a table there always seemed to be a spare seat where you would've sat, assigned now for my misery so plain to see, as if it were wearing a large red hat.

At the beginning, grief and tragedy are ripe dinner-party fodder.

'Her father died. It's such a horrible story, he had a nasty fall and was left brain damaged. Completely out of the blue! There one day – gone the next.'

'That's just awful.'

'Yeah, it completely paralysed him, he was in and out of consciousness for months, so they weren't really sure how much was, you know, going on up there . . .'

'It's so sad.'

'Terrible.'

It's much easier to empathise with the unpleasantness of a recent tragedy – proximity to the present is the real marrow. Lurking in the corner of your reality, you feel it in the room and the fear is that it could decide to pick you next. In order to preserve yourself, you must hold it up in your hands and acknowledge its very horribleness, tell someone about it in a bid for it to stay far away from you, for as long as possible. Because pain gets us all in the end, doesn't it? We all must suffer eventually. The only question is: when?

'Oh no, he left her. Did you not hear? He just got up and went one day, no explanation – he just walked out the door. And she's heartbroken. In an absolute hell of a state. We've been talking on the phone but it's like she's run out of things to say.'

I'm relieved when they stop asking me how I'm feeling, leaving me to indulge myself under a cloak of shame. Much unlike horror, the best way to prevent shame from attaching itself to you is by ignoring it entirely. Better in than out. Break-ups and death are commonplace, and you're accustomed to the rituals surrounding them. You watch them in films; you read about them in books. The retellings of an old, timeless narrative in which one etches out one's humanity. You know what to do with the anguish that immediately seeps from an ending – sudden or slow: you have been taught. It's the ongoing and ebbing sadness that continues afterwards that we all find a little dull. Unworthy of a story, perhaps.

'Were we really in love or did I just imagine it all that time?'

'Of course he loved you. That was clear to everyone,. We all saw it.'

'I should have done more when my dad was ill.'

'You did what you could. You did your best.'

'Why did he have to go?'

'Why did who have to go, Mathilda?'

I am immovable in its dark swamp, stuck. A *stuckness* so suffocating, a paralysis so ubiquitous that I almost forget to breathe. There's only so long those who love you can dampen their own happiness out of sensitivity for your misfortunes. Eventually they must resume their lives. So I smiled when they told me they'd met someone; I raised my glass to their promotion and celebrated their new show; I clapped my hands when they got engaged, and I didn't mention that a diamond was an unethical symbol of male ownership; I didn't even begrudge ordering a Virgin Mary on a Sunday afternoon when she got pregnant and he stopped drinking to support her. I kept partaking in their happiness, and the waves of joy that swell from their lives keep me going, making sure that my sadness doesn't strangle me, the swamp engulfing me entirely as I let out a final loud burp of disdain.

Eyebrows

Wrestling my key into the lock, I push into the door and swing with it into the warmth and light of the hallway. I drop my bag to the floor, it squelches, sodden like my raincoat. I struggle to hang it over the chaos of faux-furs, windbreakers, trenches and leathers. The television is on in the living room. They're all home.

'Heeey!'

'Hi.'

I wring out my wet hair and follow the chorus of greetings to where the three of them are sitting under blankets on an L-shaped pink sofa. There is a pink neon sign above an old tiled fireplace, which reads: *Everything Is Shit Except You, Love.* Ivy is biting her nails, Ekua is engrossed in her phone and Georgia's legs are crossed, her laptop resting on her knees, as she sips something hot from a mug that has 'unt' written on it, following the C-shape of the handle.

'Hey, how's everyone doing?' I push for a smile.

'Fucking fantastic,' Ivy says, raising her wild, overgrown eyebrows.

When I called Georgia six months ago to ask if I could move in, she'd already let the large room to a girl she'd found on idealflatmate.com, which sounded suspicious to me. Surely you undercut yourself on the qualifier of being *the ideal* flatmate in claiming to be one. Georgia knew how miserable I was, but we'd been friends for years so she was duty-bound to find this more acerbic me amusing. She offered me the remaining room.

'How did the shoot go in Budapest?' I ask Ivy.

'Poorly orchestrated and devastatingly boring, but the casting was fucking fantastic.' She looks up at me from beneath a seventies Jane Birkin fringe, dramatically arching her back off the sofa. 'And how've you been?'

'Fine.'

Through the Oslo filter from which I'd exclusively viewed her prior to moving in, Ivy's life did look fantastic. She was thin, beautiful, had a host of cool friends, a private-school education, and a following that enabled a swipe-up function. She had a wavering modelling career but was often staying in lavish places in Bordeaux or on the Amalfi coast. Yet in the moments I'd observed her here, in this new space, she looked sort of sad.

'You're back late.' Georgia eyes me suspiciously.

'I've been to see Constance.'

'Ah, how is she?' asks Ekua, gleefully.

'She's good. A little tired today.'

'You're a much better person than me,' she says, in her northern twang. 'I were genuinely annoyed today at having to give my seat to a pregnant woman on the tube. All I've achieved since then is that notification Netflix sends to check you're still watching. You know, to see if you've not died.'

'Oh, now, come on. Don't be so down on yourself. From what I heard last night you have your own way of being . . .' I lather on a seductive tone '. . . *very* giving.'

She bites a plump bottom lip and grins.

'Who was the lucky man?'

'Giovanni, he's from Rome,' she says, rolling her *r*s and pushing her head back into the settee.

'Yeah,' I reply flatly. 'I picked up an Italian vibe from the unashamed moans of ecstasy.'

'Christ, Eks,' Ivy balks, 'have you ever dated someone who doesn't sound like they starred in *La Dolce Vita*?'

'Do you remember Margherita?' Georgia chimes in.

'Yeah okay, she was a bit catty,' Ekua teases, before someone else makes the disclosure.

'She was only *catty* because she was so hungry – the irony of that when you're named after a gooey carb.' I frown.

'She was emaciated,' Ivy states matter-of-factly. 'I've seen pictures in your room.'

'If Ivy thinks she was emaciated, that's really saying something.'

Ivy lifts a middle finger and pushes a long tongue out at Georgia.

'Oh, give over.' Ekua tilts her chin up. 'D'you really want to have a discussion about how we should be casting our nets further afield, Tilda?'

Ivy side-eyes me.

Georgia squints, sussing our unspoken exchange, trying to translate.

'Who were you out with last night?'

I look up and pretend to search my mind. 'Umm . . .'

'She was with Freddie.' Ivy drops the mic.

And I prepare my exit.

'At least she's getting some rather than lying around the house moping.'

'True,' nods Ivy.

'Harsh,' I spout defensively. 'I need to go and get changed – I'm soaked.'

I don't make eye contact with Georgia. You wouldn't have been happy about me going back to Freddie either.

Crow

In the kitchen I make a pot of fresh mint tea to warm myself up. The dark-grey tiles are freezing under my feet and there's a draught coming from under the back door, which leads to an overgrown garden only ever used for cigarette breaks and house parties. I pour the boiling water as Georgia walks in. She watches as I pluck the leaves off the stalks and throw them into the belly of the teapot.

'Do you want a cig?' she asks, zipping up her puffer jacket.

'Yeah, okay. How is it that you still look so damn sexy in sweats?' I puzzle at her. Her cashmere joggers bunch up over a pair of trainers and her brown hair flows over the high collar of her hood.

'Shut up,' she responds. 'Don't try and butter me up.'

'Got it.'

'Maybe you could consider wearing something other than those dungarees at some point in your life.'

'I don't know what you're referring to.'

'You've lived in them for the past three months, Mathilda.' She says this like I've lost my mind, rather than been lazy with my sartorial choices.

'Well, now I'm not going to wear anything else. No.' I put my hands into the deep denim pockets and shrug. 'I'll wear them just to irk you.'

'You needn't use the dungarees for that. I know it's normal to stop caring about your appearance when you're going through a break-up but, like, they're really starting to drag me down.'

I wait patiently after pouring my tea, blowing on its surface as she wrestles with the aged rusting lock on the back door.

Georgia and I met at university and our friendship intensified, then receded in the years that followed – different goals in terms of our careers, boyfriends who didn't particularly gel, and a small handful of those other unimportant reasons that push you apart. Despite this, a thick thread was tied around our respective waists, an invisible rope that kept us attached to one other. We were careless with our friendship a lot of the time because we trusted its durability. Our rope was tough and hard-wearing, and unlike the many plant metaphors of other relationships, ours didn't demand a single drop of water. I didn't have any other friendships like it.

It's cold in the garden and we huddle together under the outdoor light that has a sensor function. Georgia's bike is tangled in ivy, and fairy lights dress the wooden trellis that lines the top of a brick wall, separating us from next door's garden. At the bottom of the long, thin lawn is a large holly bush but it's too dark to see it now.

Georgia's tone softens. 'I just want you to know that we're all here, if . . . well, if you need to talk.'

I was bored of this conversation. The one where she stresses my heaviness, grappling for a more constructive way of saying: you're carrying something dark around that neither you nor I can seem to make sense of.

'And Freddie. Seriously, Mathilda?'

I knew this was coming. 'Ah, come on, don't start. What does it matter to you?

'Of course it matters to me. You're my friend and I care about you. He's such a twat.' She's irritable. 'Rebound, yes! But not with Freddie. Why would you go back there?'

'Because when someone makes you feel like you're not good enough for them you become completely consumed by the task of disproving their theory. I want to see the look on his face when the epiphany hits and he realises I am in fact the most incredible and inimitable woman he's ever met.' I flick my head back for emphasis.

She rolls her eyes and sighs.

'You know what I mean?'

But Georgia has no idea what I mean because she'd decided Henry was the man she'd marry the very first day she met him. Which was in sixth form when she was co-educated for the first time. While her peers were unnerved by the sudden joint-gendered venture, Georgia has three older brothers and became a lighthouse serving navigational aid in those dangerous penis-filled waters. Her reward was the pick of the litter.

'How is Freddie, then? Which campaign is his latest ex-girlfriend the face of? Burberry, Yves Saint Lau—'

'Don't be an arse.'

She lifts her head in acceptance and looks down at the floor, taking another drag from her Marlboro. We enjoy the quiet for a moment or two and then I say reluctantly, 'She's actually the lead in that new Netflix series Ekua likes.'

'*Noooo!*' She laughs, becoming more animated. 'That period drama?'

'Mmm.' I take a long drag of my cigarette and flick the ash to the floor. 'How's Henry?'

'He's fine. Don't change the subject. There's something going on with you.'

I roll my eyes.

'It's not just the break-up, or your dad.'

'Look, I'm trying my best to fix things—'

'Fuck that. You don't need to "fix" yourself,' Mathilda.' She uses her fingers for quote marks, her cigarette wedged between two of them, and I pull a white feather from mounds of her hair that has escaped from the innards of her jacket.

'You're perfect the way you are. You just need to face your shit. He didn't break up with you because you did something wrong.'

'Well, that's useful to note,' I say drolly, sipping my tea.

'He's the idiot. I mean, look at you. You look like Julia Roberts, just with a smaller mouth.'

A plumper Julia Roberts more like, with imperfect teeth, robbed of her flawless smile. I blow the last of the smoke from my mouth with a titter and put out my cigarette on the brick wall, shivering in damp clothes.

'Why did he break up with me then?'

Her pregnant pause turns into a barren land where no words can propagate.

'Do you want to come to yoga with me tomorrow?' I ask, filling it.

'No, I don't. Seriously, I came with you last week and the noises that were coming from you made it sound like you were about to give birth and—'

'Fuck off. The instructor said it was okay to make noises.'

She laughs, then, 'Yeah, and therein lies my point. The instructor felt the need to come over, tap you on the shoulder and reassure you about that weird racket you were making.'

'I wasn't embarrassed,' I say coolly.

'Good for you. I was.'

'I just really want to improve my Crow and I have weak shoulders and skinny wrists.' I show them to her playfully, cigarette in one hand, careful not to spill my tea, which is in the other. 'See? I'm at a disadvantage to a lot of people.'

The light above us goes out and I grin at her through the

darkness. She waves her hand to provoke the sensor and the light comes on to outline the concern on her face.

'Do you not think that some of us are just too fucked up? People settle down and find each other, like you and Henry. Or they don't, and what's left are the broken people.'

'You're not broken.' She sighs. 'I'm so tired of the broken-woman narrative. But it's not just the break-up, is it? There's something else. There's always been something . . .'

The comment stings at the back of my throat but I don't let on. 'Look, I moved in here because I needed a place to stay, not a judgemental eye unpicking my every Crow,' I quip, opening the door, and she follows me back into the kitchen.

'Go and get cleaned up, then.' She smiles gently, then takes off her coat and heads back to the living room to join the others. 'You pair are never going to guess who's in that new period drama,' she calls.

I laugh and shake my head, topping up the tea in my cup, making the green leaves dance. I look around. This house has the potential to be breath-taking but it's rough around the edges, unlike Georgia. She got it in the usual way a millennial living in London acquires property: her parents bought it for her. Of course, there's always the death of a relative or the meeting of a wealthy lover to assist in the acquisition of a home, but I must say those weren't working out for me either. The crockery in the cupboards is mismatched – a collection of whatever her previous tenants left behind. I look up at the art on the walls, which clashes – a signed and mounted Anthony Burrill sits next to a cheap Picasso print wedged into an Ikea frame. The long pine kitchen table in front of me is better suited to a country house and there are two Swiss cheese plants on the floor – one dying and one thriving – each beholden to their individual owner's green-fingered care. I nudge one with my foot and breathe in the inharmonious charm that only shared houses have, comprising clashing styles and jarring tastes, brought together in a way that things are not supposed to be – much like the women who live in them.

Tongue to Toothache

Perhaps I've overegged you: maybe you're not as great as memory serves. Or perhaps the great thing about you was actually something silly, like the fact that you didn't drink milk. The handbook on shared living endorses small-talk after a long day and tells you not to get mad when someone drinks all your almond milk and replaces it with semi-skimmed. You used to make allowances for me when I came home from work. You'd say a light hello, then leave me to lie on the bed or take a bath, to stew in the remnants of it until I had decompressed.

I go upstairs to my bedroom, taking in its familiar smell of lavender and fig, which eases the angst in my tummy. Eden made me throw out all traces of you before I moved in. We haven't fucked on these sheets; you've never spilt black coffee on this throw; and I light incense hourly because it no longer matters that you don't like the smell. There's a cream carpet that has terrible foundation marks in the corner from the last girl who had this room, but the history here is not ours.

I undress down to my underwear and quickly run across the landing to throw my damp clothes into the washing basket that lives in the cupboard. I'm craning over it, establishing whether I need to do a black or white load tomorrow, when, suddenly the bathroom door swings open. Ivy raises an eyebrow at me, silently waiting to pass down the stairs.

'All right?' I say awkwardly, sucking my tummy in and scurrying back to my room.

There is something about her that I find unsettling. She always seems to appear from nowhere, like she's deliberately trying to catch me off guard. I close the door and look at the girl staring back at me in the mirror. I turn my body to the side slightly and replicate the same craning position over the basket to see how the rolls form on my tummy. I look at the stretchmarks on my bottom and ponder whether they really are 'tiger stripes', something beautiful, something I could love.

'Oh, enough.'

The words don't sound like mine as the sallow-skinned face in the mirror stares back, black bags nicely shaded in and burnt-auburn hair dulled and less intense than it was. I go into the bathroom and it smells a little of sick. I run a bath, pushing my feet into the soft mat, which has different types of breasts drawn over it, as I wait for the tub to fill.

As I step in, the warm water feels good on my body. I wonder where you are and what you're doing. After you left, the loss felt futile, a bit like losing my keys. I'd move around our flat, expecting to see you in all the places I would normally find you: in my dressing-gown with the morning sun on your face; in my coat pocket with last night's receipts; sitting up in bed blowing on hot black coffee; underneath the discarded mail gathering dust on the dresser; standing in front of the fridge, jaw bones edged by the light; down and in between the sides of the sofa fraternising with a pound coin. I couldn't help but feel that I would find you eventually, that you'd be there, right where I left you.

I picture your broad shoulders and all of your soft white skin stretching over the arches of my body. My imagination takes me to another dark and rainy night when you came into our bathroom still dressed in your suit. 'How was your day?' I asked. You responded, taking off your jacket, undoing the button on your cuff and gently rolling up your right sleeve as your knees dropped to the floor next to me. You put your hand in, glided through the water and pushed your fingers up inside me, kissing my sweaty cheekbone as I moaned, pushing my head back against the tub. A wave of self-hatred interrupts the orgasm – one rarely comes without the other now. Taut and tight and beating anger clashing with desire for you.

Think of something else, Mathilda. Anything. I wash my hair with some of Ivy's fancy shampoo, inhaling its medicinal scent. But my mind circles back to you, like a tongue to toothache, I pull back the soggy shower curtain and step out onto the bathmat's perky boobs.

Freddie

Despite the girls' protestations, that weekend I arrange to see Freddie again. 'The best way to get over someone is to get under someone' is a complete and utter load of bollocks, but I'm giving it a go anyway.

His name is Frederick Malkovich. It's not *quite* as bad as it sounds. I won't go into any salacious detail here, but Freddie is what I like to call a life-span regular. We met years ago when I first moved to London and I'd been keen to wrap my heart in tissue paper and hand it to him in a velvet box topped with a silk ribbon – I'm classy like that. He, on the other hand, had been a little less enthusiastic. Freddie was the type of guy who thought he'd be a fool to settle down when there were so many beautiful women to sleep with and parties to get high at. Despite this, we have spent a significant amount of time hooking up in the interim spaces of our adult lives – like in the months before one of us was moving to another city; after a boring party that ended earlier than we had expected; during periods of dating famine; or when either of us felt completely and brutally alone. Our phases of singledom were often oddly and beautifully timed, and the sex was cosmic.

We met at a party, but as we don't have mutual friends, one of us has to actively initiate contact each time. This always feels like a painful phlebotomy, except it's my dignity that the needle draws out. It starts with some 'liking' on social media. I know, *enchanting*. Move over Austen. An Instagram like here, a comment there, and the other would get the signal that the respective life-span regular is unattached. If both of us were available, we'd match this enthusiasm for the other's content and eventually one of us would slide into the other's DMs. A drink that week, straight into bed that night, dates for several weeks (sometimes even months), until it felt serious and he'd pull the plug, telling me he wasn't sure I was the one, and I'd lie and say I wasn't sure he was either.

The pursuit of male rejection is something you embedded in me. But unrequited love has its own central nervous system: you pine; you desire; you get; then you regret; you retreat; and then you wait to relapse. The most intoxicating and damaging relationships are often those that transcend us in a frozen state of hope – we can have a small part of that person but never enough to satiate our appetite. They will never give themselves to us so to taste them is to accept a perpetual pang of hunger. That was Freddie. He kept me perpetually starved.

The long and short of it is I'm sleeping with Frederick Malkovich because my heart is broken, and he knows but doesn't mind. Freddie has always been endlessly pleased by the notion of there being plenty more fish in the sea, which has been matched by an endless list of women interested in him. Outside our hook-ups, Freddie's sex life is more mesmerising and colourful than the Great Barrier Reef – at least from where I'm swimming. It's a site of remarkable variety and beauty, bustling with girls – all thinner and significantly sexier than I am – who sit against a backdrop of rich cerise pink sofas, with potent orange drinks. He makes me feel validated and completely empty all at once. The oscillation between those two feelings happens so speedily that it's taken me some years to decipher the difference.

He's the character who appears in every piece of women's literature ever written – the place where we always wrestle with you – the unobtainable and seemingly immoral character whom the protagonist will eventually realise is her one true love. But in this story, as in real life, we don't end up with our Mr Bigs or our Mr Darcys. It's a cruel trick that's been played on women. Repeatedly promised that therein lies our happy ending, we follow an ill-written script. Those karmic partners who ebb and flow from our lives are sent to teach us a very difficult and painful lesson about ourselves. Not a soul-mate but a plan for the demise of our ego, here to show us what's holding us back.

'There she is.' He smiles at me as I approach the bar. 'She'll have an Old Fashioned,' he tells the bartender. I sit down on the high stool in front of him, the familiar liquorice and pepperwood smell of expensive aftershave trickling in. 'God, it's good to see you,' he says.

No, I wasn't done battering myself with Freddie yet.

The Couples

The following Monday morning Georgia and I get the tube together and sit in comfortable silence as I watch a couple in the carriage soak up every last moment with each other before the daily grind of the working week tears them apart. He uses one large hand to hold the rail and steady himself, the other to encase her. She's small, petite and girlish. She looks smart in a well-cut trench, but her blonde hair is a little disordered, a classic sign she's not had access to the necessary hair appliances at his place. She nuzzles into his broad lower chest and from the back, if I squint a little, she looks like his small child, not his lover.

'Did you see Freddie this weekend?'

I don't answer.

'I know what you're thinking,' whispers Georgia.

'No, you don't,' I say pragmatically.

'You're thinking, why is that small woman guzzling greedily from a diminishing fountain, nay dribble, of tall available men in London?'

'No, I'm not—'

'Why is she frolicking in the lands of the high and mighty when she could date any five-foot-seven Tom, Dick or Paul?'

'That wasn't what I was thinking,' I say earnestly.

The man cranes his neck to smell her crown before whispering something in her ear – it must have been good because it leads to a doughy-eyed snog.

'Oh, Jesus Christ, they're touching each other's faces.' I scrunch my lips together in distaste.

Georgia laughs. 'Public displays of affection at this hour are offensive.'

'You too? PDAs feel like a personal attack. I'm glad it's not just me.' I scowl at the couple, catching the small woman's gaze, which flips my sneer into a scrunched-nose smile. 'Shit, she thinks we're weird for looking at them now.'

'I wasn't looking.'

'Yes, you were, Georgia. You clearly were.'

'No, it was just you.'

The average single person is forced to get through a dark and dreary Sunday evening alone, but the couples must drink their own dose of reality on a Monday morning when they have to get off at different stops to meet the demands of their day jobs. I glance back at the midget and her Goliath and feel a pang of sadness as they laugh into each other's faces.

'Yuck,' concurs Georgia.

'Yuck!' I repeat. 'I hate couples.'

'Henry and I are a couple. You don't hate us.' She turns her head to look at me, breaking London Underground social conduct.

'Yes, I hate you. You and your couple community.'

'Ooh, we're harmless, really.' She sits back in her seat.

Despite Henry instigating a small handful of breaks over the last decade, the plot dictated that they would always wind back to one another.

'No. Don't give me that.' I shake my index finger at her. 'You are the most repulsive of all human specimens and this city is heaving with you,' I gesticulate, 'rubbing it in the faces of poor heartbroken people like myself.'

'The city isn't divided between the couples and the heart-broken.'

'Yes, it is.' My eyes widen. 'Couples writhe into every social situation. There's nothing worth attending that they've not already been invited to. Their smugness smells like moist Sunday-morning sheets sacrificed to too much foreplay.'

'Gross. Don't say moist.'

'Moist,' I bellow down the carriage.

'Is there such a thing as too much foreplay?' she ponders.

The man sitting next to me coughs.

'There's not,' I say, turning my head to look at him. 'But that doesn't change the fact that I'm forced to sit opposite these couples on the tube when they use each other for headrests. The other day I was subjected to them kissing in front of a Marina Abramović at the Tate. And they don't just rub against one another in front of seminal feminist art, oh, no! They do it in coffee shops when I'm patiently waiting for my flat white, and in pubs when I'm harmlessly drinking a glass of red, minding my own business.'

'We're not so bad. Think of us as talismans – little beams of hope for your future smug self.'

'See? That's such an optimistic and couple-like thing to say.'

'No, it isn't.'

'It is. A heartbroken person would never say that. The other day, you and Henry swapped out each other's broccoli for cabbage right in front of my face, without even speaking. It was a horrible thing to witness.' I fold my arms, my face crumpling at the memory.

'Sounds wretched.'

'Well, it was no talisman, that's for sure. It was a reminder of the extra portion of delicious red cabbage that I'll never see again. And that's not even the worst of it.'

'Surely it must be,' she humours me.

'Nope. The worst of it is that you stake your claim on one

day in the yearly calendar and on that same day, every year, you publicly congratulate yourselves on your togetherness.'

'Outrageous.'

'I know. And no one ever questions your conceit.'

'What ghastly beasts we are.' Georgia laughs.

'This is my stop. I'll see you later?'

'I'm afraid not,' she gloats. 'I'll be busy doing my coupling.'

'You disgust me, Georgia Bailey, you really do,' I kiss her cheek before dashing out of the carriage.

Shoes

When I come out of the station, I head down the street towards the studio, impatient to get on the mat. You used to like exercising when I was a young child, but just as with most things you liked, your relationship with exercise became obsessive. As a little girl, I remember sitting on the lawn and watching you through the window of the shed, lifting weights for what felt like hours and hours while I'd thumb through books of sweaty men with glistening olive skin and vacuum-packed muscles decorated with flesh-coloured veins. I was so disturbed by these smiling men with teeth so white they could light a small village. That was the lesser evil in terms of your addictions. The second-hand-shoes obsession sticks out. There were bags, boxes and suitcases filled with them. Endless rows of shoes, all different sizes and styles. Brown leather brogues, black suede loafers with tarnished gold buckles, dusty lace-up workman's boots, worn-in red bowling shoes and, most unforgettably, a pair of wooden clogs with a hand-painted windmill on them – each pair old and scuffed. You collected them. You'd pick them up from charity shops and car-boot sales or you'd buy them on eBay. Most of this footwear wasn't even in your size. Did you wonder about the men who'd walked in those shoes? The new jobs they'd strolled into, the wives they'd walked out on, the cigarettes they'd extinguished and the things they'd tripped over?

I follow my own black desert boots down into the warm fitness studio, pulling off my scarf as the heat hits me. A smiley receptionist waits at the bottom of the stairs. I question whether her teeth are also whiter than they should be. And am I the only person left in London who hasn't had her eyelashes done? She's sitting behind a vibrant orange desk that's got a large clashing bouquet of calla lilies and pink roses. Alongside it are rows of protein balls and leaflets advertising new classes.

'Hey there!'

'Hi, I'm here for seven-thirty yoga.'

'Oh, wonderful,' she says, through her nose. 'Here's a towel, lovely. Have a great class today!'

I force a smile and go into the changing room to hang up my coat and scarf. I tuck my gloves into my gym bag, then place it in the locker. There are a few other girls in their underwear with towels around their heads, rosy-cheeked from the class they've just done. I observe the detail of their bodies, the smoothness of their curves and the ink on their skin, comparing the width of their thighs to that of my own and taking a mental note of any rolls that appear when they bend over to pick up their shoes. One of the girls is modelesque, a bone structure forged in generations upon generations of good genes. She bends over to retrieve her Gucci mules: not one roll of fat. Huh. She looks happy. I wonder if beauty-stamped approval is really a salve for female pain.

I'm early, and wisely turn my attention to the lives of more women who look happier than I feel by scrolling through Instagram. The success, pleasure and vitality of these women refreshes more quickly than my feed. Another promotion, another podcast launch, another understated anniversary post accompanied by an underplayed caption about their *seventeenth* year of being together. I click onto the search bar and type: Olivia Wool.

And there she is, just missing the centrefold in a fashion editorial about working mothers set against the backdrop of her Scandi-inspired living room in her east London home. I scroll right on the carousel to a close-up from the shoot. There are several thin hoops in each of her ears and she's wearing a milky oversized blazer and matching cream linen pants with a honey-coloured bralette: 'Flattered to have been included in this month's issue <3.' I sigh and tap the like button.

It's dark and even hotter in the yoga studio next door. I collect a couple of blocks and find a mat among the several other people who are already on their backs, hugging their knees to their chests and rocking back and forth slightly. Yoga has been part of my life ever since I was a student but now it's something I need to push me away from more destructive habits. I lie down, stretching my arms and legs as far as they will go, and take a deep breath, then let out a heavy sigh. I think of your old-fashioned shoe boxes piled up on top of one another; about you, sitting heavily on my chest; about what happened with Freddie the other night.

'Morning, yogis, how's everyone feeling today? Are we feeling good on this dreary Monday morning or what?'

A few people allow some British-sounding responses to rebel through pursed lips.

'Okay, let's get started.' The instructor gives up.

The music gets louder and I close my eyes as we start the warm-up in the Cat-Cow pose. On all fours, I breathe in deeply as I tuck my chin into my chest and push the top of my spine to the ceiling. I breathe out again as I lift my face to the sky and arch my back. Repeating this movement over and over, I feel the energy start to build in my body.

'Now, everyone make their way into their first Downward Dog,' she instructs, over the instrumentals. I push my body-weight into my hands and stretch out the backs of my legs, pushing the soles of my feet into the floor and away from me, lengthening my spine. My body commits itself to one pose after the next. I feel strong and my mind slows as my muscles work to fulfil the flow, and the weight of you lifts.

Cursed

After yoga I go to a nearby coffee shop with the intention of doing some prep for this new campaign but find myself back on Olivia Wool's Instagram. She was an old school friend of yours you loosely kept in touch with and she'd become an acquaintance to me when we were both on the same intern programme, before you and I even met. I catch you sometimes in the corner of her screen. I go to scroll down to the familiar picture of you drinking wine in her living room at one of her Christmas parties, then stop myself. Olivia Wool's life feels like a film at the cinema we didn't quite catch. So close I can almost taste that life – the one you ran away from. I put my phone on aeroplane mode to concentrate, and when I turn it off a few hours later it reveals three missed calls from Eden. That isn't like her. There's a WhatsApp message: *Frederick Malkovich. Are you fucking kidding me!!?*

I sigh and press my thumb on her name. The phone rings out for a couple of minutes and I'm about to hang up when—

'Sharon! Is that you?'

'Hiya, Kath!' I say loudly and enthusiastically.

'Ohhh, Sharon! I miiiiiss you. I miiiiss this beautiful voice.'

I hear her smiling down the phone.

'How is it that you moved to Paris years ago but the amount I miss you makes it feel like you just left?'

'I know, don't make me feel guilty. Are you working?'

'Trying to, yes. I've got that Hatch gig today. Look,' I say wearily, 'I really don't want to talk about Freddie.'

'Me neither,' she asserts. 'Are you sitting down?'

'Yes.' A small flitter of panic rises in my chest. 'Why?' It's a familiar feeling, one that flares up when Eden calls me at an odd time of day.

'Everything is fine, but I have something weird to tell you.'

I instantly feel calmer. Weird things to tell me falls into Eden's daily routine. 'You're not pregnant, are you?'

'Yes. Alex impregnated me with her rampant, sperm-packed ovaries and we're expecting our little darling in the spring.'

'Good. What's up, then?'

'It's sort of hard to say.'

'Come on, out with it.'

The last time she called me out of the blue was to tell me about the life-changing effects of Liposomal GABA – an oral remedy to facilitate a calming parasympathetic response to the nervous system. She now sends it to me in the post quarterly.

I think about the small pump bottles gathering dust somewhere in a basket under my bed.

'You know Alex's family are a bit of a . . . well, they're a little spiritual, I suppose. And you and I are quite open to that kind of thing – aren't we?' she asks, slightly hesitant.

'What kind of thing?'

'You know, *spiritualism* . . .' The *mmm* sound echoes down the line.

'Wait. Is this about your Reiki woman? Because, honestly, I'm starting to feel jealous of how close you two are getting.'

'No.' She chortles. 'This is about Alex's aunty.'

'The one who lives in New Orleans?'

'Yes! Exactly. You remember. Okay good, this is good.' She takes a deep breath. 'Well, she's been in Europe for work and flew out to stay with us.'

'That sounds nice. Isn't she like a psychic or something?'

'Sort of. She's a voodoo priestess.'

'Fair enough,' I say, in a dry tone, and signal to the waiter for my bill.

'She does readings and she did one for me yesterday.'

'Uh-huh. Any good?' I say, holding the phone to my ear with my right shoulder as I pull the coat off my chair behind me and push my left arm through the sleeve.

'Yes, actually, very good. She does remote readings too, sort of like doing it for someone *through* someone else . . .' Eden goes quiet.

'Oh, no, you didn't—'

'I'm just a bit worried about you at the moment, that's all.' She shoots up an octave. 'You seem a little . . . and I know that's to be expected, but—'

25

'Oh, that's perfect. More great feedback.' I roll my eyes as the waiter sets my tab down.

'What other feedback have you had?'

'It doesn't matter.'

'Was it about the dungarees?'

'Oh, for Christ's sake! You lot are unbelievable.'

'I told them. I said, "She's grieving. She needs to be comfortable to grieve"'.

I place my elbow on the table and rest my face in my hand, 'What did she say then, Eden?' I sigh loudly.

'I asked her if she could do a reading for you *through* me and she said if we were close enough she could. So, we gave it a go. Okay. It's really difficult to say this so I'm just going to come out with it, and then you can be all po-faced and sarcastic afterwards, *d'accord*?'

'Sounds splendid.'

'Well, she knew things about you. About your dad passing and what you did for work and—'

'That's nothing you couldn't (a) Google (b) learn from my Twitter account or (c) find out from Alex.'

'You said you'd let me say my piece.'

'*D'accord.*'

'She knew we call each other Sharon and Kath. How would she know that?'

Eden and I had known each other since we were playing with Barbies, and fighting over who'd get to be called Sharon – the pinnacle of adult coolness and the height of sophistication. The runner-up would be left with Kath, not quite as urbane but a solid moniker all the same.

'She knew about your relationship history, strange details. Not their names exactly, but their role in your life. She knew about Freddie – bad news, goes without saying – and she obviously knew about—'

'Please don't say his name.'

Eden stops talking. My shoulders tense and I sit back, open my wallet to retrieve my card and place it in the shiny metal dish.

'So she knew about Freddie, did she? She actually said his name?'

'No, of course not. She *said* a man keeps reappearing in your life and that the relationship isn't helping you. Just hear me out. She said there's some sort of curse on you. A strong curse. It's something from your past but it's still affecting you now. She could see it. She said it's all over you. It's in your hair and in your mouth and your ears – it's clinging to you. She said you were happy once, really, really happy, but you're blocked and this thing, this curse, you need to deal with it. She talked about your dad. She knew he drank, how difficult that was for you growing up. She said you need to get rid of this negative energy that's stuck to you . . .' Eden's voice is now stressed. 'Hello, are you still there, Mathilda?'

'Yes.' The waiter is in front of me now and I stare at him blankly as he faces the card machine towards me.

'She said you need to do a banishing bath.'

'Jesus Christ.' I hand the phone to him and mouth, 'Swapsies,' signalling at the card machine in exchange for my handset. He smiles awkwardly and shakes his head. Fair enough. I put the phone back to my ear and hear a ruffling of papers.

'Aunt Maya gave me a list of stuff you can get. Oh, here it is!' She's victorious. 'Okay, you need to bathe in it for an hour every day for seven days. Just an hour. Only one small hour out of your day, okay? I've written it all down. It's just some goat's milk soap and this thirteen-herb mixture and some oils and stuff. It will uncross and reverse the negative work that's been done.'

'Did you just say *negative work*?' I arch an eyebrow as I type my pin into the machine.

'There's a shop in London where you can pick all of this stuff up. Hang on one sec, I wrote it down somewhere too.' More ruffling.

'Does this woman have shares in this shop, might I ask?' I tut at the waiter.

'No. I just told you, you can get it all in London,' Eden says, with a whiff of frustration.

'So, you've genuinely called me to say you think I've been hexed,' I clarify drily.

'Yes.'

'Brilliant,' I whisper, under my breath.

'I'm glad you enjoyed it,' says the waiter, as he hands me my receipt and dashes into the crowded café.

'She's been right about so many things in the past. She's predicted things in Alex and her mum's lives. Births, job losses, opportunities in new cities, relationships that weren't going to last . . . and I'm as sceptical as you are—'

'No, you're not. You live for this stuff, Eden. You sound like you've been guzzling the voodoo juice.'

'How could she possibly guess I'd ask her to do a reading for you?'

'And what does Alex make of all this?'

'Alex asked me to call you. Voudon is a part of her culture and her family history. It's not the evil stereotype the Western world has made it out to be. It's how her mum and her aunties make sense of things. Maya cares about us – she was just trying to help. And you *have* had a lot of bad luck.' Her voice comes louder and clearer. 'If you have a few baths, light a candle or two and feel a bit lighter for it, what's lost?'

'This is a surreal conversation.' I feel a tear roll down my cheek, which takes me by surprise. I wipe it away.

'You don't need to decide anything now.'

'No. I've been cursed for years by the sound of things, so what's another night or two?' I look up to the ceiling and purse my lips, forbidding more tears to make the jump.

'I don't know if this is something to joke about any more,' Eden says seriously. 'You should do the uncrossing baths as soon as you can. She said your path has been tampered with.'

'Look, thanks for calling, Sharon, but I need to go or I'm going be late.'

'Okay, I love you,' Eden sounds tearful.

'I love you too.' I hang up.

I adore Alex, which is a blessing as much as a relief. The severance when a close friend falls in love induces a rhythmic leak in the gut, a constant reminder they aren't wholly available to you any more. She can't hang out because she's being introduced to their friends at the pub that evening or she's going to stay at their parents' place for the first time that weekend, and just like that there's an entire new continent in her world that you'll never get to roam with her, as you had everywhere else, tracing by foot the intricacies of her cities, her places of worship, her internal roads. Alex had made every effort to see that this transition was easier for us both when they'd met.

You used to see psychics, I remember. I wonder if they warned you of your painful and slow end. Perhaps you didn't listen when they told you the devil was knocking on the inside of a whisky bottle, each drop on your pink tongue making you more frustrated and unlikable. Your little girl is almost thirty now and she still sleeps with the blanket pulled up over her head. Even on the hottest summer nights she sweats into the sheets as she breathes through an O-shaped hole she makes in a duvet that covers her face, her mouth and her ears. And she still doesn't know why.

Hatch

I was told I came strongly recommended to Hatch, but they never said by whom. After obtaining a first in English and French at UCL, I got onto a top graduate programme at one of the largest advertising agencies in the world to pay off my mountains of student debt. Although I was a terrible account woman, I quickly found my feet on the creative side of the floor. I built up a portfolio throughout my twenties, then stepped off the ladder and into the world of freelance. Now I do branding, copywriting, directing, and whatever else comes my way. I'm good at it – not that you ever asked me about my job. I've won a few well-regarded industry awards for some of the scripts I've penned. I get asked to speak at conferences, and sometimes I sit on panels and people ask my thoughts on the industry and how it ticks. I'm not sure I've made it. But I've managed to earn enough money to live the life I want. To have my freedom. To be able to have nice things instead of second-hand school jumpers or my cousin's hand-me-downs. To be completely independent (well, financially at least), which is to carve out and hold space for oneself in this world. Which is to be noticed and taken seriously. Total savings: *nada*. Which is why it's such a shame you spent any small inheritance on old shoes.

The lift opens directly onto the open-plan office, which I've been to only once or twice to discuss my portfolio and pitch for this freelance job. I'm greeted by a sea of faces that all shoot me a courteous glance and, seeing it's only me, look away again. A ginormous sign reading 'HATCH' hangs from the ceiling – each letter is a sickly pastel colour and as tall as me, lilac, eggshell blue, toothpaste green and Pepto-Bismol pink. A guy with a man-bun and a beard – which feels like a bold combo – paces around a table talking loudly on his phone.

'No one else is doing anything like this in the space. It's a brave move for the brand, Daniel, it is. I hear you. But these are courageous times, and if you don't act and move with them, you'll get left behind. You can be one of the first soft drinks in the game to lead with this approach, or you can call me back in nine months asking if I can still create this campaign and be just another sheep in the flock. What are you, Dan? A lion or a sheep?'

I roll my eyes and remind myself the pay is good. I wander over to the 'break-egg area' – stop it, I know. Several large white eggs that are about seven feet tall rotate slightly with the weight of one or two people encased inside them; each has a brightly coloured sitting area and a round desk. Next to the break-egg area a space has been designed as an open dozen-egg box. It has a long, thin table running down its middle, just the width for a MacBook and a keep cup. People seat themselves in small egg-shaped grooves, leaning against pillows in the shape of things like lightning bolts. An egg spins around suddenly to reveal Edward sitting in it, his long, skinny, Jack-the-skeleton legs folded underneath him. Hatch had been his baby, but he'd predictably just sold to a famous global ad agency and was contracted to hang around to ensure the seamlessness of the merger.

'You're late, Miss Mathilda.'

'Am I? I thought the meeting was at ten.' It was 9.55 a.m.

'Yes, but at Hatch,' he draws the *ch* sound for a moment too long, 'we arrive fifteen minutes early to a meeting so everyone can make small-talk, sort hot drinks for themselves and settle. We want to make the most of the hour-long box slot.'

'Box slot?'

'Yes. We've got the egg box booked out for an hour.' He signals with his head, tutting at my ignorance.

I look at the people lining the box making small-talk – and when I say people, I mean men. 'Apologies, Edward, it won't happen again.'

'Call me Eddie,' he says, uncrossing his legs, which seem to have their own mind as they lead him pelvis first to the themed table.

I follow him.

'Now, guys, this is Mathilda. She's been freelancing with us for a few weeks and she's been brought in specifically for this project because she—'

'Has a vagina,' I jest.

Edward frowns and continues, 'Because she has a lot of experience in producing female-focused content, particularly when it comes to women's politics. Welcome, Mathilda.'

Edward looks me up and down, beckoning me to get inside the box. I step over and find myself a small egg-shaped groove to insert myself into. I am often the one woman shipped in to rescue campaigns or digital brand strategies when it's all gone tits up. I don't remember this being a conscious choice in my career, but it seemed I'd carved out a niche.

'Now, Max, I know you've been doing a lot of work on this in the past week and you've hit upon an idea that you're ready to present to the team this morning. The box is yours!' he adds, with an open-palmed flourish.

'All right, thanks, guys.' A New Zealander. Aptly he has a kiwi-coloured shirt on, tweed trousers with bright orange socks and brogues that look like they cost more than my entire outfit.

'So, I've been on a bit of an idea safari, guys, and it's taken me to some unexpected places.' He says this earnestly. 'I hit some dead ends along the way, of course, but I think I've finally got somewhere.' He rests his weight on two index fingers placed on the long, thin desk in front of him.

Man-bun struts over, filling the air with a suffocating haze of masculine mist. He sits down in the groove next to me. 'Hey,' he says, looking down at my tits.

'Hello,' I say, also looking down at my tits.

Max continues: 'Women want to be strong, these days. It's not about being skinny any more – heroin chic is a thing of the past – it's about being a strong, independent woman.' He pushes a button on a small egg-shaped remote control – they've really taken this theme too far – and a screen appears from nowhere as it starts to make its way down from the ceiling to position itself opposite the box. Max clicks through reams and reams of research from the planners and talks us through image after image of social influencers, squatting and smiling with protein shakes in pink packaging that have things like 'sugar free' written across them.

'So then it hit me,' he says over-zealously. 'It needed to be smarter, but it still needed to be feminine. It was going to take a merger of these two ideas, to have women in the old-fashioned trad roles but rather than the frail, skinny bodies,

33

they're replaced with strong pumped-up physiques. For example,' he clicks the egg and uses his index finger to push his glasses up his nose, 'you could have a woman dressed as a waitress but instead of her skinny arms holding a tray with drinks, the drinks will be kettle bells and she'll have muscular, strong upper arms.'

A woman with long hair and large breasts smiles at me in an apron with badly superimposed weights on her tray. Max clicks the egg and I stare at him, bamboozled by the six-figure salary he'll be taking home.

'Motherhood is huge in the fitness scene, as we've just heard. The mums wanna shed the baby weight, so we'll have a mum on the school run pushing the pram, a kid holding the side of it,' his accent grates, 'but her legs will be stacked. She'll have bulky quads that you'd never associate with a stereotypical mother figure, and the line will read, "She's not just pumping iron at the school gates."' The woman on the screen is winking to camera and he clicks the egg again. 'And we want to capture the single women's market too. Mathilda, perhaps you can help with that.'

Rude.

I apparently don't conceal the horror on my face because Edward follows up with, 'Yes, what do you think, Mathilda?' His legs barely fit into his small egg indentation.

'Well, I feel a little . . . scrambled, Edward, in truth.' I struggle to contain myself.

Edward frowns deeper into his face and nods. 'Eddie,' he corrects me, 'but continue.'

Max puffs out his kiwi-coloured breast defensively and Man-bun steals another look at mine.

'You want to use stereotypical sexist set-ups for women, but in place of "frail" and slim bodies insert muscular, body-builder-esque statures?'

'It's a play on imagery,' Max says defensively, flipping his wrist over. 'It's mocking the fact that women have been suppressed for hundreds of years and their strength underestimated.' He takes a serious and worthy tone. 'It's a comment on how today women are stronger than ever.'

Yes, I understand the concept, Max. It's just not a very good one.
'I see.'

Man-bun is looking at me and a few other heads at the other end of the table turn to see if the new girl has more than two syllables to share with the group.

'I'm just not sure this is the best approach,' I say more loudly.

'Why not?' Edward questions, in his posh voice, his frown line in the middle of his forehead becoming a crate that could house a family.

'Because these women are super-muscular, but not in an achievable way. You're just offering women yet another unattainable body type. It's the same problem you're perpetuating, just the other end of the scale. These women you've shown will go to the gym twice a day and eat nothing but protein. A working mother doesn't have that kind of time.' I look at the women's sweaty, sexualised bodies, fake tits and beaming smiles to cover their dead-behind-the-eyes, vacant stares. 'And, besides, this isn't how the majority of women want to look. Were all these images shot by male photographers?'

'What's your point?' Max shoots back defensively.

'Well, judging from the research you just presented, you're trying to imitate the imagery of fitness influencers online – which I don't think is the way to go – but that aside for a moment, at least those photographs are taken *by* women *for* women. They're

35

representative of the female gaze. It's an entirely different composition and representation of the female form—'

Max rolls his eyes and starts talking over me: 'Eddie, why don't we try this direction with a female photographer?'

'That's a nice idea, J.'

'Well, it was my idea, actually.' Two rows of heads down the table turn and stare at me. Everyone is silent for a moment.

Edward continues. 'So it was. I think you and Max should team up on this one and work on developing the idea together. Fitness Now have three hundred and fifty-five branches up and down the country, and they want more women inside their doors. It's our job to get them there. This is big business. We need to hatch *the* idea. They've already said no to two of our pitches. If we don't get it right this time, we'll lose the client.'

Everyone nods and starts to get up, chatting among themselves. I look over to Max, who is showing the guy next to him something on his phone and laughing.

'I hope you have fun on Maximillion's idea safari,' Man-bun scoffs.

I was wrong. This job isn't paying enough.

Oyster Bay

That night, I follow the fishy, garlicky smell downstairs and into the kitchen. 'Oh, my God, it smells *delicious*, Eks.'

There's steam on the windows that face out onto the garden, and a blurry yellow mist shines through them from the fairy lights.

'If it weren't for me, you lot would never sit and have your tea together. We're having veggie soup to start with crusty white bread – which, yes, I've baked myself.' Ekua turns to me. She's got her red oven mitts on, which are cradling the fresh loaf. 'For main, it's a crab and mushroom gratin and for dessert we have chocolate fondants!'

'Mmm . . .' Ekua turns to me, the deliciousness of her words enveloped in a northern twang. 'Yummy. I've got my period, I'm craving sugar.'

'*Noo*, I were kidding. There's nowt for dessert. I opted for more wine instead.'

I laugh and pour us both a large glass of white wine, adding soda water and one cube of ice to Ekua's because that's how she likes it. She smiles and we cheers. The cold crisp liquid slips down my throat and I start to feel a little more chipper about this evening.

'Still no word from Fuck-face, then?' she says, looking down at my dungarees.

'I don't wear them *that* much.' I tuck my hair behind my ears, something I do when I feel defensive.

'I didn't say anything.' She raises her spare hand into the air in her defence.

'Have I heard from the man who ripped out my heart, mindlessly sat on it, compressing the thing until it burst, disseminating into the wider atmosphere like blood-red confetti?

'Never let it be said she's dramatic.' Ekua's wearing a short red dress, which is heavily patterned and sits on the edges of her smooth shoulders.

'You look really nice by the way.' I play with one of the large, ruched sleeves.

'Thank you, doll.' She touches my arm. 'It really is time to move on, though.' She smiles kindly, with a wide mouth that

37

takes up most of her face and a diastema I've always envied. 'It's been six months.'

'I know. And I am. I'm really trying.' I tuck my hands into my pockets and shrug.

'I just wish I didn't remember him as so . . . I don't know, good and handsome and just, bleh!'

'Well, he were handsome,' She says, matter-of-fact, salting the garlicky dish that's cooking in one of her pans, 'but he's also incredibly insecure and intimidated by you. Then again, most people are.' She doesn't meet my eye and I know she's avoiding indulging me in the same conversation we've had countless times over the same bottle of mid-week Oyster Bay.

'Good,' I say, turning my saggy denim bum to rest on the work surface and swigging my wine. 'Do you need help cooking?'

'Hell, no! I'm not having you take any credit for my chef-d'oeuvre!' She smiles, her teeth framed by her signature bright tangerine lipstick, luminous against her dark skin.

Ekua has made me a lot of consoling hot meals these last few months. Since the day I met her in our shared intercollegiate halls, she'd thrived on being maternal. In fact, when we first met, that had been the very subject matter of her art. Her dad Teddy said she was conceived somewhere between a Northern Soul dance hall and the back of his Saab 900. Her mum fell pregnant with her at just seventeen and, after battling post-natal depression and trying to kill herself twice, she left. Ekua was three years old.

'It's like I've idealised him in my mind, forgotten any bad or irritating traits, and he's retrospectively perfect.'

'He weren't.' Ekua scrunches her nose and shakes her head.

'You need to try and stop masturbating over him too. That's not helping.'

'I'm not masturbating over him!' I say, widening my mouth with horror.

'Umm-hmm . . . I can tell. It's not gonna help the dungaree sitch neither. And, quite frankly, you need to find someone new to sleep with because having sex with Freddie is not a good look, hot as he may be.' She puts her wooden spoon down and takes me by the wrists. 'Repeat after me: I need to flick my bean for someone new.'

I laugh at her to dismiss the subject and lift my arms towards my chest as she clings on.

'Do you remember that time when we were all at the pub for G's birthday and we had to leave because I wasn't feeling well?'

'Yeah I remember, you had a terrible migraine,' she says, already bored of where this is going.

'That's right, I did. And we stopped at a supermarket to get painkillers and I waited outside because I couldn't bear the brightness of the lights. And he emerged with a new cure he'd learnt from a woman behind him in the queue.' I smile into the memory. 'He always gave strangers the time of day, ya know?'

'Maybe it seemed that way because you try to forgo as much interaction with people as is humanly possible.'

'Only people that aren't you.' I pull my arms free. 'Anyway, when we got home, he ran a hot bath and asked me to put just my hands and feet in the water, and then he placed this ice-pack on the back of my neck.' I run my fingers along my nape. 'And it worked! He was always so kind to me. Not in a grand or performative way—'

'Just in a really mundane uneventful way.' Ekua frowns at me, disenchanted. 'I mean, sure. That's a nice thing to do. But walking out on you with no rhyme or reason, is that kind? If you get a migraine, I am more than capable of running some water in the bath and holding some frozen peas on your 'ead. So if that's a reason to continue harbouring feelings for him, maybe let that one go. I got you.'

'Are you stalking his social media?' A new voice enters the conversation from nowhere, and Ivy is in the doorway, her back flat against its wooden frame, arms folded. There's a well-known rush of unease and it makes me feel lightheaded.

'He's not on social media.'

'Shame. I'd have liked to see what all the fuss is about.' She sinks her deep-set gaze into mine. She's undeniably striking, bones shaven down in all the right places.

'The right question to ask is: is she still stalking Olivia Wool?' Ekua incites.

'No.' I break eye contact and dart my eyes towards Ekua, protectively.

'And who is Olivia Wool exactly?' Ivy runs her bony fingers across her fringe to reposition it. A mannerism I've noticed her perform when she's pretending to be uninterested in a conversation.

'She's no one,' I say bluntly.

'She's the one mutual friend her and the ex share.' Ekua throws her head back in my direction.

'Well, then, let's look at her profile.' Ivy walks over and leans into me as she reaches up to the cabinet to get herself a wine glass. I hesitate.

'Well?' She lays her palm flat then, gesturing at me for my phone. I look into Ivy's eyes and it's as if there's a melancholy cloud tied to her, exposing her online happiness to be made up once again. It's uncomfortably familiar.

'No.' I shake my head.

'You need to let it go!' says Ekua, emphatically, turning her back to us to stir the large silver pot.

I resent that comment. It's easy to say, 'Let it go, Mathilda. Move on,' but the reality is much harder to execute. Ekua – for all her issues – doesn't understand what it's like to be choked by the rejection of men, over and over. Fathers create a ripple effect and intoxicate the waters. They infect the small exchanges we have with other men – from the CMO you can't stand at work to the cute guy at the Espresso Hut who makes your morning coffee. They contaminate lovers and threaten to drown them in a deep, endless void. A vast, oceanlike space for men to fail to fill. Teddy worshipped Ekua, and I often wonder if that makes male validation pale in comparison. She certainly seems to lean into her sexual orientation for women more than she leans into her desire for men, on the basis that she finds women far more interesting and emotionally literate. Perhaps I envy her that choice. Maybe some small part of me even hates her for it. It's an uncomfortable thought, but her tangerine glow and those words on her lips – 'let it go' – lead me to rest on it.

'God I hate him.' I push my head back and hold my wine glass out for Ivy to refill.

'Do you, though? Is he the right place to house all this hate?' She tops up my glass and props herself against the countertop next to me.

'What do you mean?'

'Well, maybe it belongs to someone else. Like, maybe you have an issue with men in general.'

The hair on the back of my neck stands up and I look for you in a dark corner of the room.

'You used my shampoo, you skank.' She stands on tiptoe to sniff the crown of my head. 'Your hair smells fucking fantastic.'

We all turn our heads at the sound of the front door slamming. Georgia is back from her weekly blow-dry. It's hard to be jealous of Georgia's wealth sometimes because of the way it came to her family, but most of the time it isn't. Her dad is self-made and built a comparison website in the noughties. Mrs Bailey traded in her marital rings for more impressive rocks when it went public on the stock market, something Georgia is still ashamed of.

'Right,' she says, from the hallway, before entering the kitchen with Selfridges bags in each hand, 'have you told them about this women's circle we're doing tonight?'

Ekua grins at me with clenched, pleading teeth. Ivy rolls her eyes.

'Well,' I say, taking a deep breath, 'before you tell me about that, I need to tell *you* something.' I relay Eden's call earlier, making gag after gag about the ridiculousness of it. But anxiety creeps in when they nod along with concern, more serious than I expected as I tell them about the curse.

Women's Circle

Ekua arranges candles around the crystals she's brought down from her bedroom into a cluster on the coffee-table. She turns off all the lamps in the living room except the neon, and lights some incense. Its perfume seeps into the room. Ivy makes eye contact with me across the table and theatrically raises an eyebrow. The smoke from the joss stick clouds parts of her face. I swallow the musky scent of cigarettes and tangy wine.

'So, remember, we go around in a circle and each person has their turn.' Ekua is standing, topping up our glasses. 'When it's your turn, you have the floor and the freedom to talk about whatever you want, without interruption. When someone is speaking you can't talk or have any contact with them whatsoever. You just listen.'

'I feel like I'm in *The Craft*,' says Ivy, drained of enthusiasm.

'You don't comfort them if they cry and you don't hold their hand or tell them it's going to be okay. All you can do is listen. Oh, and you can't get angry if they say something you disagree with or don't like. The whole point of this ceremony is that each woman has her chance to be heard.'

'Are we *meant* to cry and say mean things about each other?' I ask.

Georgia and Ivy start giggling. Ekua ignores the question.

'Comforting someone when they cry can actually suppress their feelings. It prevents them from leaning into the emotion and what it is that they're feeling. And, yes, it's fine to giggle. This is an unusual situation, and so it's a little uncomfortable.'

'Okay, but how do we know when the person's done with their turn?' Georgia asks sincerely, stretching her vowels. A typical Virgo, who hates getting things wrong.

'The person will just stop speaking and, umm . . . I don't know. You can just tell they're done, doll.'

'I'm not sure how many times you've seen Ekua cry,' says Georgia to Ivy, 'but once she gets going, she really goes for it.'

'Yeah, we could be here all night,' I say, with a straight face. 'No one else might get a turn.'

Ivy's smile is ominous, lit by the pink glow of the neon behind her.

'Oh, shut your gob!' Ekua retorts. 'The point of this is to be

43

open-minded and supportive. It were dead good when I did it on my artists' retreat in Munich. Now hold hands.'

Ekua's hand is thick and clammy in mine compared to Ivy's noticeably cold bony fingers.

'Now breathe in and hold it for five, four, three, two, one, and breathe out.' Ekua's voice is now tranquil and syrupy. 'Breathe in, five, four, three, two, one, and breathe out, five four, three, two, one. Continue with your eyes closed.' The room is still but for the rising of our chests and the only sound is of our synchronised breathing. I feel a little dizzy but I'm calm, my mind starting to empty. We continue like this until I stop counting and breathe without thinking. Ekua lets go of my hand and we release one another in a domino effect. I open my eyes instinctively. Ekua goes first.

Women's Circle: Tower of Babel

'I'm feeling really grateful that we're doing this, and incredibly lucky to have women like you in my life. I hope you all know that. I value that we can be vulnerable together, that we aren't afraid to share things about ourselves. Maybe even things we feel ashamed of.'

She pauses then and we all smile at her. This feels good. Unexpected.

'So, yeah, I wanted to express that to you. My gratitude. I've decided my next show is going to be about romantic intimacy. It seems to be even more poignant at this stage in our lives, doesn't it? We're just into our thirties and have never placed much importance on "the one". But sometimes I worry we're on the cusp of middle-age and settling for our lot, the fire in our bellies extinguished by bourgeois boredom or something. Romantic intimacy, what is it really? I wanna assess intimacy stripped back when all that's left is the carcass. So, I've started dating people but without talking to them – no dialogue whatsoever. It's called,' she says, moving her hand across the air with each word, 'the Languageless Dating Project.'

Georgia rolls her eyes at me, hair perfectly blown out and running over angular shoulders.

'I saw that, Georgia Bailey! Okay, fine, the title needs work. But, honestly, it's dead interesting. No words, we just exist together in a small corner of time and see what happens. It were inspired by the Tower of Babel. I want to remove the confusion and misunderstanding language creates.'

Church had played an informative role in Ekua's life because Teddy's parents had been the stars of her childhood show: her grandmother held a handwritten recipe book passed down from her own mother, imprinting on Ekua the social power of cooking; her grandfather took her to church on Sundays in her squeaky patent Kickers and implored the bigger questions in life. Despite turning against religion in her teens, it was still a framework she sought out to make sense of the world.

'I've been on seven dates now – some of them have been electrifying.'

Well, that's a rarely used adjective when describing modern dating.

'I copy and paste a short paragraph about the project and the terms of engagement on Hinge or Tinder, and then we agree a time and a place to meet. It can be a little awkward at times, sure. But that's where the meaning is – a residue of truth – a thin film of consciousness, something that we'd otherwise suppress in verbal niceties and etiquette. *That which we do not bring into consciousness appears in our lives as fate.* That's what Jung wrote. Meaning that which I do not allow myself to process I then create out of all that's around me.'

She pauses for a moment and I try to connect the dots.

'I met this one girl in Costa.'

Ivy lets out a laugh.

'And not long after our drinks arrived, she started crying. I sat and watched. I didn't try to comfort her, just tried to see her. To acknowledge her without resorting to any meaningless cliché like *It's okay. It'll be okay. Don't cry. I promise everything will work out.*' Ekua's face creases with each concerning phrase. 'Her cries got loud and heavy, like she started disturbing the people sat around us and that. The barista had to come over to see if she were okay – but they scooted off when met with our silence.'

Huh. A date without speaking.

'Sure, some people have misunderstood the brief. Kevin followed me into the pub toilet and blindsided me with his penis. "Please, Kev, put that away," I said. He looked disappointed. That was the end of the date. I went on another with a guy last week. We wrapped up and sat on a blanket in the park, shared some Comté and a bottle of Pinot Noir. It were nice. But after the edible props perished, we looked at one another and reached the unspoken and mutual conclusion that there was no real attraction. But, yet, it were the most connected I've felt to another person in a long time. Don't you think we place too much importance on words? Words are not always helpful. Sometimes, in fact, they get in't way.'

We all sit still, very consciously still. The energy in the room vibrates, wordless thoughts exchanging in the atmosphere.

'I've seen the girl again. Lucia's her name.'

I purse my lips, resisting the urge to make a joke.

'Yeah, I know. She's Italian. Three dates and we've still not said a word to one another.'

She stops speaking and looks at Georgia, who nods in acknowledgement at being the next person to talk.

Women's Circle: Pressure

'I feel pressured. If there's one word that could sum up my human experience, that would be it. There's pressure to have decided on who I want to be and what I want to do with my life. I have this house that my parents bought me, and I do know how lucky I am for that,' she follows up, almost in pre-emptive defence.

Georgia's feelings of luck are more of a public-facing event; privately they're more complicated.

'So now what? Marriage and babies? And then what? My life feels like a treadmill, an inevitable never-ending movement. Everything is the same. I'll have the same birthday party next year, celebrated in a similar London pub, where I'll be given handwritten cards with the same sentimental messages as the year before.'

Well, *that's* rude. I always put a lot of thought into my day-of-birth musings.

'If I blink for too long, it'll all be over. My life will have unwrapped itself when I wasn't looking. I'll be left, this woman frozen in a picture that I don't even remember painting. We're not twenty any more, you know. It's not about "seeing how it goes" or "feeling our way". It's not cute to make mistakes. Or to make the wrong move and hurt people. We must know better

47

now. I love Henry, I do. Of all the uncertainty I feel, he is the one thing that I am sure about. But he's asking me to step into this next chapter with him and for some reason I don't feel ready. I'm less adventurous now. I don't feel the urge to leave things or break things just to see what will happen.' Georgia pauses. She's playing with a wine-bottle cap, flattening its edges and stretching it out to its original shape again. She repeats this movement as she stares at the floor, her long hair falling all around her, like a willow tree's branches, concealing her face. Performing the universal female affliction: to hide.

'I should ask you girls to move out and I should ask Henry to move in. You've all said it to me. And I know he wants to. I can hear him almost ask me across the table in restaurants after too many drinks. But then I distract him or change the conversation – talk about a funny thing one of you said the other day, say I'm worried because one of you is having a hard time.'

I look down at my hands, cheeks burning from the wine and the idea of myself as a burden.

'I've told him I want to marry him and have babies, but if I'm honest, I'm not sure I do. Fuck. That's the first time I've said it out loud.'

This was something I could have told Georgia years ago. She has never had a motherly compulsion. Her own experience of the maternal was complicated and losing her mother's attention in exchange for material goods had made her resentful.

'I know I need to take that next step, but I'm so sad about letting all this go – the smell of burnt hair and Elnett, passive-aggressive notes stuck to the fridge and our Facebook group with the annual documentation of our Halloween parties.'

We all chuckle at this. I'd gone as a Freudian slip last year.

'Once he moves in, I'll probably never live with my friends

again. And I'm mourning that. Grieving the end of it. I should stop buying shoes and get a new kitchen fitted. At the very least do some research on my energy suppliers and get a cheaper tariff. Because that's what grown-up women do, isn't it? I'm scared he'll move in, and when I wake up, you'll all be gone. The house will be quiet and empty. All except for Henry outside in the garden fixing his bike or mowing the lawn, for goodness' sake. My mother busying herself with an interior designer, cooing over South American folk art and asking if I want built-in bookshelves in the nursery. Jesus.' She laughs unexpectedly. 'And I'll think, Is this it?'

Resisting the urge to reach out and touch her is harder than I expect. She wipes a tear from under her eyes. Pulling her long, dark hair up over her head and twisting it into a bun that self-holds, she readjusts her sitting position. When she stops moving it's clear that she's finished, and we all look to Ivy, who bears the weight of our silent stares.

Apranihita

The next day, I sit in the break-egg area at Hatch feeling slightly seasick as the large egg rotates every time Max mansplains something to me or reaches for his coffee. He's wearing the same slightly high-waisted tweed trousers but has switched his orange socks for yellow ones, pairing them with a navy silk shirt, which he's tucked in.

'I've pulled together a list of brilliant female photographers for us to go through,' I say, positioning my laptop so he can see my screen.

'Yeah, nah,' he replies dismissively. 'It's golden. My mate Clara has already said yes to doing it.'

'Your mate Clara?' I ask, openly mystified.

'Yeah, it's all good,' he says, with his Kiwi lilt. 'She's done heaps of stuff like this and I've already put her work in front of the client – the other night when we were having drinks.'

'Okay. But that's not really the process. We haven't finalised the direction yet and we should consider someone who has a genuine interest in fitness.'

'Yee-ah,' he says, unperturbed. 'Clara works out. She's fit.'

'Okay, Max, we need to have a little talk.'

He tweaks his round tortoiseshell glasses, which I'm convinced aren't prescription, and puffs out his chest as I scare him off with the 'beach-body ready' ad and warn him that this gym campaign could cost him his career and reputation. 'Who did that campaign, Max?'

He stares at me thoughtfully.

'You don't know. That's because no one knows that dude's name. And D&AD aren't going to hand out a Pencil Award to someone who missteps and is responsible for another thought-less campaign, and it's so easily done in this day and age. Like you just said, people are oversensitive.' I bite my tongue. 'If we lose this client, a head will roll. You're invested in Hatch and I'm just a freelancer. Why not let me take that risk?'

He relinquishes his involvement by midday, and I start working on a new idea with one of the female art directors and Man-bun, people who have actually been inside a gym. We work on the campaign all day, and when I finally take a break and reach for my phone, there's a voice note from Eden.

Helloooo, my little crab-apple. How are ya? How's your day going? Tell me all the things . . . I'm just on my way to court now and I absolutely cannot be fucked. I had lunch with Sal yesterday – you know my Reiki healer, Sal? I think we're going to do a project together, some sort of series of events for queer couples. Anywa . . . Pardon? Oh. Non, désolée. *No, I'm afraid I don't speak French. I'm not from here. Sorry . . .*Long pause with Eden's stamping heels* The fucking Champs-Élysées, it's a breeding ground for tourists. What was I saying? Ah, yes, Sal! She was telling me all about this Zen teaching, Apranihita! It means aimlessness in Sanskrit. Look it up. It's a form of meditation. It's the belief that you already are who you want to become: I already am the successful, married, brilliant mother with a fulfilling career and a goldmine of a self-start-up idea* and *a summer home in the South of France. Sal says, 'You'll have all those things that you want because they're already yours.' And it made me think of you. I mean I'm always thinking of you but I just thought . . . Well, isn't that lovely? This idea that you are already validated and you are already complete. All the things you want in life are yours. You are whole and you have nowhere to get to and nothing to strive for. You can just be . . . *Police sirens and beeps etch a backdrop for a drawn-out silence* I told Alex about it too, in a desperate bid to push her baby demands back. I'm like, darling, you already* are *a happy mother of three, that is who you shall become. Just not in this decade. She doesn't seem convinced but we're going to try some couples' meditation. Sal recommended it. Speaking of which, did you book your Reiki appointment with that guy she suggested? He's in Clerkenwell, isn't he? Mm . . . I really think you'd get a lot from it, you know. And where are we at with the curse, please? Have you ordered the banishing-bath stuff yet because Georgia told me you haven't and— Oh, fuck, is that the time? I'm late. I'm so late. Love, I have to go. You should book an appointment! Love you, Sharon.*

2.03mins

I take my headphones out and sigh. 'I'll be back in a minute,' I say to the rest of the team as I walk over to a quiet part of the office. I press the microphone button down on my screen and lift the phone to my mouth.

Eden. I don't need any Reiki in my life, okay? Would you stop pushing it on me? And Georgia is a Judas . . . What is with you both at the moment? You need to dial it down with all this spiritualismmmmm. You're such a ray of oracle-giving sunshine at the moment. It's like you've joined the Hare Krishnas or something . . . Have you? You'll need to invest in some bold earrings to counterbalance that bald head, ya know. I love you deeply so I'm going to tell you the truth: orange isn't your colour. *Man-bun calls me from across the office* I have to go, Man-bun is beckoning me. But you should stop being a massive dick and help people with directions. You've lived in Paris for five years and you speak fluent French. The 'I'm sorry I'm not from here' line surely doesn't wash any more. Just imagine you're reincarnated as someone who's always getting lost. Which I understand is a philosophy you subscribe to now, O bringer of curses and new-found spiritual guidance . . . I'm not feeling very freaking Apprantita or whatever the hell it is . . . I'm cursed, remember? You're the one who told me. *Man-bun calls me from across the office* I'll ring you later, okay, Kath? Byyyyeeee.
57.75 seconds

Eden is typing . . .
Book the appointment you massive bell end.
I laugh to myself. I'm not booking that appointment.
Eden is typing. . .
Man-bun sounds FIT. Shag him?

Constance

I'm standing on the doorstep with a tote bag full of pineapples, getting drenched. I feel comforted by the brightness of their shells and their lustrous verdant hairstyles, but the spikes are digging into my underarm. Everything else is grey. I should invest in an umbrella.

I crouch down and shout through the letterbox. 'Constance! Are you here?'

Nothing. I stand up and sigh, looking around the empty dark side-street.

'Constance! It's me!' I push my face close to the door, trying to get as much shelter as I can from its narrow frame. I've been here for what feels like half an hour and the rain, hurling itself onto my back, is starting to take its toll. I close my eyes and breathe in the wooden smell of the chipped pale-blue door. My coat is soaked and heavy, the weight of the water pulling it down past my ankles. I'm starting to worry: I'm going to have to call my service manager if she doesn't answer. What was her name again? Amanda? Ami . . . Amika! Yes. My hand scrabbles at the bottom of my leather bucket bag. I pull out my phone and search for her number, resting my back against the door. I put the phone to my ear and wait for the ring tone. Suddenly there's a rustling from behind and I fall backwards onto the ground. I'm looking up at Constance, who's smiling down at me.

'Oh, it's you!' she says, as if surprised. 'Are you all right, dear?' She tilts her grey bob to the side.

'Yes, I'm fine.' I giggle a little, heaving my body forward in a bid to get up. 'I've been waiting outside for ages. I rang the bell and I was shouting through the letterbox. Didn't you hear me?' I ask, in disbelief.

'No, no, I didn't.' She turns her back on me and makes her way down a dark, narrow corridor that leads to a low-lit room.

I breathe in the familiar sweet and musty smell of her ground-floor flat and close the door behind me. In her living room the plastered walls are covered with framed art and bleached cloth that have been Blu-tacked into place. Each is a piece of her art. A lot of them are pencil sketches of her past, pictures she drew of her two children playing and portraits of her husband, unaware that his likeness was being taken. Constance has lived her entire life without the convenient abomination that is the smartphone and she's only ever shown me drawings of her loved ones, with the exception of a photograph of her daughter, which lives next to her bed. I knew she had died young so I didn't pry. I also didn't ask if her photo of a dead relative shook and clanked in the night. A resourceful soul, Constance makes collages from dried fruit and plants, which she sews to old cloth she finds, then bleaches to make it more interesting to the eye. She is the purest kind of artist.

'Look at this!' she says, from the corner of the small room, lit by a tall metal lamp placed next to a sofa that's covered with green blankets. She walks over to me with the palms of her hands open, and inside is a painting still drying. It's Francis Bacon-esque with a misshapen figure created in dark reds and burgundies, and streaks of white that run over the image.

'It's good, Constance.' I pore over it. 'There's a sadness to it but something that I find reassuring too.'

'Do you think so?' She stares down at the piece, smiling. 'I wasn't able to get out today with the rain. I thought it best to stay indoors. The last thing I need is another fall.' She pauses, then says, 'I didn't think you were coming.'

Not this again.

'Why not?' I use both hands to tuck my long hair behind my ears. 'I texted you earlier in the week to see if I could come today and you said it was fine. You even sent me your list.'

Constance had made it her business to master an old Nokia 3310, which seems noble given I've accepted I'm already too old to learn TikTok.

'Yes, I did. But you didn't come last week so I didn't know if you were coming this week,' she responds curtly.

'Well, I didn't come last week because you asked me not to. You had plans to watch a film with Iris at the community hall, remember?'

Constance's memory is a little shaky but that's to be expected and she always remembers the important stuff. I've been seeing her every week for several months now, and I've only ever cancelled on her once. She gets confused and quite often cancels on me, though.

'Yes, they were showing Paolo Sorrentino's *The Great Beauty* and Iris has never seen it.'

'Was it good, then?'

'Was what good, dear?'

'*The Great Beauty.*'

'Oh, I didn't go in the end. It's a very long film and Iris felt too tired.'

'Right.' I sigh, and she doesn't pick up on my tone. 'Have you had a good week?'

'Well, it's been very quiet. I haven't been out much. I'm very tired, these days, but I shan't complain. I'm lucky enough.'

Other than the lamp and the two-person sofa, which faces a small flat-screen TV, there's a full bookshelf pushed against the wall. It is overflowing with all manner of subjects and genres – so much so that she's started several piles of books that tower messily on the floor in front of it. There is also a much shorter set of shelves, hand-painted in a pale green. On these are trays full of leaflets, pieces of paper, and what looks like an entire life's worth of admin. The top is used as a side table where she keeps her monthly calendars, which are hand-drawn on A4 sheets. Each day has something scrawled in pencil, and I look down at today's date and see my name followed by four dramatic question marks, underlined three times. I shake my head. There's a desk pushed to the left-hand corner of the room with a little stool that has a round, hand-embroidered cushion on it. That's where she paints. The furniture she has is quaint and a little worn in; her most precious belongings are her art and her books.

'Did you get wet? Would you like a towel?'

'Yes, please,' I squeeze the water out of my hair and it drips onto the floor.

She potters off and I remove my coat and hang it on the top of the living-room door to dry. I feel so giant in her flat – everything in it seems miniature.

'Here you go!' She walks back into the room and hands me a hard, rough towel. I sit down on the chair and place it over my knees, tucking my hands underneath to warm up. She follows my lead and sits too.

'Have you been very busy, then?' she asks pointedly.

'Um, not too bad. Lots going on at work but I'm enjoying it, so . . .'

Despite this being a 'loneliness' scheme, Constance is actually quite busy. There's Iris who lives next door, her son who visits quite often, and all manner of friends from the local galleries and community centre. I think you'd like Constance a lot. Sometimes I feel it's a shame you left before you got the chance to meet her. But then, I probably wouldn't know her if you hadn't.

Sitting around feeling sorry for myself felt great at first. There's something strangely calming about not being able to get out of bed, not wanting to move from under the duvet and having no desire to see the day. Your life slows down. The day is barely day before it starts to get dark and the night merges with the morning so gently that it's hard to trace the difference. There's no need to keep up with the news, face the commute or have an opinion on which mid-century coffee-table someone should get – not caring about anything, including yourself, can be liberating. I had no energy. It was like you'd taken it with you when you went. One morning I'd felt so tired that I couldn't get out of bed. I just about managed to get up and have a bath later that afternoon. When I stepped out of the soapy water I felt heavy and tired and made my way back to our bed, where I sat on the corner of it with my hands either side of me, shivering. The heating was off because neither of us was usually home at that time of day. I was so cold, but I couldn't be bothered to move so I just sat there, naked and shaking. Focusing on physical pain was a reprieve: the coldness brought with it some relief. Eventually the suds evaporated and I was bone dry. I sat like that for hours, completely still, trying to stop or freeze myself out of existence, vaguely aware of the hum of the radio in the background. Until I heard an elderly woman being interviewed about whether she received enough support from her local council.

Presenter: *'Is it true that you haven't had a bath in over* three years?'

Mrs Gladwell: *'Well, yes, that is true but only because my poor carers have so many people to get through that they don't have time to bathe me, so a shower must suffice. But I'm kept clean and they do the best they can with the very little time and resources they have. I'm very grateful for that. And in any case, I'm not concerned about having a bath! It would be nice but it's certainly not the worst thing about being old. Ha!.'*

Presented: *'What is it that concerns you most about the level of care you receive from your local council, Mrs Gladwell?'*

Mrs Gladwell: *'The honest answer to that is company. I can't remember the last time I shared a meal with someone. My carers come and make me something to eat but they're too busy cleaning and sorting my medicine to sit and eat with me. I haven't shared a meal with someone in years. That's the thing I miss most. I suppose if I'm honest I'm a bit lonely.'*

Her voice was spent and sunny, and she said this without a sprinkling of self-pity. There was warm water on my face, and I realised I was crying again. This time not for myself, but for the woman who just wanted to sit and have some dinner with a friend. It was such a simple ask. Who wants to eat spag bol on their own? No good is going to come from a Chinese for one. And why the hell would you go to the trouble of making a single portion of fish pie? I wept. There I was feeling sorry for myself because you'd decided to bugger off but there were people out there who were actually *really* lonely. Not just sitting self-indulgently blubbering in a bathtub listening to Kate Bush. I was pathetic. I got up and dug to the bottom of my drawer, where I pulled out my favourite pair of soft thick pyjamas and got under the covers with my laptop. I went straight to the AgeUK website, where I registered for a befriending scheme in our local borough. One phone call, two meetings, and a very boring day-long training course on the hottest day of the year with Amika and her team, and here I was. Constance and I had been paired for two reasons: our postcodes and our love of literature. We had found each other in this world because she needed someone, and I desperately needed to be needed. And as I'd grown to know Constance, I'd become incredibly fond of her. I'd started to really care about her and in doing so, was forced to consider caring about myself.

'I'm sorry we missed each other last week, Constance, but I'm not at all busy with work so I won't need to miss another week for a really long time.'

'Well, don't you ever prioritise me over your work. That's a lot more important. You call and let me down anytime. I don't mind! You know this,' she says, with a pointed finger.

'Did you enjoy the book I lent you?' I ask.

'Which book's that?' She squints at me, frustrated she can't recall.

'*All My Friends are Superheroes* by—'

'Oh, yes!' Her eyes light up, 'Andrew Kaufman. I know! It was beautiful. What would I do without you and your beautiful books, Mathilda?' She smiles so openly at me. 'I so enjoyed all of the different superpowers he describes his characters having, how some of them are magical and others are basic human traits. It reminds you that we all have our own superpower.'

'Yes, we just don't think of them like that, as powers, I mean.'

Perhaps your superpower was to put me in a trance so utter I sidestepped memories too painful to remember.

'What's your superpower?' she asks, her hands cupped

together, resting on grey checked trousers. She's wearing the lavender jumper I gave her. I'd picked it up at a charity shop but had never worn it. One of the scheme's rules is that you're not allowed to give presents to anyone you befriend, but it'd been a cold winter.

'Do you mean a real trait I have and consider a power, or a fantasy superpower?'

'Both.' She raises her eyebrows, enthused by the challenge she's offered.

I look at the thick, rough stitches where the arms of the fluffy jumper meet the shoulder, realising that she's cut it up and re-sewn it together so that it fits better. I marvel at her resourcefulness.

'Well, if I could have any superpower it would be the ability to just look at a book and have read it. In that one look, I'd take in all its knowledge and feel every single emotion the author wanted to provoke in me. I'd live the story and afterwards I would remember it and carry it with me.'

'Oooh, that's a good one,' she says, with a mischievous smile. 'And what about your real-life superpower?'

Making light of the utter tragic mess that is my life.

'That's a harder one,' I say. 'I'd need to give it more thought.'

'Oh, come on, don't be dull,' she grumbles.

'Okay, put on the spot I'd have to say it's my ability to make sad things funny. Or at least to give it a good go.'

'I'd say that's true.' She nods.

'What would be your superpower?'

'Time travel, of course. To be in control of time would be the greatest power for me. To go back and relive the best parts of my life, to really savour the precious moments with those special people. And also to be able to speed time up at less pleasant times. To fast forward the end when it's less exciting.' She smiles, gazing at the floor.

'Would you speed up this chapter of your life?'

'Yes.' She looks at me all blue-eyed and glazed.

'Well, that's offensive. I trek all the way over here with your tropical goods and get absolutely soaked, only to be told I'm in the fast-forward section. Charming! Next time you can get your own milk and pineapples, okay? I'm not bloody doing it. And why do you need so many anyway? Honestly, I don't know what you do with them.'

She laughs. I make my way into the tiny kitchenette that's attached to her living room and start to unpack the groceries. I see it's been a while since the bin has been taken out. She mumbles something from the other room.

'What's that?' I say, poking my head around the door.

'I've left the money on the side next to the kettle.'

'Yep, I know. Thank you.' I go to walk back into the kitchen, but before I do, I stop and swing my head back around the door so that I can see her face.

'What's your real superpower, Constance?'

'Ah,' she says. 'You'll have to figure that one out for yourself.'

'You're unbelievable.'

'Oh, stop your moaning!'

'Well, come and put the kettle on while I take your bins out. I'm gasping! I could use some warming up. Make an effort, please. I don't come here for the benefit of my health.'

But the truth was, I did.

Women's Circle: Shame

Georgia stops moving then to signal that she's finished, and we all look to Ivy, who bears the weight of our silent stares.

'Fuck. I guess it's my turn. Well, shit. I thought I'd have time to think of something to say, but you're a lot more interesting than I gave you credit for.' She grins facetiously.

There's something performative and controlled about Ivy. It's glaringly obvious now I've watched Georgia bare her soul. Girlishness and indifference are oxymoronic, but that is her way.

'So where to start with it all, really . . .' She tails off and I watch her push her tongue against the back of her teeth as she lifts her head to the ceiling, sighing loudly.

Another long pause.

It's awkward because none of us knows Ivy well. I feel a bit pained at being unable to step in and make a cheap joke. I look at Ekua, who leans back on the rug with her hands behind her, indicating that we need to be patient. We sit in silence for a while and I'm anxious. Are toilet breaks allowed? As I muster the confidence to interject this ceremony with my human need to pee, Ivy starts to speak.

'I'm not going to tell you about all the weird and wonderful undeserving men I've been fucking in a bid to ease my bitter self-loathing. Much like Ekua's ugly crying, you don't need to have lived with me long to work that one out, do you?' She gives Ekua a playful wink. Georgia had had a word with Ivy about the different guys she kept bringing home, telling her she didn't appreciate seeing the same red kimono encasing a different man in her kitchen three times a week. Ekua would raise an eyebrow at me over a crumpet as Georgia made a painful attempt at polite small-talk with the poor lamb.

'I went to see Slavoj Žižek speak at the Royal Festival Hall last week and he talked a lot about shame. He said shame was interesting because it was the place where the self and society cross. I know what you think of me, silly, narcissistic Ivy, a model embracing all the clichés. Taking drugs and shagging men more interested in being seen with me than really *seeing* me,' She stares me in the eye until I turn away.

'Don't look so guilty. We're all superior in what we think are the right choices. We all judge. Each of us has judged everyone in this room in order to feel better about ourselves. It's only natural. But you don't always have to question everything, you know.' She looks accusingly at Georgia. 'We are the generation of women who have been told that we can have it all, raised in a time of Thatcher and Disney – well, what did we expect would happen? I don't remember ever asking for it *all* – do you? I don't want it *all*, I just want my portion.'

She picks up her wine glass from the table and takes a slow, controlled sip before placing it back on its coaster. Ekua does the exact same thing, showcasing some kind of allegiance to her.

'My father slept with his receptionist throughout my parents' entire marriage. I imagine sometimes she challenged him on it. My mother, I mean. I have this fantasy that she marches into his office and makes a whole fucking show, humiliating him in front of everyone. But that's ridiculous because she would never have had the guts. Much better to hide at home behind us.'

There's a chill in the air and I pull my arms around me.

'He'd still be sleeping with her now if she hadn't died.'

The atmosphere shifts.

'Breast cancer, stage three. They caught it too late and we all pretended like he wasn't grieving for her. As if his level of anguish was a rational response for a man who'd employed a woman for twenty-odd years.'

I stare through the empty bottle of wine on the table.

'And I was glad,' she says, through gritted teeth. 'I felt so goddamn glad.' She starts to laugh manically, and a few tears roll down her cheeks. 'I was actually happy that she was going to die.'

She picks up her glass from the table again and downs the remaining white wine. This is the first time I've seen Ivy cry and she breathes out the burn of the alcohol. Ekua downs her wine in symbiosis. I look around for a clock, trying to determine how long we've been sitting here. Ivy lets it out: she sits and cries. Intermittently there's laughter until she gives a wail that's sharp and shocking to endure. We all sit and watch, until her sobs eventually slow into deep breathing. She makes no attempt to wipe away the thick black mascara running down her face.

'It's so much of a cliché I feel embarrassed, but's that's what clichés are built on, right? Populist truth. My mother got plucked, waxed and facialed, preened, steamed and blow-dried, while he picked his nose in public and bored us all to death with right-wing politics. She went to Pilates five times a week while he lightly jogged up and down a pitch every Sunday with his paunch in his hands. What a fucking liberty.' Her rage shimmers. 'I'd go into her bedroom sometimes in the mornings and she'd be there in perfect matching lace underwear. What did he do for her? She starved herself into the perfect body, and for what?' Ivy shouts.

She looks directly at me and I'm grateful I don't have to

answer her question. I can't offer any reassuring coos. I think back to the bathroom and the smell of vomit. I focus on her breathing, which is getting faster.

'Do you know what keeps us so contained, ladies? Do you? It's shame. Your shame and my shame. It keeps us tempered. We perform a role – a lot of us learn that performance from our mothers.' I sense Ekua flinch. 'Well, fuck that.' Her delicate skinny arm raises her empty glass into the air.

I wonder if our wholesome women's circle is turning sour or whether it's exactly as it should be. It's hard to tell if we're doing it right. Is alcoholic dead dad better than lying, cheating dad? But you lied to me too, didn't you? I feel you in the room now, your presence overt and dense as if you've been summoned. Invited. I look down at my hands and start to feel a little sick. When I look up, I feel your gaze on me. Watching. And now the eyes of Ivy, Ekua and Georgia. It's my turn.

Ghost

I'm tired after another long day at Hatch. I meet some friends at a pub afterwards but only stay for one, then head home. Cars rush past in the darkness, coursing through puddles so black they look like oil. The smog is blocking out the stars. I pull my oversized coat around me and start walking towards Hackney Central Overground. I think about the curse and how ridiculous it is. I think about the darkness, this black cloud. The only light seems to come from the traffic lights: red, amber, green, amber, red. A broad-shouldered man cycles past me and muddy water splashes against my shins. He's wearing a red helmet and it's like I've seen a ghost.

I feel that way every time a man of your vague weight and colouring cycles past me in a red helmet. You seem endless and haunting. You aren't just in blood-red helmets, you are in the man sitting across from me at a café making his friends belly-laugh with ease. You are in the shy guy with an awkward half-smile waiting to get served at a bar. I drive past you at night in an Uber and you're arm in arm with a blonde stranger, rushing through the streets in the rain. You are in the window of the pub I walk past, drinking a pint of Guinness. You haunt me from the art in the picture frames at our favourite brunch spot. You lurk in the milky nape of men with curly hair, pushing it back off their faces. It seems you are woven into the fabric of me. You are in the water of the scalding-hot bath I deliberately force myself into. You are in forehead kisses and hard fucks. You are in the mouth of my six-year-old nephew, who asks why you're not there at Christmas. You're in crunchy peanut butter, *Game of Thrones* and Hackney; in fact, you're the entire borough. If I were a sponge cake you would be in every grain of sugar, marching through me. You are sweet and salt, pain and perpetuity – inextricably linked to any semblance of hope. Another car flashes past, more water splashes up my legs.

When I get back to the house that evening it's quiet. Ekua is out with Lucia again and Georgia is with Henry. Lord only knows where Ivy is. All the lights are off except for the one in the hallway, and I stare up the dark staircase reluctantly. I am tentative. Is it you? I can't shake your presence and my chest tightens. It feels heavy. I go upstairs to my bedroom and flick off my dungarees. Without washing my face or brushing my teeth, I whip on my nightie over my vest top and leap into bed.

I look around the room for you. I'm being ridiculous. But perhaps you miss me, perhaps you don't feel we got the chance to say goodbye. I turn the light out and pull the covers over my head, and after a few moments of silence, like clockwork, it starts.

The first Father's Day after your death, a friend got a photograph of us printed, a thoughtful attempt to frame some comfort. I rested the rectangular frame on top of a set of drawers. But the damn thing haunts me. The lamp had started to shake at night, its black iron stem clanging in the darkness. It starts again this evening: your photo bangs gently against it, a desperation or urge that's starting to feel like a threat. I feel like I'm choking on my heart. It throbs, meaty in my throat. *Ding. Ding. Ding.* I close my eyes, willing myself to ignore it. Think of something else, Mathilda. I'm sweaty – suddenly and all over. My hair sticks to the back of my neck, my nightie sticky on my legs. I need a glass of water. I push my hand out from underneath the duvet, flick on the bedside light and emerge, cautiously. There is no one here.

I go downstairs and sneak softly along the hallway into the kitchen to get myself a glass of water. I don't turn on the light, not wanting to disturb the presence I feel in the air. The single-glazed windowpanes shake and wind whistles under the kitchen door. It's dark outside and the light from the hallway shines behind me – someone could be looking in. I pour myself some water. When I turn off the tap the silence is deafening, but for a flatline humming in my ear. Something moves in the living room. I sense it. I reach for the knife block and pull out one of Ekua's sharp butcher's knives. But it's silly to be afraid of you, isn't it? Fuck. I hear it again. Something taps against the window; I shoot around to face the garden. I think it was just the wind.

My mind plays another trick on me. So close as if you're breathing down my neck. Hot, whisky-soiled breath. Can you smell that? Someone is here. My mind resists but I force myself to make slow steps back down the hallway towards the front door. Eyes bulging with adrenalin, teeth clenched. There it is again. There's a rustle, some gentle movement. I force one more step down the hallway towards the noise, my red socks sliding reluctantly across the laminate flooring. My whole body is rock solid, a block of ice hardened by the tension. I close my eyes for a moment and freeze in front of the open doorway. My senses focus on sounds. Nothing. It's silent again.

'Hello?' I say. 'Is someone there? Ivy, is that you?' The knife shakes in my hands. No response, but for another rustle. It's menacing. 'Hello? Who's there?'

I resist the urge to open the front door and run down the street. I swing my body into the living room, flicking on the light, the knife held out in front of me.

There, in the corner of the room in a small black crate, is what can only be described as a hairless dog-slash-rat, fidgeting in a taco-shaped, sheepskin-lined bed.

'For fuck's sake. You almost gave me a bloody heart attack!' I flop down on the sofa with relief, knife still in hand. 'Who the hell are you?'

The creature looks up at me, asking the same question. It starts to jump around in the crate, moaning and whining, pleading with me to be released. I set the knife on the coffee-table and open the crate door. It shoots out, running around my ankles and jumping up at me. I stare bemused and a little disturbed, gently pretending to pet it while making as little physical contact as possible with its bare skin. Still alarmed, I pluck up the courage to pick the little rat up and pop it back in its crate. It tilts its head and watches me as I exit the room, turning the light off behind me. How strange. One of the girls must be looking after it for somebody. Most likely one of Ivy's weird friends who thinks ugly dogs are *en vogue*. I text her and ask if she's aware of the intruder.

I post the knife back into the slit in the block, pick up my water and make my way upstairs. I go through each of the girls' bedrooms to put myself at ease. I open Ivy's closed door first and turn the light on. It's sparse but for a few slim books on the nightstand, a metal rail full of expensive clothes and an unmade bed. A half-eaten Pot Noodle rests on an old chest at the end of the bed. 'Gross.' My voice echoes back at me in the empty room. I close the door behind me and go to Ekua's.

The entire back wall is covered with large metal mood boards besieged with press cuttings and reviews from her shows. There are photographs of her and Teddy, of us and other friends, and an explosion of magazine cut-outs, postcards from the shows of artists she admires, or conversely hates, strange receipts and tickets, photographs she's taken of sculptures in parks, and reams of illustrations denoting quotes on the subject of love. I smile to myself, taking her in. Confident no one is in here, I walk up a few more steps to Georgia's room. The door is already open.

The bed is made, and everything is immaculate. Expensive perfumes line her dressing-table and each makeup brush and lipstick is housed in its rightful place. It's noticeable, the pride and detail applied to her room compared to the rest of the house. I turn around and look at the huge, king-size bed in the centre. I drop to my knees and look under it. Nothing. My eyes shoot straight to the skirting board on the other side of the space. Those who have the luxury of not having to store anything under their bed must sleep more soundly. My entire life is crammed underneath mine. Next to the bed are two matching glass bedside tables that reflect my own black outline back at me; on top of one a glass milk bottle is stuffed with deep purple lavender from Columbia Road flower market. It's pungent and the room has a charming floral scent. Happy no one is lurking under her bed, I tuck myself back into my own and pull the duvet over my head, wondering if it's all in my mind as I listen to your photograph clang against the lamp.

Ding. Ding. Ding.

Jeremy

The next morning, I don't bother reading my WhatsApp messages and instead lose almost an hour to what feels like a ten-minute flick through Instagram. And not to general thumb scrolling, informed by algorithms. No. I forgo being present in my own existence to observe the life of Olivia Wool, specifically. Nothing new. Olivia still has the perfect life. At least, that's what her feed would have you believe. Although our careers started on the same internship, I stepped off the corporate ladder while she stepped up it and is a now a highly sought-after creative director at a top agency. She was excited when she found out we were dating and made suggestions about dinners and double dates that never came to fruition. On top of this, Olivia has a gorgeous husband, who has a touch of the John Travolta about him, a beautiful baby girl, with whom she sometimes wears matching clothing (striped Petit Bateau, Gucci logo T-shirts and the like), and a five-bedroom house in Hackney with a stoop, and ivy dressing the front door. She's made it. I trace back her every move, inch by inch, square image by square image, trying to decide if her face looked different before she had her baby. It did.

I scroll so far back that the face of her beautiful husband vanishes off the scene entirely. You're peppered in this chapter of her life, in photographs of festivals and at large group gatherings. Your image sets off heart palpitations. Three and half years and she's seemed to turn it all around. Who's thinner *after* they've had a baby? I wonder what made her dye her hair from ash blonde to brunette – maybe she felt more like a mummy with a chocolate bob. I observe the expensive pieces she recycles each season, like her woollen YSL coat, her Vivienne Westwood pirate boots and her Celine tote. I notice the trend-led pieces that make it on to several squares only over the course of one spring. Olivia Wool has the kind of style that money can't buy. I wonder if she's happy with her life or if she sometimes feels disappointed with the reality of having a baby, the one who stole her weightless smile – the kind of smile that belonged to a girl who hadn't yet made up her mind. It's strange, I wanted to be just like her and now I'm completely terrified of her: I like her most recent post, a selfie of her on a beach with a pink and lilac sky.

I put my phone down and let out a long sigh that brings my mind out of social media and back into my body. That's enough Olivia Wool for one day, eh? I look around my room. Not so much flat lays of peonies harmonising with a rose-gold MacBook and a manicured hand lightly pincering a porcelain teacup as yesterday's mugs, a few crumb-kissed plates and a crusty half-empty bowl of porridge – the reality of working from home isn't as pretty as Olivia would make it look. I pull myself out of bed. I really need to have a shower. It's gone 9 a.m. already.

I glance up at you across the room. You look different in the framed photograph. A man not yet afraid of himself. Someone without a shadow on their life. Last night it was as if you were in my bedroom with me, lurching over me in the darkness, completely still – no breath expanding your lungs, no human tremor in your hands, no blinking. Your presence so palpable I could smell you, could hear you shaking against the stem of the lamp. Scared of what might happen if you leave me.

'I'm fine,' I say, into the empty room. So that if you are there you might accept this plea.

Then, suddenly, I hear a scream. It's Ekua. Shit, not another mouse! I leap out of bed and run downstairs to find her and Georgia in the kitchen making gleeful screeches and *ahhing* sounds.

'Ahhhh!' Ekua screeches again. 'What will you call him?'

'What will you call who?' I ask, skidding into the kitchen. And from behind one of the wooden chairs the bald, ugly dog from last night steps out. It has long hair on its head, but absolutely none whatsoever on its body, with the exception of some hairy white slippers more apt for a nineties seductress.

'What the hell is that? It scared the shit out of me last night.'

'Didn't you get my text? IT'S MY PUPPY.' Georgia beams.

'Your puppy?' I look across at her.

'MY PUPPY.' Georgia beams at me again.

'Her puppy,' Ekua joins in, to help the concept hit home.

'But why? When? And you left him at home last night.' The confusion's not easing.

'I've been thinking about it for some time now. Henry and I had tickets to this restaurant opening. I only left him for a few hours. It's good for them to get settled in their crate anyhow.'

'News to me. Is he all right? He looks a bit troubled.'

She tuts at me. 'He's not troubled, he's perfect. Aren't you?' She coos at the thing.

His tongue hangs out loosely, like he has brain damage and has forgotten what to do with it.

'What kind of puppy is it?' I ask, eyeing its concrete-grey, spotted skin.

'It's a Chinese Crested Dog.'

'A Chinese what now?'

'Crested Dog.' Georgia frowns like I've lost the plot, which at this stage feels a little hypocritical.

'Is that a pure breed?'

'Yes.' She's curt.

'Oh, yeah. He's lovely.' I play along.

She walks across the kitchen and picks him up, handing him to me.

'Oh, I can feel his skin,' I say, taking him in my hands, gawping at Ekua for help.

'Yes. They're a hairless breed.'

'Is that so?' I hold him at a distance from me, my arms out straight as if I were about to mimic driving a bus. His legs dangle in mid-air. 'Yeah, I think there was one of these in *Edward Scissorhands*. Or was it *Labyrinth* maybe?' I give Ekua the side-eye to check that we're on the same page with this puppy business. We're not.

'Isn't he adorable?' Georgia says, ignoring my insinuations.

'He certainly is.' I nod in agreement. 'What will you call him?'

'Jeremy.'

'That's actually a really good name,' I nod approvingly, before placing him back on the floor, where he proceeds to do a shit much larger than you'd imagine his tiny bowel would allow for.

Women's Circle: You

I feel you in the room now. I look at my hands and start to feel a little sick. When I look up, I feel your gaze on me. Watching me. And now the eyes of Ivy, Ekua and Georgia. It's my turn.

'I know you all think Freddie's a bit of a joke. And, in truth, he is. I know you think he's bad for me and you're right. You were right all along.'

I see Ekua nod from the corner of my eye, a subconscious reflex. Georgia offers a half-smile: welcome to the party, Mathilda. The air is thick with vulnerability and the sweet, woodsy smell of *nag champa*. Something is brimming on the surface of me, something that's tingling across my skin, like hard, crusty glitter and sticky Pritt glue. It is difficult to verbalise or understand that event, wrapped up in the physical: it was some translucent exchange or power. Some spoiling, some dirty residue that can't be constructed into letters and hung together to create meaning. This thing that evades me. It's hiding from me, like a small child who knows it's in trouble. It manifests itself in the discomfort of crusty hard glitter between my fingers, rubbing down my fleshy webs like sandpaper.

'It was . . . I mean I'm not really sure how I feel about it, but . . . It's hard to tell whether . . .' The words trip over them-selves on my tongue and get lost in the excess saliva filling my mouth. I feel sick. 'It's hard to describe, I suppose, and I'm not sure if there's really anything to say.'

Ivy looks at me and we hold one another's gaze long enough that it should feel uncomfortable, but it doesn't: there is an imparting of power, a loaning of strength she drips into me like fuel.

'I saw Freddie. It was Friday and we'd been out. Not together, we hadn't gone out together, but we'd met in a bar. Around ten p.m.' We often meet there. It's the sort of bar that offers the promise of another wave of evening when you want more from the twenty-four stripes of a day. 'He was waiting for me at the bar and he ordered my drink. I knew he was high.' I flash back to big square blocks of ice, pretty girls with long hair, spindly like spiders, scuttling in dark corners, bartenders in brown aprons mixing drinks. Sitting on bar stools, the backdrop of Alex Turner singing in harmony with the metal spoon swirling around and around in the Old Fashioneds. 'I had a drink, we did some coke, he sobered up some. We got a taxi back to the house. You weren't here.'

I look up at their faces, confirming each of them is still in the room alongside their respective absence that night.

'It was late, and no one was home. We drank some wine, did some more coke. We chatted and then we rowed. He left to get some cigarettes from the shop, took a walk. He came back, we smoked and chatted. I talked about the break-up, what happened. I got upset. Talked about how sad I was, how lonely. I didn't want to have sex. He tried but I wasn't feeling up to it. We went to bed with two cold plastic bottles of water from the fridge, one with a blue cap and one pink. Silly . . . but I remember them. We slept, for some time, I think. I woke up. It was dark still, in the early hours of the morning but still late. He was on top of me, I had no knickers on. I'm not sure where they were. He'd taken them off. I found them at the bottom of the bed the next morning. It's a strange feeling to wake up to someone inside you, isn't it? Sleep is so solitary and penetration so . . . I came around and started to move and open my eyes. He was moving back and forth, he seemed so tall, like he was really high above me. "Go back to sleep," he said. "Pretend you're asleep." I didn't move. I remember making noises, ones of receipt. I didn't say anything, just lay there. I didn't ask him to stop. I didn't say, "Stop." I think I was in shock. When he was done, we both rolled over and he went to sleep. The next day I had this feeling, but it's like a chameleon – it won't stay the same colour long enough for me to name it. The only way I can describe it is like sand. Yes, like sand. Like wet itchy sand between your fingers, when it's so uncomfortable and irritating that it feels as though it might never go away. Like you might never experience the sensation of having soft, clean hands again.'

I look up at Georgia, who is crying, and I'm confused by this. Ekua has her legs stretched out, one crossed over the other, and she is staring at her shoes, belligerent. I look at Ivy, who smiles at me, sympathetic, then unplugs me from her power source.

You. Yes, you. We've had enough of you. We will no longer tolerate you. You, who break us like we're china dolls. You, who hurt us. You, who make us afraid when we're alone with you in cabs or outnumbered by you on buses. You, who impose yourself on us. You, who fuck us without our consent. You, who push our legs back. You, who rape, pillage and maim us. You, who pin us up on billboards and in magazines to show us we're not good enough. You, who shroud us in pain and violence in porn. You, who steal our education from us. You, who tell us we cannot vote. You, who tell us we aren't women because we weren't born that way. You, who wedge us into ill-fitting boxes. You, who catcall us on the street. You, who ignore our cries of 'No!' You, who put your hands up our skirts on trains. You, who call us sluts and slags and whores. You, who tell us we cannot have abortions. You, who assume ownership over our bodies. You, who mutilate us and throw acid in our faces. You, who kidnap us and hide us away in basements. You, who traffic us and pump us full of drugs. You, who humiliate and shame. You, who create fear. You, who fail. You, who say nothing to defend us in the pub. You, who talk over us in meetings. You, who think we were asking for it. You, who believe women are equal now. You, who watched and waited until we were just drunk enough. You, who beat us to a pulp with your fast fists. You, who slowly and emotionally undo us, piece by piece. You, who think we are weak and vulnerable and defenceless. You, who are mistaken. You, whom we will bring an end to and burn down the trees of your former glory, ripping up the roots of your power as we rage against the bark, tear it down with bloodied hands and scald the earth where you planted your poison, which spawns and soaks into the fabric of our lives.

Hospital

'Come in!' I shout.

Georgia walks in with the rat in her hand. She sits on my bed, placing him on her lap, and then spreads her hands behind her, holding up the weight of her body as her legs stretch out, one foot placed over the other.

'What are you doing?'

'Nothing, I've just had a shower,' I reply.

'Fair enough,' she says. She pauses, then lets out a forced sigh, her brunette mane flowing around her, accentuating the narrowness of her waist.

'Are you all right?'

'Yeah. I just bought a puppy, Mathilda.' She looks at me like I'm mad, 'I'm great.' She lies back on the bed now, interlinking her fingers and putting them behind her head so her white elbows poke out either side of her.

'How much did the little guy set you back, then?'

'About a grand.'

'I'm surprised they weren't giving them away.' He shuffles his bald little body around on her lap. 'He won't pee on my bed, will he?'

'Well, if he did, I wouldn't blame him,' she says, widening her eyes. 'I thought you'd like him.'

'Did you?'

'I thought he'd cheer you up.' She frowns, disheartened.

I feel bad and walk over to reluctantly stroke his naked flesh. 'He's very sweet, G.'

'Do you really think so?'

'Yes,' I lie, in kindness. 'So he's definitely a Jeremy, then?'

'Yeah, it suits him, doesn't it?'

I nod approvingly.

'Would you like to come to puppy-training class with me?'

No. 'Errr, isn't that something Henry might like to do with you?'

'No, it's not. He's not *our* dog, he's *my* dog.' She strokes him. 'That's why I got him before Henry moves in.'

'Oh, okay.'

'So you'll come, then?'

'To puppy-training classes? Oh, right. Yes. If you'd like me to then of course I will.'

'What could be better than a room full of small, gorgeous puppies? It's enough to lift anyone's spirits.' Happiness reigns in her eyes.

'You didn't buy an ugly dog to lift my spirits, did you, Georgia?' My question is cosseted in concern.

'No. Absolutely not.' She shakes her head over-zealously.

'Because that would have been a mistake.'

'I didn't.'

'Big mistake,' I gesture the size with my hands.

'I didn't buy a dog to cheer you up—'

'Huge,' I interrupt.

'I wanted a dog.'

'You wanted a dog?' I'm unconvinced.

'Yes.'

'Since when?'

'Since for ever. My granny had one of these when I was a kid.'

'Granny Marge?'

'Yes.'

'A fine woman.'

'The very best of women.'

'Well that's a relief. Because if you were to have bought a dog to cheer me up, at the very least you could have treated me to one with real fur.'

She laughs. 'Shut up, he's adorable. You'll love him. You'll see.'

It's quiet between us for a few minutes and I enjoy the delicate consonance of two women sharing comfortable silence. I do up my black lace bralette and swivel it around my body, pulling each strap over my shoulders. Georgia is watching me from the bed as I roller deodorant under my arms; I wonder if her gaze is admiring or comparing.

'We need to talk about what you said in the women's circle last week.' She blurts this out as if to say it quickly, before losing the courage.

'Urgh! G.' I tilt my head back and look up to the ceiling, 'I don't want to talk about it any more. We talked it to death after the ceremony. Don't make me regret telling you.'

'Please don't say that. It's important that you told us.'

I gaze at her. My eyes feel weighty as the familiar heaviness seeps into my body, slowing even the lightest of facial expressions. 'I don't know what more to say. It's too complicated. Freddie and I had a very active sex life for a long time. And sometimes we did wake up in the middle of the night and start having sex.'

'But this time was different. You didn't consent and you weren't in the right frame of mind to have sex. You didn't want to.'

I cross my arms then, my black underwear harsh against my white skin. 'Georgia. I'm okay. I'm not going to see Freddie ever again. I've blocked him on everything. Now, please, change the conversation.'

'You look thin.' She delivers this like an accusation.

'Thanks, I guess.'

'You're being very controlled at the moment.' She kicks off her trainers and pulls herself further up the bed so she's leaning against the headboard. An assertion that she's not going anywhere until we've had this out. 'You never seem to go anywhere or see anyone.'

'Don't be so dramatic. I'm hardly a hermit,' I say, flicking my wrists at the air. 'I'm just trying to stop running away from myself. I'm trying to sit with myself and deal with what the fuck it is that's happening to me.'

She raises her voice. 'And what is happening to you, Mathilda?'

'I DON'T KNOW!' I shout across the room at her, body lurching forward, cheeks hot. We're both shocked by my outburst.

I push my face into my hands and rub my eyes firmly, breathing out. I walk over to my drawers and pull a thin red woollen polo neck over my hair. I reach for my black dungarees, which are where I left them last night, thrown over the back of my circular rattan chair. I put them on and pull the buckles over my shoulders to do them up.

I catch Georgia grinning from the corner of my eye. 'What the fuck is so fucking funny?' I turn to face her with crossed arms and a hip tilt.

She laughs. 'I'm sorry. It's not funny. I'm not laughing.'

'Well, yes, you are. That's exactly what you're doing.'

'No, I'm not.' She uses her hand to cover her smile with an uncharacteristic girlishness. 'It's just this curse business that Eden was talking about. Ekua thinks it might have something to do with the dungarees. She thinks we should burn them.'

'You're unbelievable,' I say, circling my head, then tucking my hair behind my ears.

She takes a sip from the glass of water discarded on my bedside table.

'I don't want you to forget who you are. You're a fun, vivacious person and you've got so much energy and life. I don't want you to dull yourself down, punish yourself for something that was completely out of your control. He didn't leave because you'd done something wrong, he left because he was weak. And your dad didn't die because you did something wrong either. He died because . . . well . . .' She pauses again.

'Because what? Go on, enlighten me.'

'He died because people die, Mathilda. It's shit but they do. And I know you had a difficult relationship with your dad and you feel guilty. Maybe you should go and talk to someone about that.'

I don't respond.

'I don't want that light inside you to go out,' she pleads.

'Well, I can't turn my light on just for your entertainment.'

'That's not what I'm saying.'

She puts the glass back on the nightstand. It's oak, rectangular, with Eames-inspired hairpin legs. I bought it from a design fair one year with some money you'd given me for my birthday. I realise now that I've never liked it. I start brushing my hair and sit down in front of my mirror, hoping that Georgia will gather Jeremy and leave. But she stays on the bed, sitting directly behind me, and we look at each other through the mirror. This act of observing each other makes it hard to ascertain who is watching whom.

My mind shifts to a memory where I visited you in the hospital. It had been a few weeks since I'd been, perhaps even a month, maybe longer. I was feeling guilty about that. I hadn't felt that way before the visit, but as I pulled into the hospital car park and turned off the ignition that knowing shame started seeping in, wrapping itself around each organ, artery and sinew, like the choking smoke that spreads through a burning house. Breathe. Or don't breathe – both options were lethal. I sat staring at the concrete enclave of the hospital for some time, contemplating you lying inside it, alone. I finally built up the courage to get out of the car. I went inside and spoke to a nurse to see which ward you were on, your full name feeling salty and watery in my mouth, strange to say aloud, having always called you Dad. When I finally found your ward, I spoke to another nurse, who was caring for you, and she showed me to your room. When I walked in your facial expression didn't change, you just stared at me.

'Hello, Dad, how are you doing?' It was a stupid question.

'It's lovely to see you.' I forced a smile. 'You're looking well.' Both were lies. Silence took over the room.

'How are you getting on here? It's a lot nicer than the last ward you were on, isn't it? The nurse said you've got quite the sense of humour.' Apparently you had obvious favourites and made no apologies for making that known. You were always considered and careful about whom you liked. I think you were a good judge of character. I sat down on a chair next to your bed and was scared to touch you, but I reached out and held your hand. You looked down, surprised by the skin-to-skin contact that you must have felt then only through clinical necessity: bed washes; bed turns; catheter changes.

'I hear you've been listening to the radio a lot.' I looked at an old, dark-green CD player on the table next to your bed. 'The nurse says she's been playing you the Beatles album – I bought you that for your birthday a few years ago, do you remember?'

I searched your eyes for any glimmer of recognition. It was undeterminable. Sometimes on my visits there was a sense that you knew who I was. It was fleeting and came in slow, cool waves. The nurse walked into the room then and I was grateful for the interruption.

'Hello there, handsome. We're having a bit of a slow day today, aren't we? That's okay, though. It happens sometimes, doesn't it? she said, in a warm Jamaican lilt.

I looked back at you and your face was beaming at her. A boyish smile filled with recognition and glee for this kind stranger who knew more about you then than I did.

'I'll be back in a few minutes with some food – it's apple crumble and custard today. Oooh, that's your favourite now, isn't it?' She laughed, as though you'd responded with a quick quip.

You were glowing, in the truest sense of the word: radiant. Your eyes beamed up at her and that smile was one I'd not seen before: it's wasn't self-conscious, more childlike and naive.

'Would you like to feed him yourself, lovely?' She tilted her head, her hands on her wide hips, smiling at me.

'Oh, umm . . . I, uh . . .'

You were looking at me then and I felt as though denying you time with that nurse would've been a cruelty. Or perhaps that thought masked a more selfish response: no, please don't make me do that. The nurse didn't wait for me to answer.

'Okay, I'll come back when they bring around the food trolleys. Now enough of this pouting from you, please, handsome. Your lovely daughter is here to visit. Come on, give her a smile.'

You looked back at me with a curious frown. Your daughter? She left the room and we were abandoned in the silence once more. Think of something to say.

'I'm doing well. Work is playing heavy on my mind. It's busy and a bit stressful but I'm working hard and enjoying it mostly.'

You frowned at me again, either confused by what I was saying or irritated by the small-talk being used to cover up what I wasn't. And just as you failed to look after a vulnerable little girl, she was unable or unwilling to look after you.

'Is the food good here?' Nothing.

'You always did love your food. That's something you've passed on to me.'

Was I the bad person, or were you?

'I'm sorry I haven't been to visit. It's difficult to get here from London but I will try to come again.'

I didn't know if I could.

I stood up and walked along the bottom of your bed towards the window. It was green and mountainous outside. Sometimes it's less painful to be inside something ugly than it is to be outside it, where you can see the full scope of its foulness. I rearranged some flowers. I hadn't brought anything for you. I hid my face, busying myself by lifting up a card on the window-sill. I didn't recognise the name. I set it down again, and as I turned my body away from you, facing a large mirror, I caught my reflection. Then my eyes shifted to the right and our gazes met. They held and you saw it: you saw that I didn't want to be there. We looked at each other through the mirror and there was anger in your face and I was scared of you. The anger shifted to sadness but acknowledging your pain was more than I could bear.

'Right, here it is, handsome! A beef Sunday dinner and a crumble for my favourite customer.' The nurse backed into the room with the trolley in front of her and a laugh engineered to give us a moment to compose ourselves.

You were handsome. Even then on your deathbed there was barely a blemish or wrinkle in your smooth, pale skin. Reddish brown hair offset against a strong jawline with matching stubble.

'I'll go, then,' I said.

'Oh, no, you don't have to,' the nurse quickly appealed.

'No, no, it's fine. I'll leave you to it! He loves his food. I'll leave him to enjoy it in peace.'

She nodded at me, smiling wide with closed lips.

'It was good to see you, though.' I walked over to the bed and kissed your forehead – salty.

You pushed your head back into the pillow, resisting the unwelcome affection from a stranger.

I picked up my bag. 'That's me, then. See you soon, Dad.'

And scurried out of your room and along the corridor, off your ward, down in the lift, across the grass and back into the car, where I sat and wept surrounded by green mountains where nobody could see.

Georgia is still looking at me in the mirror and I look over her head to the framed photograph: you're smiling back at me, youthful and unaffected. You remind me of a Jack Kerouac character, sort of beatnik. You're uninhibited, childless and boyish. Sitting on a stripy deckchair in the garden that's faded from the sun, wearing stonewashed jeans and a white T-shirt that's tight on your upper arms. Your ginger hair is wet with gel and slicked back. And you have this smile on your face that implies anything could happen next.

I hold her gaze in the mirror for a couple of moments and say nothing. I break eye contact to pick up my pencil and start to shade in the right eyebrow.

'It's as though you're punishing yourself. You let men hurt you repeatedly – and why? It's as if that's just the sort of behaviour you've come to expect from them. And then you look me in the face and tell me you're trying to heal.'

I don't say anything, and this stirs a new anger in her.

'He raped you.'

'Is it rape, though?'

'What do you mean?' The air fuses with her exasperation.

'Well, I didn't say no.'

'You didn't give your consent. You woke up to him having sex with you in the middle of the night, after you'd told him no earlier that evening.'

It was true: I hadn't given consent. But the word 'rape' felt so loaded. It belonged to women worse off than me, to women who experienced violence and pain, to women with bloodied thighs who were attacked by strangers in dark alleys or coerced by obnoxious bosses at work. I'd usually enjoyed having sex with Freddie, hadn't I? I knew the definition of rape. I'd read the feminist essays and partaken in the Me Too tidal wave; I'd read the cup-of-tea analogy, debated the Aziz Ansari article over dinner with friends. I'd done my homework. I knew what rape meant, but still I couldn't attach it to the situation, at least not permanently, at least not to myself.

'That's fucked up, Mathilda. I don't need to tell you that.'

Neither of us says anything. I put down the pencil and look up at her in the mirror again. I feel angry with myself when I see how sad she looks. You didn't set the highest standards when it came to men, did you?

'I think you should do this banishing bath.'

'What? I thought you agreed it was complete tosh.'

'Eden won't stop hounding me about it, and maybe she's right. You're not in a good place right now.'

I watch and as she walks past me her hand gently massages the top of my head. My hair stands on end at the loving touch of another person, a rush of affection releasing in my body.

'I'm here for you,' she says, 'whatever you need.'

You met Georgia once, but I doubt you'll remember it. It was the day after my twenty-fifth birthday, the year I bought that ugly nightstand. A few friends were coming over to my place for a meal to ease our hangovers from the night before. Georgia was in the kitchen drinking wine and watching me butcher a lasagne, pleading for a takeaway. She answered the door to our first guest.

'There's a weird man at the door asking for the birthday girl,' she said, with a puzzled expression.

A weird man? I stopped stirring the lumpy béchamel and made my way to the front door, Georgia following.

'Oh, hi, Dad!' I sensed her shrivel in embarrassment behind me at that three-letter word. You'd come to drop off a birthday card – neither of us was ever that great with dates.

Adorabile

I open my eyes. Why is it dark? My mouth is dry and tacky. How long have I been asleep? I reach for my phone somewhere under the covers. It's 17:41. Shit. My screen is awash with WhatsApp messages and missed calls, mostly work-related stuff, but I don't have the energy to face it. It can wait. I've slept the whole day. I reach across and turn on my bedside lamp, pulling the back of my hand over my eyes to shield them from the bright light. My muscles feel weak. I use both arms to slide myself up. I need to get into the shower or I'm going to be late for Constance.

I muster the energy to walk out of my bedroom and past Georgia's. There is a lamp on, but when I peer in, she's not there. Someone is cooking. I go down a few stairs and pass Ekua's door, which is half open with the light on. I go to walk in but then see a girl I don't recognise sitting on her bed.

'*Il tuo posto è adorabile, mi piace moltissimo.*'

It's Lucia. Ekua comes into view, smiling. She doesn't speak a word. She keeps saying she's going to learn. I watch her walk over to Lucia, who is tall and lean. Her navy cardigan hangs off her left arm, revealing an olive shoulder. She's pretty in the effortless way that Italian women often are. Her t-shirt cinching in at the exact right spot on her waist. Her face bare but for rouge on high cheekbones. She smiles at Ekua, who sits herself down on the bed next to her.

'*Sei adorabile. Tanto più bello di quanto tu sappia.*'

I took a few Italian classes at university. I'm a little rusty but not so much that I can't determine her musings: Ekua really was so much more beautiful than she would ever realise. She smiles back at Lucia but, uncharacteristically, doesn't say anything. I pull my towel more closely around me and veer into the scene. Lucia lifts her hand, her fingers almost entirely covered with gold sovereigns, rubies and other decorative gold bands. She places it on Ekua's face and the jewellery glints and beams against her skin. Lucia tilts her head ever so slightly and Ekua dips her chin. Their heads move in towards one another, so slowly it's as if they're not moving, as if with each blink of the eye, their faces have always been that close, their lips always about to touch. I feel their longing and the heat flushes in my cheeks. There's a shooting pain in my toes.

'OWWW! Jeremy, no! Get off!' He bites at my feet, growling, his teeth like needles. I lift my leg and he comes with it, his fangs attached to my toes, bum hovering thirty centimetres off the floor. I glance through the door – Ekua and Lucia are staring at me.

'Get the hell off!' I shout down at Jeremy, who growls at me.

'Jeremy! Come here, baby. Come to Mumma,' Georgia shouts, from the bottom of the stairs. 'It's not his fault. He can sense the curse on you.'

'Georgia, control this bloodthirsty runt!'

'Jeremy, kill!' she shouts up at us.

I hover awkwardly in front of Ekua's door, trying to shake him off without letting go of my towel. I hobble down a few stairs, Jeremy still attached, and Georgia creeps up on her hands and knees to retrieve the hairless villain from my foot.

'She's brought Lucia home?' I mouth silently.

'I KNOW!' she mouths back, raising her eyebrows and pressing her lips together in unison.

Urn

'The point of the urn is that it teases Keats out of thought. The poem is about him looking at the images on an old piece of pottery, but they coax him out of the mundanity of life, of his reality, which is fleeting and ever passing. Whereas the scenes on the urn, the images of the people that decorate it, are frozen in time,' Constance says, pulling her glasses down to the tip of her nose and studying me over them.

'Yes, I suppose,' I respond weakly.

I was finding it hard to concentrate. There was a ball of angst in my stomach, and the more I ignored it the more it tugged at my gut. Even reading with Constance wasn't easing it. We'd started our own little book club and would read certain collections at the same time so that we could discuss them together.

'The urn's beauty is a double-edged sword because on the one hand the never-ending imminence of those moments is what's so wonderful about the whole thing. The anticipation! It's devoid of melancholy because there's no end, you see. But on the other hand there's something cold and perhaps sterile about being trapped in a single moment for all of time.'

I don't respond to this and Constance continues: 'The question is, are you really feeling if the emotion and experience don't crescendo or complete themselves?' She rests the book on her lap for a moment. 'What do you think?' she asks then, more directly.

I can't shake this blasted curse from my mind. Ekua was on my case about it now too, and Eden was voice-noting me daily on the subject of spiritual bathing. Even Ivy texted me from a job in Milan:

I've been thinking about it and I think you should do it. But there is no point in you bothering if you're just going to do it for Eden and the girls, it needs to be for yourself. It doesn't matter whether or not you believe in witches and cauldrons, you should do it because of the sand stuck to your hands. Ix

The idea of the curse was divisive, but the assertion that I wasn't myself and had, for some time now, 'been laden with something dark' was disconcertingly unanimous. I wondered if this was something you also saw in me, if that was why you left. As if my inner child were made of glass, frozen in time and damned to silence. Through her, the light refracted, creating at first an enticing rainbow display, red and yellow and pink and green. But this bait inevitably drew in the wrong men, and then you saw what really lay behind the vibrant magic trick: darkness. And in the blackness, we were exposed. Sometimes it's mutual trauma that draws us to our lovers. The scars on our hearts draw out the same patterns. The way you left broke the most delicate part of me. You knocked this child down on your way out, smashing her into tiny pieces, and I sit here with her, mouth full of shards, and bloodied hands that snap, crackle and pop as they clench around the sharp edges of her pain. My pain. So what if the vase breaks?

'You're away with the fairies today!'

'Why don't you read me one of your poems instead, Constance?' I say. She was right. I was distracted.

'What's wrong with Keats? I thought you liked Keats,' she asks accusingly.

'I'm not sure I ever said that.'

'Oh, goodness gracious me. What is wrong with you today, my girl?' She takes the glasses off her nose and glides them onto the top of her head. She's wearing a teal mohair jumper. It's a hand-me-down from a friend she met at art college, and it makes me smile because it's far too bold and attention-seeking for her taste. With the green sofa, the green books pop on the shelves behind her and everything in the room seems iridescent.

'What if the vase breaks? Then these delicate images of lovers almost embracing or of melodies never heard and animals almost to the slaughter would be smashed into oblivion! That should put an end to the tension, eh?' I lift an argumentative eyebrow.

'And is that how you experience this poem, through the tension?' She leans forward slightly.

'No,' I say sternly. 'What I'm experiencing is something very goddamn unrealistic. It's romantic that the lovers are frozen in time – why? So they never start to look haggard? So we never have to see them get sick of one another, tire of each other or grow resentful of the compromise demanded in a real relationship. We don't have to see the love come to an end, which it will because all things have a beginning and an end. So smash the vase.'

'Well, it's an urn, dear.'

'Smash the urn, then!'

'Well, I didn't know Keats got you so riled up.'

'It's not Keats. It's just . . . I don't know, I have a lot on my mind, that's all.'

'Mmm . . . is that so?'

She pauses for a while, and I sit sulkily.

'Have you by chance heard of *kintsugi*?'

'That's a *kintsy-no* from me!' I marvel, with a cheeky grin.

'It's a Japanese word,' she says, tilting her head to the side and looking at the ceiling, unamused.

'Well, Keats's urn is Grecian, so I don't know where you're going with this one.'

'*Kintsugi* is the art form of repairing broken ceramics with a gold lacquer. It fills the gaps and makes what's broken central to an object's design, visible for all to see.'

'We can lacquer the lovers' lips together, then.'

'No. It's a philosophy, really, a metaphor for overcoming suffering and bringing to light not the loss itself but how it shaped an object . . . or a person. Imperfection and broken pieces can define beauty. It became what it is because it was broken. Through its repair it is defined.'

I sit for a while with that thought and Constance shuffles through the Keats collection on her lap, pretending to read other poems when, really, it's me she's reading like a book.

'Is there something on your mind, dear? Because if there is, you can talk to me about it.'

If anyone is going to help me navigate this curse, it's Constance.

'Do you believe in curses?' I ask, with a hint of desperation.

'That seems like a strange question for you to ask me.'

'So that's a no, then?' I roll my eyes and reach for the cup of tea on the table beside me.

'It's certainly not an outright no. Tell me what you mean by curses.'

'Well, it's sort of embarrassing to talk about,' I say, circling my fingers over the childlike illustration on the Joan Miró mug. She'd bought it at the retrospective we went to a couple of months ago. I notice for the first time that the inside is painted green.

'There really is no need to be embarrassed, dear. I'm a hop, skip and a jump from the grave, so even if you are, I'll be dead soon and the whole thing will go with me into the ashes.'

'I wish you wouldn't talk like that.' I frown.

She drinks from her own mug, which is white and has 'BADASS' written across it in black capital letters. I'd given it as a Christmas gift and can't fathom whether it's her favourite mug or if she only uses it when I'm here.

She points her finger at me, puts her mug down, then crosses her arms in front of her.

'Okay, fine.' I start talking again, but this time I don't make eye contact with her because it feels easier that way. I tell her about the curse, and she nods me along encouragingly and says things like 'I see' and 'Okay, dear'.

When I've finished, she looks at me through those squinting blue eyes. 'Do you think you're cursed, Mathilda?'

'Well, I've not been very lucky in love. In fact, I'd go as far as to say I've been incredibly *un*lucky.'

'And do you believe the problems in your romantic life are down to this "work", as you called it?'

'I am in part responsible, of course. And it's not just about getting dumped. There's something else. I honestly don't know what's wrong, but I know that something is. The idea of being cursed seems ridiculous, yet the idea is plaguing me. I've been using things to paper over it, but it's getting bigger and harder to manage. This feeling . . . I don't know, energy . . .'

'Now there's a better word for it.'

'What?'

'Energy. Let's drop all this curse business and think of it as that, shall we?'

'Okay.'

'That's all we're made up of,' Constance takes a deep breath. 'We're just energy. And there's good energy and bad energy, and it's something we recognise in one another. Sometimes we're drawn to a person and we can't explain why. We might feel joyful and uplifted in their presence. Or there might even be something curious and intriguing about the way a person makes us feel, something that unsettles feelings from our past.'

Ivy comes to mind.

'We might see this energy as a conduit to reconciliation. Sometimes it is. And we can also be repelled by someone's energy. We might not know why that is either. We're just uncomfortable and don't enjoy being around them. Did you know that after death a human body weighs twenty-one grams less? Some people believe that is the weight of a human soul. Others think it's down to a rise in temperature when the lungs stop receiving oxygen and cooling our blood, which results in excess sweating. Either way, energy can't be destroyed, so arguably when we die it must go somewhere.'

'Twenty-one grams seems light for the weight of an entire soul. Mine feels a lot heavier than that.'

Constance laughs.

'I know what you mean, though. It's a bit like how sometimes you don't want to go into a room, or you might not want to stand in a certain corner of your house.'

She nods at me. 'Go on . . .'

'It's just a feeling, a sixth sense that you don't feel good when

95

you're in a particular space. I've felt like there's been some weird energy in my house recently.'

'You mentioned that you cleansed it with . . . What was it again?'

'Yes.' I smile. 'With sage. Much to Georgia's distress.'

'So isn't this bath ritual the same thing? You're removing the negative energy that's built up around you. Whether that's from bad relationships or some curse.'

'Yes, I suppose you could look at it like that. You make it sound so simple.'

'I don't understand why you've made it so complicated.' She lifts her chin. 'If you have an instinct to seek something out, Mathilda, then you should. And if it means leaning on more . . . *unconventional* methods, shall we say, then that's okay, isn't it?'

I smile at her and realise the wrenching anxiety in my tummy has eased, at least for now.

'Now,' she says, pulling her glasses back onto her face and picking up the book that's still resting open on her lap, 'shall we continue with Mr John Keats and the more romantic notions he concerned himself with? Perhaps *he* will inspire more luck in your love life, eh?'

Puppy Class

Georgia, Jeremy and I wander through Dalston towards the vet's. I breathe out and the condensation floats from my mouth.

'Should you be smoking near him?' I ask wryly.

'What do you mean?'

'Well, isn't it a bit like those babies in the backs of cars, passively breathing in their parents' deadly smoke?' I smirk as she computes this.

She looks down at Jeremy, who is hooked over her forearm, tongue splaying from his juicy gums, eyes unoccupied. 'Well, I don't know. I hadn't thought about it.'

'Yeah, I think it's the same thing. He's just a baby, isn't he? Baby lungs 'n' that. Your smoking is probably killing him,' I assert.

Georgia looks horrified. 'Can dogs get cancer?'

'Yeah, of course they can.'

'Ah, shit.' She drops the half-smoked cigarette and puts it out with the ball of her foot.

'Would it be the worst thing in the world if the little guy didn't stick around for too long?' I laugh.

'All right, that's enough! Don't come with us if you feel that way.'

'I'm joking! I'm joking! Jeez.'

I'm not.

We step into the warmth of the surgery and there are already two puppies with their owners inside. One Japanese girl with slick black hair stands next to an indie guy in a band T-shirt. I don't recognise the band. She has in her arms an unfathomably small toy-something. It looks like a teddy-bear, all fluffy, brown and button-nosed.

'That's cute,' I whisper to Georgia. 'Why couldn't you get a teddy-bear like that girl? Look what a lovely life she has, how happy she is.'

'Hi, hello there, hi!' Georgia's British politeness kicks in and she starts introducing herself to the other owners and their dogs. 'Oh, what a darling, what's he called?' she says, walking over to people.

'Yuck! This place is full of couples.' I pretend to put my fingers down my throat.

Georgia pushes past, ignoring me. 'This is Jeremy!' she says, approaching two men who look just like one other.

'A Chinese Crested,' one says. He is long and lean with a pointy noise and round thick-rimmed glasses. His brother is wearing an almost identical pair.

'Great spot! You know your breeds.' Georgia grins, elated someone has recognised the little bag of bones.

'Yes, Nigel knows a lot about dogs,' the other man joins in. 'We did a lot of research before making such a big commitment, didn't we, Nigel?'

'That's so nice.' I smile. 'Unusual for two brothers to share a dog, isn't it? But what a lovely idea. It's nice to have someone to share the responsibility with, I think.' I widen my let's-like-each-other smile.

'Actually,' says Nigel, his large, bony nose protruding forth, 'this is Daniel, my husband.'

'Right,' I say, nodding.

Georgia is looking at me with horror.

'Well, that's great. Yeah . . . makes sense. They say like attracts, though, don't they?' I look around for nods of reassurance. Nothing. 'My ex-boyfriend looked just like me in fact.' I pause momentarily. 'He was an ugly bastard.'

'Mathilda!'

'And who is this little guy?' I smile down at the puppy in Nigel's arms, taking Georgia's cue to move the conversation on.

'This is Sheila.'

'Oh, course she is. She's darling. Shih Tzu, is it?' I hazard a guess.

'Italian Greyhound.'

Okay, Nige, there's no need to be smug.

'We'd better go and sign up before the class.' Georgia clasps me by the forearm. 'It was lovely to meet you both,' she says.

'Yes, and little Sheila!' I add, as she pulls me over to the counter with her.

'Why did you have to say that?'

'Say what? They look *just* like each other. It was an easy mistake. Anyone could have made it. To be honest, I was pondering whether or not they were twins. The question that they might not even be brothers never crossed my mind.'

'You knew that wasn't a Shih Tzu. Just try not to be rude or piss anyone off, can you, please?' Her hair is propped on her head in a smooth, fat bun – the cherry on top of a disappointed face.

'Yes, okay, I'm sorry. I won't say anything else.' I hold up my hands.

'AND HELLO!' a woman bellows at us from behind the counter.

'Oh, wow.' I push a finger into my ear. 'At least there's the other eardrum.'

'AND WHOOOO IS THIS?' she questions, with all the condescension she can muster.

'This is Jeremy.' Georgia beams back, an A-star pupil.

'Ah, yes, lovely. Lovely, lovely, lovely. Let's take a look at him.'

The woman is wearing a purple turban, a long purple skirt with a flower print and a purple angora jumper. It's a lot of aubergine for one person.

'It's his first time,' Georgia interrupts the woman's fusses 'We're really excited and we have quite a few questions.'

'Yeah, like does he look okay to you?' I push my arms forward, putting him under the lady's nose.

'Sorry?' the woman says.

'Well, there's nothing wrong with him, is there? Aren't you a vet?' I ask, a concerned expression on my face.

The woman folds her arms and smiles at me curiously. 'I am a qualified dog trainer with a certified commendation of excellence in dog training from Goddard's Kennel School, the oldest, most established centre for dog training. I have twelve years' experience—'

'Here are Jeremy's forms,' Georgia interjects. 'Thank you so much, err . . .' She stumbles, realising she doesn't know the woman's name.

'Miriam, dear.'

'Miriam. Well, thank you so much, Miriam. My name is Georgia, and this is my friend Mathilda and we are, as I said, really excited about tonight's class.'

'That's right, we are.' I swing my hand around Georgia. 'It's a pleasure to meet you, Miriam.' I try out the let's-like-each-other smile again and Miriam squints back at me.

After Georgia has given me another telling off and the rest of the class arrives, we're taken behind the counter to a room that backs on to the main reception. A selection of seats is set out in a circle. We all sit down, and I position myself on a stool with wheels.

'Oooh, look at me.' I whoosh back and forth. 'I feel like someone out of *Grey's Anatomy*. Scalpel?' I hold out my hand.

Georgia tells me with a glance to keep still.

'Well, you did *ask* me to come,' I say back to her stare. 'I can see it's going to be a fun and light-hearted evening.' I tut and roll my eyes.

'Welcome, welcome. Thank you all for coming along to this

evening's puppy-training class.' A man takes centre stage in the middle of the room. 'My name is Dave and I'll be running today's session but do go easy on me as it's my first time. I'll start by telling you a little bit about how I came to work with Miriam. It's a cautionary tale.'

'Ooooh,' I say, enthusiastic for story time with Dave.

'I attended one of these classes with my own puppy and I didn't take on board any of the things Miriam told me. I didn't come to the follow-up sessions and I didn't learn how to handle my dog. I wanted him to be happy and have everything he wanted. But the puppy grew into a big dog. Because that's what happens, folks.' He lets out an awkward chuckle.

Dave is in his late forties. He's wearing a grey T-shirt that's a little too big for him and tucked into some pale-blue denim jeans that are held up over his hip bones with a black belt. His salt-and-pepper hair is starting to bald, and he has a grey beard shaved close to his skin. I notice a jade beaded bracelet on his left wrist and a thumb ring on his right hand.

'In the end, he was so unmanageable, it was ruining my life. And it was my fault. I hadn't learnt how to discipline him. He jumped up at everyone, chewed everything and didn't have any training at all. So I called up Miriam one day and we had a little chat and then some one-to-one sessions to help with my situation. I hope you all learn from my mistake. We've got some lovely puppies here today and I recognise a few faces. What we'll do now is work our way around the circle and you can each introduce yourself, your dog, and say how many sessions you've attended. Sound good?'

Dave's eyes edge back and forth. He looks a little nervous. I can't help but think it didn't work out with his dog, given he didn't share a name or a happy ending. He looks at the Japanese girl holding the teddy-bear and says tentatively, 'Um . . . might you like to go first?'

She gleams back at him. 'Hello, my name is Mei and this is my Teacup Poodle, Bobbi. This is our first time and she is twelve weeks old.' She pauses. 'Oh, and this is my best friend, Sam. He's here to learn, too, as he helps take care of Bobbi sometimes.'

Sam lifts a hand to the group, offering a shy-guy wave.

I slide into Georgia's ear, 'Sam's been friend-zoned.'

Georgia turns her head away.

'He's clearly in love with Mei.'

'Sssh,' she says.

'Who wouldn't be?' I whisper. 'Look how shiny her hair is.'

'Lovely to meet you, Mei, Sam and . . . Bobbi.' Dave looks relieved that he's remembered all three names. Good job, Dave.

The next person starts introducing themselves. 'Hi, this is Frank and he's an English and French Bulldog cross. My name is Alysha and this is my boyfriend, Dave.'

'Oh, another Dave!' the trainer chirps excitedly, giving his reluctant namesake a double-wave.

'Frank is fifteen weeks old and this is our first time too.'

Frank is a sight to behold. His eyes are incredible: one is bright blue and the other a contrasting light brown. He has a marbled black and brown coat and I've never seen anyone look so unimpressed with life. His chops are pulled downwards in a caricature upside-down smile; above his eyes there are wrinkle upon wrinkle of frowns. We make our way around the circle and Georgia proudly introduces Jeremy, who wags his tail back and forth as if he's trying to hypnotise the group. I'm a little embarrassed by how weird he is but I offer him a warm smile when Georgia introduces me, wanting to show I'm as dedicated a friend as indie Sam. Jeremy responds by gazing despondently into the circle. Nigel and hubby Dan introduce Sheila, who shows off her perfect grey-and-white tuxedo markings. It's their third time to the class and Sheila sits on their laps elegantly and calmly, as smug as the men who created her. There is a very petite couple with a giant Labrador puppy, almost five times the size of Jeremy. It's their fifth session and they look like they're really struggling. They both have black bags under their eyes and the Lab struggles to escape them. It lets out high-pitched attempts at barking throughout the introductions and they try but fail to settle it. Last but not least is a family of four, which seems excessive but let's move on. The dad is wearing very tight cycling shorts and a high-vis jacket done up to his chin. He has a very posh accent and his wife sits next to him, slender and well-groomed. They look muscular and athletic. She's already raised a manicured finger twice to ask a question. Dave tells her we'll get to that later in the session. They have two little girls, around eight or nine, who have proved themselves to be a little precocious.

'Hi, my name is Kish, and this is my wife Manpreet. These are our two daughters Hana and Ami, and our dog is a Chihuahua—'

'No, she's not, she's a Chorkie!' the two girls shout.

'A Chihuahua *mixed* with a Yorkshire Terrier.' Their mother rolls her eyes comedically and smiles at the rest of the group. Kish has shown her up and he's going to hear about it later.

'Oh, that's right.' He covers his eyes with his hand. 'She's a Chorkie.' He gazes longingly at the Labrador. 'She's twelve weeks old and this is our first training class.'

The two girls giggle at their hopeless dad, stroking their little pride and joy. 'And she's called Cookie,' they say.

'Yes,' Kish looks at the floor in shame, 'and she's called Cookie.'

You can tell Kish wanted a proper dog, a real dog. Something dignified he could take out with him on his morning runs. Not Cookie, a small, fluffy lapdog unlikely ever to scale a mountain or accompany Kish on a sixteen-mile hike. I nod at him sympathetically, understanding his disappointment.

'Right, well, thank you all for introducing yourselves. And welcome, welcome,' says Dave, swinging his hips in a camp fashion and rubbing his hands together. 'Now I'm pleased to say that most of you did introduce yourself and the human – or hu*mans* – joining you for this evening's session. But some of you introduced your dogs first, which I'm afraid to say is the wrong way around.' He wags a finger at us.

Georgia's smile drops – annoyed at herself for getting the first thing wrong.

'Now remember—'

'It's humans first and dogs second!' Miriam appears from behind the wall, a giant human grape.

'Uh, yes. Thank you, Miriam.' He chuckles nervously. 'It's humans first and dogs second always because you don't want your pups to think they're more important or the head of the pack. So when someone comes over and tries to stroke your puppy, what should you do?'

Manpreet shoots her hand up.

'Yes.' Dave points, signalling her to speak.

'I read that you should always make sure when answering the front door at home that the person coming in greets you first before they acknowledge the puppy.'

'Yes, that's right,' says Dave. He starts going around the room testing the dog owners. He reaches out – reluctantly I imagine – to stroke Jeremy, and Georgia takes his hand and shakes it.

'Hello, it's lovely to meet you. I'd love you to pet my puppy but I'm trying to train him, and it would be really helpful if you could say a quick hello to me before stroking the dog.'

'Very nice!' says Dave, emphatically.

'Perfectly done.' Miriam's head pops from behind the wall again and Georgia looks pleased with herself, which I can't help but find adorable.

I watch the poor couple wrestling with their Labrador and feel sorry for them. Miriam goes over to lend a hand and Dave stops what he's doing and follows immediately.

'It's all right, Miriam, all under control here.' He forces another chuckle.

'I am just showing them how to put him in the de-stress position,' she says bossily.

'Yes, I was coming to that. Not to worry, I'll get to that now, Miriam.' Dave tries to shoo her away by lifting the puppy out of the lap of the guy holding it. Miriam walks out of the room again.

'Now we're going to try the de-stress position. This is a great hold to pop your dog in if he's getting agitated or is having a manic moment and you can't get him to calm down.'

'How long until he should sleep through the night?' the tired Labrador owner asks desperately, and off-piste.

'Uh . . .' Dave stumbles over the question and there's an anxious expression on his face. 'Uh, Miriam?'

'Yes?' She appears from behind the wall almost immediately. This is her moment.

'How long until the puppy should sleep the whole night through?' Dave asks her.

'Well, how old is she?'

'Yes, how old is she?' Dave repeats the question to the guy.

'Five months.'

'Five months,' Dave says back to Miriam, as if she's not standing less than a metre away from them.

'Well, really she should be sleeping through at four months.'

'Yes, she should really be sleeping through at four months,' parrots Dave.

The guy gives his girlfriend a concerned look.

'Here, look, you're not quite holding him right. Let me show you the de-stress position.'

'No. No, Miriam,' Dave says assertively, his tone on the cusp of exasperation. The rest of the group stops and looks at him. 'We're just getting to that. I'm just getting to it.' He smiles at her nervously.

Miriam ignores him and carries on helping the struggling couple.

'Right, everyone, look at me!' Dave says competitively, waving a hand in the air to get our attention. 'This is how you put your dog into the de-stress position. Lay your pup on its back and place it on your lap so its head is resting on your chest. Hold your hands across the tummy of the dog, so your fingers touch in the middle.'

'Hold them tight and don't let them go,' says Miriam.

'Yes. Hold them tight and don't let them wriggle out of your hold.'

'This won't hurt them,' says Miriam.

'It won't hurt them,' confirms Dave.

I look around at the group. Kish and his wife seem to be finding this as amusing as we are. Others go on in blissful ignorance. Nigel and his husband are obviously used to it, what with this being their 105th session. Dave walks over and positions himself in front of Miriam, who is still assisting with the Labrador, blocking her view of the rest of the group.

'Your dog is learning from you all the time. If he can wriggle out of this position, he will know going forward that he can perform until you set him free. You need to let your dog know from the get-go that you won't set him free from the de-stress position until he's stopped fidgeting and trying to escape.'

Frank seems to take to the position okay. Cookie is trying to bite Kish so Dave assists and shows him how to pop his hand under the dog's chin and hold its head back so it can't bite him. Sheila basically lowers herself into the position without being asked and Jeremy lies on Georgia aimlessly. She kisses the top of his head.

'Nice work, Jezza,' I say, stroking his tummy.

'Oh dear, oh dear!' says Miriam, rushing over to us.

'Oh, damn it!' shouts Georgia.

Dave rushes over to see what all the fuss is about. Jeremy has pissed all over Georgia, who is wearing a long cream cotton dress over a cream roll neck.

'I've got it,' says Dave, racing Miriam to the front reception for some wet wipes.

'It's fine. I've got them.'

'Miriam, please, let me.' They wrestle with the wipes in front of us, both pulling at them.

Georgia is standing, holding Jeremy under one arm as the wee – a shade of yellow that suggests Jeremy had a big night out – continues to trickle down her dress.

'Oh, give them here!' She snatches the wet wipes from them. 'I'll do it myself.' She hands me Jeremy and stands soaking up his warm urine as Dave and Miriam look at her in disbelief. The class is quiet, watching the commotion, all except Sheila, who has her back to us because she's above all this. And then I start to giggle. It comes from nowhere, and I feel the rest of the class's eyes on me. The giggling gets louder and turns to laughter. Then the laughter in my throat makes its way into my tummy and Georgia starts laughing with me. I laugh harder and harder, moving back and forth with Jeremy on the stool, the noise vibrating in my tummy. Georgia bends over in her sodden dress, screeching for some air as she laughs uncontrollably with me. The scene starts to blur with the tears in my eyes as we continue to shriek together. The rest of the class watch bemused.

'Come on, let's go,' she says, still laughing. 'Thank you so much. You've both been really helpful.'

I roar – I can't help myself.

'Goodbye.' She reaches for my hand, stifling a snort.

I manage to squeeze out a 'Bye!' to the wider group as we walk away, arm in arm, pissing ourselves with Jeremy all the way back down the street.

Fish and Chips

We were sitting outside the fish and chip shop, the wind noisy in my ears, and my hair blowing violently around my head. On the corner there was a shop with a blue and white striped awning, its entire front covered with large sticky liquorice allsorts in the way of colourful knickknacks and whatnots. There were blue-yellow-and-red-striped windbreakers for sale, every colour of bucket and spade, and yellow rubber dinghies hanging from the awning in small, medium and large. On the floor were rows of shiny plastic windmills – red and yellow and pink and green – twirling in the breeze. I breathed in the briny sea air, the thick salt crunching in my hair, my ears, my nose, meshing with the sound of the crying seagulls, their beaks as yellow as egg yolk.

'Are you enjoying your food?' you asked.

'Yes.' I looked down at the vinegar-soaked paper and prodded another bloated chip, its soft innards squeezing out of its golden sack. 'It's delicious, thanks.'

You nodded briefly and turned your attention to your own soiled paper. I watched you peel apart the cod, ripping the crunchy batter as you bit into the white flesh, grease wetting your lips. 'How's work?' I asked tentatively.

'Good. How's school?'

'It's great, yeah. I'm really enjoying it, actually. I'm doing pretty well,' I said confidently, looking up at you.

You nodded and tore another piece of flaky fish, your fingers shiny.

I tried again. 'Uh, in fact, I'm sort of glad you asked. My teachers think I'm going to get straight As in my A levels.'

You nodded, looking out to sea, watching the gulls dance and soar and leap and fall.

'It's a pretty big deal . . .' I said, under my breath.

The wind made up for the silence that settled between us.

'So, Dad, they think I should apply to university. I'm one of three in my year group expected to get those grades. And, well, I'd really like to go.'

'That sounds expensive. Who's going to pay for it?' You lifted your wooden fork and scooped the mushy peas into your mouth. Another scoop. And another. And then another. A spectacle of green.

'Well, there are grants I can apply for. And Nan said she's got some money saved.'

'What? A few hundred quid?' you mocked, scraping the polystyrene cup for the last remnants of peas. 'That won't go far, girl.'

I bit down on the wooden fork, rubbing my tongue across its smooth back.

'What do you intend to study exactly?'

'I'd like to do English or maybe English and French . . .'

'And what are you going to do with this piece of paper, this degree?'

'Get a job,' I said, as if you'd asked a stupid question.

You scrunched up the paper in front of you, shaking your head.

I took a deep breath, leaning back on the wooden bench that sat adjacent to the glass-fronted chippy. Folded my arms across my chest, mirroring you as I exhaled heavily. The rounded dip of our noses was identical, the slope of our wide philtrum just the same.

'I'm going to London,' I said, deliberate and assertive.

'Cheezsh! And you're confident you'll get the grades to go somewhere in London, are you?'

I nodded furiously.

'I can't pay your fees. I haven't got the money, you know that.'

I looked down into my arms, guilt *en pointe* pirouetting in my stomach. I shouldn't have asked.

'But I can give you three hundred a month, if it'll help, for food 'n' that.'

My eyes shot up at you.

'Just for three years while you're studying and then you're on your own, girlie.'

'Oh, my God, Dad!' I flip my legs over the bench and come over to you, stretching my arms. 'Thank you thank you thank you. Oh, my God, Dad. Really, thank you. You have no idea how much that will help.'

Your body tensed and you tried resting your head on mine, rhythmically patting my arm, which stretched across your chest, my hands clasped tight with relief at your shoulders.

The morning I was due to go to London you were too drunk to drive me, so a friend borrowed his dad's car and took me instead. You paid me three hundred pounds every month for three years on the exact same day and continued covering the cost of my mobile phone contract, which neither of us ever mentioned. This is the last time I remember us hugging. Our hair embroiled, the exact same colour.

Ragù

Hello, Sharon, I have just woken up and am enjoying the most glorious lie-in with Alex. Ahh! What heaven! What utter delight! What have you been doing with your weekend? Did you see Constance? How is she? Did she ask after me, ooor? I know it's against the rules of the scheme 'n' all but I really think it's time she and I met. I don't like there being a person in your life who I don't know. It feels strange. I must be enabled all-access to every corner of your life. That's the commitment you made to me when we became best friends in 1999. What else have I got to tell you? . . . We're

going to take the dog for a walk and get a coffee later and then I'm going to make a wild boar ragù because I'm a very, very good wife. *Ssh, Eden. Stop making so much noise. Alex groans in the background* Yes, Alex is thrilled about it too as you can probably hear. Alex, stop that! Unbelievable . . . I remember when she used to wake me up with oral favours and now it's elbow jabs in the ribs. Ouvre la bouche! **Alex laughing* Amazing what a decade with the same person can do to you. Anyway, what did you decide? On the banishing bath, I mean. I really think you should make a decision one way or the other and stop letting it hang over you, or rather over me. So, yeah. . . what are you thinking on that one? Let me know. I'll send you pictures of my ragù later, darling. Have a gorgeous Saturday and send me a photo of your face. I miss it dearly. Byeeeee!*
1.59mins

I send her a voicenote back.

Hello, ragù. Your Saturday sounds delightful. And I miss your face. A lot today, actually. Not having the best of days . . . just feeling a little bit blue, I suppose. I really wish you were here . . . No, actually, I wish I was there to eat your ragù and walk Bardot with you. Speaking of which, Georgia got a dog. Yep, you heard me correctly. Georgia Bailey got a dog. Well, I don't even know if you could call it that in truth, it's more in keeping with the rodent family. It's a strange little creature – sort of part dog, part pigeon. It doesn't seem like it has a lot going on upstairs . . . She calls it Jeremy. Oh, how I miss Bardot and his fluffy fawn coat. I miss Alex. I miss you. God. I'm not good, Eden . . . It's not easy to say that to you. I need to do something about it. Dad. The lamp thing. I know you say it's all in my head but it's starting to get to me. I feel like you think I'm making it up . . . Maybe I think I'm

making it up . . . And the Freddie stuff, I feel like that's unearthed something. I feel like a turkey stuffed to the brim with feelings, all sage and onion and fear. And I get this feeling on my chest. This weight of panic, it's like trepidation. And I can feel it, physically, in my body. And sometimes it just gets too much, too heavy . . . The other day, I, well . . . I had this feeling, so overwhelming and I just couldn't ride it out. Not that time. So I went upstairs into the bathroom and turned on the tap and I let the water run hot, boiling hot. And I pushed my hand under it and held it there. I just needed to not feel what I was feeling. I'm sorry, that's really heavy for a Saturday before you've even had your breakfast. Fuck.
1.46mins

I look at my screen and watch the second tick turn blue. My phone starts to ring.

Idiot

The last day I ever saw you, you were still in bed when I left, head and hair under pillows, shielding your eyes from the early-morning light as I got ready for work.

'I'll see you later, babe.'

'Hey, give me a kiss before you go,' you said.

My knees pressed into the mattress as I stretched across the bed to meet your face. We kissed.

'I love you.'

'I love you too.'

That same evening, you thought I'd be working late. I worked late a lot then. I suppose I still do. I was in such a fantastic mood, though, I decided to finish early. I walked along the pavement clutching a paper bag from our local deli, filled with all of our favourite things: cold cut meats, truffle Gorgonzola, figs, a bottle of nice wine, fried cannoli and the good olives. I was so light, all the world's cares and disturbances seemingly passing through me. Translucent in joy. We had built a small home together, spent Christmas with one another's families; you knew how much lost-pet signs affected my mood and I knew not to push you on why you were always late for everything. I'd play jazz on Sundays to wind you up and you'd tickle my feet at night to wind me down. I turned onto our street. Outside our house, a white van was parked, and our stained-glass front door was open. I walked through it, and then the secondary door to our flat. The unused keys made the familiar *clank* when I dropped them on the console, the punctuation mark for the pile of cardboard boxes in front of me in our hallway. I opened a box and inside were some of our mutual possessions – books, a lamp and the Apple TV – folded in bubble wrap, defeated.

You hadn't expected me to come home. I went into the living room, but stepped instead onto a set of our home, unfinished, incomplete. The fitted bookshelves I'd adored until that very moment, half empty. And where was our coffee-table? I continued listlessly under the archway into our kitchen, where you'd taken photographs out of frames and left them hanging on the wall. The blue ceramic bowls we'd bought in Cape Town were missing from the cupboard and the last remnants of dignity were peeling from the lining at the back of my throat.

I heard footsteps coming down the stairs. When I walked back into the hallway your face dropped.

'Mathilda.' You'd never said my name like that before, like you hadn't bought me a Kinder Egg Surprise from every garage you'd ever stopped at to get petrol.

You sat down on the incriminating box, the one housing our record player. Crouching over, you rested your dark head of curls in your hands.

'I thought you would be working late.'

The guilt in your voice winded me. 'What the hell is going on?' The shock kept my voice calm and steady.

You didn't say anything.

'Have you packed up all your stuff?'

'I have, yes.'

'Are you leaving me?'

'Yes.'

When I asked why your facial expression was pained at having no retort. When I asked if there was someone else, you lifted your head and rebuffed, 'Don't be an idiot.' Your face was flushed, filled with something much deeper, more chaotic than sadness.

'But you can't leave. That's insane. We're happy. *You* are happy. We've not even had a fight . . . I . . .' I looked around me in disbelief, then back at you, waiting for you to get off that fucking box '. . . I . . . please,' I started to cry, 'we love each other.'

You looked away. 'My heart is broken too, you know. But this is for the best.'

'You can't just say it's for the best and go. That makes no sense. You need to tell me what's happening.'

Nick appeared in the doorway then. Nick, whose birthday party we were at the first time you said I love you. Nick, whose wife had booked us on a couples' trip to Lisbon next month. Nick, who whimpered like a baby that New Year's Eve he got so drunk he wet himself and I helped him find a change of clothes and disposed of the evidence. That Nick.

'That's the last of it, buddy. I'll take these, and you can meet me in the van when you're ready.' It was only at this point that he finally dug up the courage to look at me. 'Hey, Mannings.' He swallowed, and tried for a smile, but his expression was too sad to give way to it. 'I'll see you in the car,' he said, so softly it was almost a whisper.

'Yeah, see you in the car, Nick!' I shouted after him as he left, an alien to me now. I turned back towards you. 'Have I done something to upset you? Did I do something wrong?'

'No.' You shook your head, dejected. Or was that remorse?

'But you can't just leave me.' The tears streamed down my face gaining momentum with rising panic. 'You need to tell me why.'

'I don't.' You stood up and gathered the last remaining box. 'I don't know how to do this,' you said.

And with that, you kissed my forehead and walked out, closing the door behind you. I heard the front door slam too. You had left, with Nick, in a white van which you'd rented that day to remove all of your belongings while I was still at work. Fear sank into me. I walked around our flat unsure where to put myself. I went upstairs and opened the vacant set of drawers where you'd kept your pants and socks, I stared into it. I opened your empty wardrobe, crawled in and closed the door behind me. I don't remember ever coming out.

Gone

There were some good days. Days where I found laughter and could ease myself into joy like a warm bubble bath. The fear stored in my shoulders dropped; the gritty darkness was less on the surface of things. My self-loathing would evaporate, hot steam rising to create condensation on a window where I could draw out a happier future. I tried desperately to cling to those moments. To find the threads that linked me back to the girls and kept me anchored and sane. I'd reach out in the murky water, scrabbling to grasp a strand that suddenly slipped through my fingers and into the dark waters out of sight, leaving me alone. Gone.

But what does 'gone' really mean? Gone away, gone dancing brb, gone girl, too far gone, he's gone too far, gone are the days, it's all gone. Gone. I say it so many times that the word starts to slip around in my mouth and lose meaning. We were going somewhere. But now you are gone. What frantically irked me was the permanence of this departure: are you gone for ever, or will you be coming back? To leave so suddenly and without cause somehow held the door ajar.

After my call with Eden, in which she tries to soothe me and suggests all the usual solutions, I spend the afternoon minding my own business moping around the house. When Ivy walks into the living room to find me spread-eagled face down on the pink velvet sofa, thinking about your gone-ness, I hear her sigh.

'Really, Mathilda?'

I try to say something, but it emerges as a stifled muffle into the pillow that's covering my face.

'What are your plans for the rest of the day?'

I attempt again to say something normal and sort of casual, like *Oh, I'm just gonna hang here and watch a film,* but instead all that comes out is another muffle echoing through the thick fabric of the pillow.

'Okay, get up,' Ivy demands. 'Get up.' She kicks my leg.

There's more nonsensical muffling. She grabs me by the waist and pulls my body up. I'm surprised by her strength as I swing upright.

'Enough.' She pushes me back into the sofa. 'He's not worth this. No person is worth this.'

'He was my soul-mate,' I whimper pathetically, tears gathering in the corners of my crinkling eyes.

'And what do you think a soul-mate is? Someone you run off into the sunset with. Don't be so naive. You've been watching too much Disney.'

It was true: I'd been watching *Mulan* a lot lately.

'A soul-mate isn't the person you end up with. A soul-mate is someone who is sent into your life to shake shit up. It isn't a person you want, it's a person you need – to hurt you. To help you. They're meant to leave. Being with your soul-mate forever isn't the point.' She smacks the top of my head with her palm.

'Owww!' I squawk childishly.

'You're missing the point! Now. Go upstairs and brush your hair. We're going out,' she asserts boldly, and I can see it's not up for negotiation.

Ivy waits for me at the bottom of the stairs while I brush and tie my hair back. I put on a geometric-patterned jumpsuit that's colourful and comfortable on my skin, with large clunky gold earrings and a pair of Vans. We're going to her friend's party, which she insists will be good for me. We step out into the street and the cold air hits the back of my lungs. I'm surprised to see it's still light.

Later, I'm in a large loft space surrounded by Ivy's friends, people who belong on the pages of fashion editorials and in music videos, all edgy haircuts, ink-stained bodies, oversized clothing with striking footwear. I've had too much to drink and I feel like the old Mathilda. She's funny and brazen and people seem to enjoy her. In this scenario, I'm able to make cheap, fleeting quips about my situation. And it's comforting to note how pain can transcend into something comical – meaty fodder for a party-worthy anecdote. Enveloped in the eye creases of laughter, a deep aching stored in the body can transition into something lighter, something that can be set free. You are converted into a story I'm well versed in performing. Sooner or later even the worst atrocities are used as a release valve. But one drink too many tips me over the edge back into that heaviness, and the party starts to play in black and white. In the midst of clashing champagne glasses, resealable baggies and overexposed photographs taken on a candle-lit balcony in Clerkenwell, I dare to utter the words to Ivy: 'Do you think he'll come back?'

I'm crippled with humiliation, not for asking but for being so desperate for the answer. Her answer. A sane, objective point of view; a signpost, a clarification, a vital piece of evidence for the case I'm building in my head, both for and against you.

'Do you think he'll come back?' I ask again, sitting in my chair, enjoying the cold touch of my two fingers pressed to my lips as I weakly draw on my cigarette.

Ivy stares at me over half-burnt white taper candles, dribbling down onto an antique candelabrum. 'I don't know.' She holds her gaze and adds to it a serious, concerned frown.

Gone remains inconceivably inconclusive.

Later I turn my attention to a couple on the sofa inside. Their legs are crossed and they're facing each other, laughing, fumbling for hands, imprinting vulnerability.

We were at a festival: I could smell the petrichor coming from the drying grass on a warm summer evening. We, too, were drunkenly fumbling, back to our tent, but we came across a hammock we leapt into, swinging our bodies in tandem as I sang all three parts – Eponine's, Cosette's and Marius's – of 'A Heart Full of Love' at the top of my voice. You'd never seen *Les Mis*, but you clapped along and played the role of gratified audience to my own stylised rendition.

'I think we're gonna be together for a really long time, Mathilda Mannings.' You smiled at me through the darkness, folding your arms behind your head as you lay back on your side of the hammock and continued watching me sing.

I leave the party. I stumble into a cab and when I get back to the house I'm alone. I put the kettle on to make camomile tea. I tap my hand against the kitchen counter, impatient. It's going to take more than that to calm me down. I go upstairs to the bathroom and start to run a bath, throwing my hands around the tub and drumming up foam with my fists as the hot water pours from the taps. She's always here, but sometimes she's more prominent. A small, dark, menacing girl. I'm scared to touch her. She is sitting in the corner of the bathroom on the floor, in a white cotton nightie that's patterned with pale pink rocking-horses. Her face is buried in folded arms with long thick hair that pours messily around her. I walk to the washbasin, grabbing its curvatures with my hands, and I look at me – look at her – in the mirror. She starts to cry. Compulsively. It gets louder and more violent. She's looking back at me in the mirror and I see her sad eyes; she's overcome with rage. I see less of myself in my reflection and more of the little girl incised with self-loathing. I feel the old familiar urge and look towards the bath where the razor is resting on the rim. I reach down for the pale, pearly blue razor and bring it back to the basin so that we can both see what we're doing. We're united in this one visceral desire to hurt ourselves – or to hurt one another.

I pull the razor's sharp edge across my skin, relishing the scraping friction, which is closely followed by a stinging sensation. The next time we push down harder and it cuts through the skin. There's more blood. We look at each other in the mirror: she's grateful, and me? I'm relieved. It seems like the only thing we ever agree on. I grate the razor against my skin again but this time she's just watching. No longer with me. Snot runs from my nose and I can hear myself howling. Thick tears blur my vision and the flashes of red and bumpy flesh are dreamlike. I can't tell if she thinks we've gone too far.

My loud sobs have become white noise and the collar on my jumpsuit sodden with tears. I drop to the floor clutching my arm with a bloodied towel. The tiles beneath me are cold on my face. Ivy pushes open the door, which hits my spine. She's left the party and followed me home. 'Oh, my God, Mathilda, what are you doing?' She gapes down at me in horror.

VoodooHand.com

I can't believe you. I genuinely can't believe you. I had a package arrive at Hatch today. At Hatch, Eden! Really! You sent ingredients for a banishing bath in the post to the agency I'm freelancing at! How did you think that was gonna go? There I am, cracking on with a brief, minding my own business on a fried-egg-shaped sofa, when one of the junior creatives wanders over. I see her all the time around the office, Eden! Her name is Sylvia. You'd like her. She's pretty and blonde and

gets underestimated quite a lot. Sound familiar? I warmed to her after watching her aggressively take down an account manager – she has a lot more anger inside her than there seems to be space for. I thought she could be someone I could make friends with. But guess what? She approached me cautiously today after lunch. 'Hi,' she says suspiciously. 'Oh, hi!' I reply merrily, and none the wiser. You know, just trying to appear warm and approachable as the new girl. And then she says, 'A package came for you yesterday and I'm really sorry but I accidentally opened it. I didn't realise we had someone called Mathilda working with us.' And I'm all like, 'Oh, that's okay! No worries! That's not a problem, Sylv! Don't you worry.' And what does she hand me? Oh, no! Hang on, I'll show you exactly what she handed me.
2.15mins

I take a picture of the receipt and send it through to her.

THEVOODOOHAND.COM
FOR SPELL SUPPLIES, TOOLS AND OTHER WITCHCRAFT PROVISIONS.

SPIRITUAL BATHING:
1x "Banishing Reverse and Uncross 7-Day Ritual Kit"
For clearing jinxes and crossed conditions

VAT: £4.67
Total: £39.99

I push my thumb to send another voice note.

That's right, folks! It's only a receipt for THE VOODOO HAND. COM. Urrgh! Are you fucking kidding me with this, Eden? Nobody

knows me at Hatch. And before I could even get the words 'thank you' out of my mouth, she dropped the large parcel and did what can only be described as, as . . . well, running away. I watched as her little silver brogues galloped courageously across the office and into the distance. And who can blame her, eh? Was her urgency due to her being utterly mortified on my behalf, or was she just terrified of the new freelancing, spell-casting WITCH? Both seem like tenable options, don't you think? URGH! I could murder you. I could absolutely murder you. Call me when you get this. You piglet.
59.45 seconds

Eden is recording.

Soooooo . . . that's a bit awkward. Yeaaah . . . That does sound really awkward, in fact. Now, I'm not gonna call ya 'cause you sound pretty angry. But what I am going to do for you in this moment is offer some words of support and encouragement – down the line. So, I actually think it's pretty cool that you have this witchy reputation now. Pretty mysterious, if you ask me. And people like mystery, it's interesting. Lean into it. What I've done there is give you an edge. You've been complaining about how pale, male and stale it is there and this is going to freak them out. Yeah. It's true. No more getting ogled by the man with the bun – those gawping days are over. O-V-E-R. Annnnnd also, the other thing is that . . . umm . . . well, they'll be even more afraid of you than they probably already were, so they won't want to cross you or piss you off. I think that's a really positive outcome. Don't you? See? It's all in how you look at things.
48.03 seconds

Banishing Bath

I sit on the toilet as the bathroom fills with steam around me. It's dark outside and the white seat is cold on my bottom. One of the walls is painted a deep red, which makes the space feel protective and womb-like. I take a deep breath and start reading through the instructions that are written on a purple, decorative manual.

Do you suspect someone has done magick work against you? Do you feel down and upset but you're unable to locate the reason why? Is there an overwhelming sense of negativity all around you? A banishing bath will uncross and remove any negative work that clings to you. Spiritual bathing is a very old form of cleansing and you can find references to the ritual in most cultures. It is mentioned in the Bible and the tradition of removing spiritual work by bathing is practised across the world. Inside this box, you'll find a pre-made thirteen-herb mixture, which includes hyssop, agrimony and rue; 100ml of a liquid parsley ointment; two bars of organic goat's milk soap; pure essential oil; hand-blended herbal bath salts; seven sticks of hand-dipped resin 'jinx-removing' incense; 'Van-Van' bath wash; and a blessed seven-knob black banishing candle.

Focus your mind on your intention throughout the ritual. You might meditate on your intention in silence or you may prefer to verbalise it. You may want to call on a spirit guide to assist you or you may call on your ancestors for aid. This is optional, and the most important thing is that you follow your own instincts when carrying out each of the seven baths. You should carry out all seven of the rituals in daily succession and aim to perform the

ritual at the same time each day. Once you have completed the
ritual you will have banished, reversed and uncrossed any danger,
negativity, destructive influences or spiritual work. Set your inten-
tion, follow the instructions step by step and drain any destructive
and harmful influences away.

'That simple, eh?' I ask, over the noise of the running water.
I'm acutely aware that this won't be worth trying unless I take
it seriously, so I turn off the sarcastic narration in my head by
closing my eyes for a moment, breathing in and out slowly and
deeply. The girls were elated when I arrived home with a box
of potions and they were even more ecstatic at the comedy value
of Eden having posted them to Hatch. I'm grateful they aren't
in this evening, though. Ekua and Ivy are at the pub, and Georgia
has gone to her yoga class. I'm very aware of being on my own
in the house. I could sense a pin drop or the sound if someone
were to make the smallest movement in one of the rooms downstairs, the whole house is reverberating at my pace and beat:
any disruption would be noted. I read through the instructions
in the manual more carefully until I feel confident with what
I'm meant to be doing.

The bathroom is filled with steam now and I breathe out my
embarrassment from yesterday's scene. I notice there's a draught
coming from the window behind me, but I open the top section
slightly to let some of the steam out. I look down at the wooden
pallet box between my feet. I lift the lid to reveal a sea of lilac
string paper covering each of the objects and the ingredients
that are described in the manual. It smells incredible. Inside a
black voile bag that's tied with black ribbon are the seven incense
sticks. I lift out a bright cornflower-blue bottle containing the
parsley ointment, then take the goat's milk soap bars in my

hands, bringing them to my nose to inspect their floral scent. They are beige and marbled with pastel colours – one pink and one blue. There are seven small muslin bags and the smell of the herbs inside them is overpowering. Each is tied at the top with brown string that I rub between my thumb and forefinger. The Van-Van bath wash is in a tiny essential-oil bottle with a label that has the image of a woman with a black hood over her head. It's hard to distinguish her expression. I finger the plastic cone-shaped bag of purple bath salts, and they crunch and crackle. Last, I lift out the black candle, gently rubbing my finger down its distinct ribbed notches. I count them with my forefinger again to be sure: there are seven. It's large and fat, heavy in my hands. It's the most dominant of all the objects in the box and reminds me of a gimmicky dildo.

I take some matches and ignite the tea lights in the holders that line the bathroom window, then a few larger candles that I've brought from my bedroom, and turn off the bathroom light. I stand up and take a look at my reflection in the mirror that runs from the window all the way across the back wall and above the bath. My cheeks are a little pink. I look at the curvature of my pale body, the angle of my hips and the gentle bend of my translucent breasts and darkened nipples. My stomach protrudes a little from the pasta bake I just ate – I didn't want to get hungry in the bath. I mean, who knows how long these things might take?

That feeling of trepidation dawns. My hands tremble slightly as I pull out the black voile bag and take one of the black resin incense sticks. I light it and waft its scent around the bathroom. Following the instructions carefully, I add each of the ingredients to the bath. A seventh of the purple salts, a seventh of the parsley ointment, seven drops of the Van-Van wash and, last, I gently untie the string around one of the muslin bags and pour in the herbal mixture, stirring the fragrant soup with my hand. I place the black candle at the bottom next to the silver taps, and light it, then turn off the water and step, one foot after the other, into the tub. It's the perfect temperature and I sigh in relaxation as I hold on to the sides to lower myself in.

Lying back and bending my knees, I submerge my head. Under I go. I can hear the popping and clicking of the pipes below. I open my eyes and look up through the blurred ripples at the slightly cracked corners of the ceiling. I open my mouth and let it fill, enabling the water to cleanse each orifice. It tastes florid and fragrant. I envisage the water flooding through my nose and into my ears, around my mouth and over the tops of my eyeballs, dimming a green speckled light that leaks from each aperture of my body: my belly button; the gaps under my finger nails; the clefts between my toes; each of the hidden crevices between my legs. And I will the negativity to be rubbed off, gently wiped away by the repetitive flow and movement of the waves I generate using my feet to motion my body back and forth. I sit up, taking a deep breath of air as I readjust to the dimly lit, red glow of the bathroom and its forgotten silence. The house is calm and quiet; I observe my solitude again.

I lie down, lean the back of my head against the curve of the bath behind me and close my eyes. I try to conjure the feeling of instinctive know-how described in the manual. Do I know what to do? Am I the first woman in my family to have performed such a ritual? I try to imagine their faces – the expressions of the women who have come before me. The great-great-grandmothers whose essence I've seen in my dreams, with the resilient and rebellious spirits of the great-aunts I was never destined to meet. Wrinkled, imagined faces appear in my mind, a swirl of grey-haired women with convictive gazes. A maternal strength with fire for guts stirs, and the room is swollen and hot.

'Take it away,' I whisper into the quiet. I feel a bit silly but try again. 'Please take this horrible thing away.'

The room is unresponsive, except for a deafening dripping that's coming from the tap. I silence it momentarily, wedging my big toe into the hole.

'Please,' I say again, 'remove this negative energy that is stuck to me. Uncross any work that has been done and relieve me of the weight I'm carrying. Take it away,' I whisper into the room. I repeat the action of submerging my entire body in the water, ensuring every fold of skin is wet and covered. I feel my hair floating around my ears, close my eyes and there's a greenish light matted in each strand. I run my fingers through it under the water, desperately pulling at something to come off. I surface for air and lie back against the tub again. I look down at the cuts on my arm and feel tears make their way down my hot cheeks. There is warmth coming from every corner of the room.

'Please make it go away,' I sob quietly. 'Take away any bad energy. Remove it, please.' Sadness overwhelms me and I let myself cry, until something inside me starts creeping out. Its slither is slow and painful, a dull ache. I'm not sure how long it's going to last.

I repeat this action and these phrases in a sort of meditative trance. I lose track of time and my ego – no one is watching. I am not aware of myself: my inner critic has gone quiet. Each time I enact my intention I feel a little lighter, a bit safer, calmer and cleaner. The green light is starting to dim, and I look down at my fingertips, which are white and wrinkled. I'm brought back into the room with a shiver. It's cold. The water has cooled and there's a strong breeze coming from the bathroom window. I'm not sure what time it is. My body looks like a skinned chicken, fleshy with raised goose bumps. I look at the candle and the top notch is only halfway burnt down. What now?

I run more hot water into the bath and push my shoulders under, grateful for the warmth again, enjoying the feeling of every muscle in my body softening. Everything is still and quiet as if there's more space in the bathroom. No longer packed with steam, there's room to think and to breathe. I look up to the ceiling at a large spider's web. It's hard to concentrate, hard to focus. I want to get out of the bath but instinctively feel that's the wrong thing to do. I'm seeking something, looking for guidance, but what? What is it you need, Mathilda? I try to refocus my mind and channel this inner desperation. It's quiet and I tune in to the dripping of the tap. Nothing happens. Classic. Come on, focus. I acquiesce and let myself float freely in the tub, the water rocking me gently.

I think of the moment I really fell for you, not the initial falling induced by lust, but the moment I let all of myself fall *into* you. That exact and precise instant. We were rushing to get out of the flat, late already for a christening at which you would become a godparent. I'd woken up to you, taut chest soft against my back, lips pleasing ears, a hand firmly writhing between my legs. We'd made love twice that morning. You made pancakes and we ate them, naked bodies on white linen sheets with blueberry stains and sweet sweat as you told me how many children we'd have: three girls, all redheads – just like me. Each different, you said, bringing with them new problems into the world for us to have to fix.

After that, we were running even later.

'Come on now, what are you doing up there? Let's go!'

You came into the bedroom to find me sitting at the end of our bed, my pale legs covered with coconut-scented moisturiser that was thick and gloopy.

'Ah, Jesus.' You laughed at me.

'Eden sent me this stuff.' I was breathless in my exertion. 'It's meant to be natural but it's like clay. It won't rub in!'

You dropped to your knees, took the other leg and started vigorously rubbing the stubborn cream into my skin with me. We moved together in symbiosis.

'Okay, are you ready now?'

'Ready.' I smiled.

'God, I love ya.' You put your hand behind my neck and pushed me with a kiss back into the bed. I fell.

The memory prompts something to shift in the air. Stirrings of a masculine energy, and the faces of other men come into my mind's eye. There's a disconnect. There are things that were meant to be mine having not come for me. Things that were written and destined being bleached out or misdirected. The faces of the men I've loved and lost make their way across my inner eyelids. The weight of regret is heavy and there's a feeling unspoken – a loss too wretched to look at. I will for it to be dispelled from me. I don't want this in my body. I envisage them rising off my flesh, evaporating this imprint.

'Take it away,' I whisper again, but this time I'm commanding. 'Take it away.'

I feel as if my skin is stretching open, finding a way for what's inside to drift up and out of me. It's as though something is merging into the steam above my body, a pure feeling, one of undoing. I lie with my eyes closed for some time. The water cooling again prompts me to open one eye and check the towering black candle. The first notch hasn't completely melted down. There's still some time left.

I lie calm and still. I'm waiting. I'm waiting for something, an instruction or a signal maybe. I listen to the wind blowing against the window, to the rattling. And then I feel it, a suggestive sensation at first and then a more potent urgency. An urge that won't be told to wait, something imminent and inevitable. What is it? I feel panic in my chest. I need to get out. I jump out of the water and blow out the banishing candle. I pull out the plug, grabbing my white towelling dressing-gown from the back of the bathroom door. I wrap it around my body tightly, frantically blowing out all of the other candles. I open the door and run downstairs into the living room.

Where is it? Where the hell is it? I remember hiding it when Eden helped me move in and made me throw all your things away. I'd not looked at it since. I go into the living room and start searching the bookcase vigorously, running my hands across the spines and examining the colours and the titles. It's not here. I turn and run frantically up the stairs, sprinting across the landing and into my bedroom. I drop down on my knees, skidding slightly, and the friction of the carpet against my skin burns. It's got to be here somewhere. I know I still have it. I keep running my forefinger across the flat back of every book, making my way up the shelf as quickly as I can, until, yes, I've found it! I pull out a dark-green cloth-covered book, a first edition of a Sylvia Plath poetry collection. I open it to the endpapers and there it is, on the very opening page, scrawled in black ink as fresh as the day you wrote it:

Mathilda, I'm still falling.

x

Something pangs as I relive the inflection of your voice. I need to burn it. I pull some black leggings over my damp legs and tug my black Dr Martens onto my bare feet. I grab an Aran wool cardigan from the shelf in the top of my wardrobe, and pull it over my naked skin. I run into the bathroom to find the matches, then straight downstairs into the kitchen. I don't stop as I grab some newspapers off the table and unlock the back door to the garden. It's mild outside and it's dark, but I can still make out the rounded bulbous top of the barbecue. I open its lid and start tearing the newspaper into small crunched-up balls, chaotically trying to light them with the matches.

'What are you doing?' a voice vibrates from behind me. I jump, dropping the book, spinning around to find a dark shadow framed in the doorway. It's Georgia, back from her class already.

'I need to burn this book,' I say, turning around and relighting bits of paper.

'Why? Why do you need to burn the book?' She sounds scared.

'I just need to burn it!' I scream at her, feeling the tendrils of my wet hair hit the side of my face. With matches in one hand and newspaper wedged under my left arm, I consider for a moment how unhinged I must look. But I don't care. I carry on with what I'm doing, and she disappears back into the house. I start to collect twigs from the grass around me to get the fire going. Jeremy appears at my feet as if to help. Nothing is working but I have to burn this book and I have to do it now. The panic rises in my chest. I can't breathe. I hear her again rustling behind me. I turn to her as she thrusts a box of firelighters at me.

'Here, you need these,' she says, struggling with a bag of charcoal. She sets it down and lifts the metal grid off the barbecue, which clatters, and the balls of paper fall with it to the grass. Georgia pours some charcoal into its bowl and I place the firelighters on top, which she sets alight with a lighter as I use matches to do the same. We stand then in silence, adding more firelighters and stoking the fire once it catches. We listen to it crackle in the darkness, mesmerised by the movement of the cajoling flames, so elegant, sweet-talking to us with their heat. I pick the book up from the ground and open it to take one last look at your handwriting. I place it open and face up on the fire and we watch your words melt into the orange embers, each vowel vanishing as the flesh of the book burns. The fire rages hard against its bones, the thicker green board taking longer to disintegrate and become engulfed in the high flames.

Georgia puts out her hand and takes hold of mine. We stand, rapt by the fire, breathing in the hot fumes of the future that was no longer for me.

Ashes to Ashes

'That was pretty intense last night.'

I open my eyes and Georgia and Jeremy are under the covers, facing me. She is resting her face on the palm of her hand, her other arm around Jeremy, who is a little spoon.

'What – your snoring?'

'I don't snore!' she protests.

'You do, and it's unworkable. I have no idea why Henry is in such a rush to move in with you.'

'Shut up.' She lifts the pillow from underneath me and hits me with it. 'I meant you cooking up a storm with your belongings on my barbecue like George Foreman.'

'I know what you meant.'

'Do you think someone put a curse on your relationship with him?'

'No. Is that what you think?'

'I don't know.' She gazes at me, her hair splayed across the white feathered bedding surrounding her.

'It's boiling in this bed. You're a human radiator – the heat coming off you is unbelievable! It's hotter than the actual sun.' I can feel the sweat sticky on my back. 'And I don't remember saying *he* could sleep in here.'

'Well, you did wear an Aran cardigan to bed, and he couldn't sleep on his own. He's just a baby.'

I look down and she's right. I'm still in my leggings and the woollen cardigan from last night. Afterwards we'd put the barbecue out, had a cigarette and crawled into bed with a cup of tea. I'd told Georgia all about the bath and feeling compelled to find the book.

'It's just so odd. That's the sort of thing I would have chosen in my list of things to save if the house was on fire,' I say, edging my way out.

'And now you've burned it. To a crisp.'

I laugh and walk over to the chest of drawers and you're sitting, leaning against the lamp, watching. I pull the thick, oversized cream cardigan over my head and pick up a stripy T-shirt from a pile of washing that's on the chair.

'Yes, I mean there's no coming back from that now,' I say. 'It's burnt to dust. Fried like a chicken. Ashes to ashes! And weirdly I feel great about it, lighter. I wonder what else I'll burn when I have my second banishing bath tonight.'

Georgia doesn't say anything, but her expression has changed.

'You'll be on hand to pyro-assist, won't you? Firelighters at the ready!' I laugh but she doesn't laugh with me. She just stares with this strange, blank expression as I crawl back into bed alongside her and the dog. 'Hey! What's up?'

'Mathilda, what's that on your arm?'

I look down at the angry cuts, which are red and sore but have started to scab over slightly.

'It's nothing.'

'Did you do that to yourself?' She looks at me with wide brown eyes. Adrenalin bolts through my body. I can't lie to her.

'It won't happen again.'

'I thought that had stopped. You said—'

'It won't happen again. I just had a really bad night, that's all. It was stupid.'

'Oh, darling, please. Please talk to me.'

'I am talking to you. This is me talking to you right now.' Anxiety spreads up my spine, colonising each vertebra with shame.

'It's nothing to be embarrassed about. Please don't be embarrassed. I'm so sorry you're feeling like this.' She blinks at me slowly, careful to make no sudden movements.

'It's okay, it's not like an ongoing thing. It's not going to happen again.'

'How do you know?'

'I just know. I was drunk, that's all. I was feeling really low and I went out with Ivy. I shouldn't have got so drunk, I wasn't in the right frame of mind.'

Georgia looks so sad, which induces a fluttering in my chest, making me want to cry. 'What do you think triggered it this time?'

She had accepted she couldn't relate to my pain, couldn't understand it. The question made me feel uncomfortable, I wasn't capable of putting into words the complexity of such a thing.

'Georgia, I know you're worried and I love you for that, but I need to ask you to back off, just a little.'

'You're right, I'm sorry.' She attempts to give me some breathing space, but then continues, 'it's just Eden told me about the tap, about you putting your hand under . . .'

I don't say anything.

'She's just worried about you, and she can't be here. It was the right thing for her to tell me.'

'I know. I'm not annoyed.'

It's quiet between us and I feel as though I could go back to sleep for a little while. I turn towards her and put my hand under Jeremy's warm, skinny body, skating him across the sheets, like it's an ice rink, and into my arms for a cuddle.

'I don't know how to help you,' she whispers, facing me and wrenching her knees up into the foetal position.

'It's okay, you don't have to.' I breathe in the puppy smell of Jeremy's fluffy head. 'You shouldn't have to. I'm going to look after myself, I promise. I'm sorry.'

'But you don't have to, Mathilda. You don't have to face this alone. You have us.'

I pull the duvet over our heads with my spare arm and we lie like that together for some time.

Ekua's Surprise

It's raining, naturally. This is England. I get drenched in showers on my way in to Hatch.

That morning we wrap up a small social campaign using

136

digital-first talent, and the Fitness Now team are happy with the results. We have our big campaign pitch in a few weeks, and I want to smash it, but there's still something that's not quite coming together for me. Man-bun spends most of the morning taking the piss out of me for being a witch, and to be fair he's a lot funnier than I gave him credit for, which I tell him before inviting his application to join my coven. As with a lot of men I encounter in the advertising world, he's stopped with the lecherous gaze now that he's started respecting my work. I leave him to finish the market-research section of the deck and head off for a late lunch with Ekua. I walk to the umbrella stand and try to dig one out that hasn't got a chicken for a handle. They remind me of Mary Poppins' parrot umbrella, only ill-shaped for the role, the bulbous chicken bodies too fat for me to fit my palm around.

I see his pelvis coming at me first. His long spindly legs rising and falling, almost feather light as he makes his way towards me in black pin-stripe trousers and a yellow roll neck.

'Mathilda, good day to you! Lovely day for it too.'

'Yes, hi, Edward. How are things?'

'It's Eddie,' he says, scrunching his nose to imply a small, unimportant error. 'Where are you going?'

'I'm just popping out to meet a friend. I'm feeling a little stuck with the Fitness Now pitch . . . Nothing major but there's still something missing. I have this friend. She's an artist and I want to run some images by her.'

'Oh, marvellous.' Over-enthusiasm is manic in his eyes. 'An artist friend, you say. Well, is she here, can I meet her?' Like a meerkat with bent arms, he looks around the office eagerly.

'Uh, no, she's not here. I'm actually on my way out to meet her for a late lunch.'

'Well, splendid. Splendid, Mathilda!' His voice rises. 'I haven't eaten either. I'll join you both and you can bring me up to speed on the campaign and your gender-fluid musings.' He reaches for the coat stand then, his long skeleton-like arm and bony finger prising out a long black coat.

'Err . . . well, actually, Edward—'

'Eddie.' His teeth almost chip on the passive-aggression.

'Eddie,' I say, shaking my head. 'I think it's an authority thing – feels a little disrespectful to call someone in a position of authority a shortening of their name.'

He buys it, smiling at me, enjoying this version of himself through my eyes.

'The thing is, I really don't want you to see the storyboard and the pitch until it's perfect. There will be time for amendments, of course. And I'd love your eye on it. I mean, we *need* your eye on it, Eddie.' He smiles again, soaking up the flattery like the natural sponge his yellow jumper likens him to. 'But I don't want to disappoint, and if you could just give me a bit more time . . .'

'Of course, of course. I understand completely,' he says, pulling his long arm down from the high coat stand continuously, as if it might never finish retracting.

'As I said, there's something not cementing it all at the minute. Something missing. And I just need to figure out what that is.'

'And indeed you shall. Go. You go!' He fans me away with the backs of his bony hands. 'Here, take a cluckbrella.' He hands me one with a tomato-red chicken handle, 'You can introduce me to your artist friend another time.'

'Cheers, Eddie!'

'See?' He fires finger guns at me. 'You're picking things up around here already. Who knows? We may even have a more permanent position for you.' He offers a drawn-out wink.

I smile and turn to press the button for the lift.

'Wouldn't that be clucking fantastic?' I whisper to myself.

'What's that?' Eddie asks.

'Oh, nothing – that's cracking.' I smile, and the lift door closes.

I put down the umbrella and shake off the rainwater as I walk into the café, scanning the room for Ekua. It's a bright open space with plants growing up and out of the brick interior walls. On the far-left wall some large wooden shelves are skinny and bamboo-like. On them are asparagus ferns, dipped rattan baskets, birthday cards, tapered candles and other trinkets for sale. Opposite, a shorter set of shelves sells confectionery in beautiful packaging, shimmering golds and pinks make up a Ganesha-like figure on some tea, and some beautifully boxed chilli mackerel catches my eye next to some fancy olives in white tins.

'Over here.' Ekua waves at me from the corner table nearby, with dried flowers in an old amber medicine bottle and two matcha lattes. 'I ordered for us. We haven't got long.' She smiles at me with tangerine-stained lips.

'Haven't we?' I say, walking over. I give her a hug and take in the familiar patchouli and vanilla scent. I feel myself relax; my clenched gut unfurls and the fight-or-flight mode from the tube starts to ease. 'In truth I was hoping not to have to go back to the office this afternoon. I thought that was why we were having a late lunch. What's on the menu?'

'I ordered us creamy mushrooms in a cashew sauce on toast. And I got you a side of tomatoes.'

'Thanks, that sounds good. How did it go with Lucia last night?' Ekua stayed at hers yesterday. 'I'm assuming you've started talking to one another?'

'Not yet.' She smiles into her latte, dumbstruck in a memory she'd never show me.

'Really? I thought I heard her whispering Italian sweet nothings to you in your bedroom the other day. You're really into her, aren't you?'

'It just works.' She grins. 'Besides, it doesn't count because I don't speak a word of Italian. And we're not here to talk about me.'

'Aren't we? But you're my favourite subject.'

'Well, I am an incredibly interesting person. But I've brought you here to talk about you.'

'Oh, God, really? You too?'

'No, not me too.'

'Georgia told you, didn't she?' I pull my cashmere jumper down over my wrist.

'Well . . .' She watches me hide myself.

'*Yes*. Don't lie.'

'I'd never lie to you.'

'Are you mad?'

'No, I'm not. I'm just concerned.'

'Oh, Jesus. This is starting to feel a bit like an intervention. You haven't bought a small gerbil to cheer me up, have you?'

'Ha!' she says loudly. 'Not my style, doll.'

'What is your style, then? What would you like to talk about?'

'Eden has kick-started some kinda modern-day spiritual quest. And I just want to, you know, help you along . . .' She hesitates for a moment and lets the smile drift off her face. 'I've booked you an appointment.'

'Sounds ominous. I hope it's not Reiki because Eden's already on that train and I really couldn't think of anything worse. Besides, I am *not* on a spiritual quest. How millennial.' I squirm as if there's a bad taste in my mouth. 'How extra.'

'No, it's not Reiki. It's a little less tangible than that. And, yes, you are a big fat break-up cliché. But you're also hurting, Tilda.'

'The plot thickens somewhat. Less tangible . . .' I contemplate.

'Less physical, let's say. Less of this world.'

'Oh, okay.' I perk up. 'Come on then, you've got my full attention.'

'Well, remember you told me you were seeing that canal boat advertising tarot readings when you were on your runs?'

'Oh, yeah!' I regularly ran down the canal and I'd seen the boat several times. It had a brightly hand-painted sign, with a phone number. 'It caught my eye. My aunty always used to read tarot cards. It sort of runs in our family, I guess. I've always been curious.'

'I know. So I've booked you an appointment.' She peers at me through long, black lashes.

'No way! How come?'

'I just thought, well, you mentioned it a couple of times and, like you've said, spiritual readings at times like this—'

'*At times like this,*' I parrot.

'Yes,' she asserts, 'at times like this. At times of loss, grief and confusion. I think a nudge in the right direction from your spiritual guides might be helpful.'

'Are you worried about the curse? Scared it might rub off on you? Because you needn't be. I'm doing these baths now, aren't I? And old Aunt Maya promised that would get rid of it. I've only got one left to do and then I'm basically curse-free.'

'If only it were that simple.' Ekua sighs.

'Fair enough.'

'I'm not worried about the curse. I'm worried you've given up. You think the best part of your life has happened to you. But life isn't like that. There are better things to come, happier times. I want you to believe that – you need to believe it.'

As I look at her now, I'm filled with admiration. Ekua has always had the ability to thrive in chaos. I always thought a simple way to explain the difference between her and Georgia was that when one of them ran back to the house to check they hadn't left the iron on, Georgia never had, unlike Ekua, who always almost always did. Ekua often left restaurants forgetting to pay, as if her experience of the world was a star-crossed exchange of people willing to do things for one another. She had a steadfast confidence in her life, that she was on the right path and that even when things were abundantly horrible and everything hurt, there would be something to gain from it. A lesson worth enduring.

'So . . .' she says, playing with her grandmother's chunky silver charm bracelet.

'Are you having one too?' I ask.

'No, ta. I had one recently when I were at that artists' retreat,' she says, in her low gravelly voice. 'They told me I were going to reconnect with my mam, but I don't much fancy that. Besides, I don't want to be greedy. My spirits have other shit to do.'

A waiter with tattooed sleeves comes over and pops the mushrooms on toast in front of us. 'Can I get you anything else?'

'No, that's perfect,' Ekua says, eyeing him up.

'Just the side of tomatoes, please. Oh, and some pepper,' I add.

'On their way.'

'He's fit, isn't he?' Ekua says, as he walks off.

'Is he?'

She tuts.

I hadn't noticed. But when he returns and sets the tomatoes down alongside a pepper-mill, I take note of his chiselled jawline, large green eyes and gelled slicked-back hair, like a Teddy boy's. But his handsomeness seems faded to me. As if everything has over it a glaze of grey that blocks out all colour. My eyes dart to the chilli mackerel in their beautiful packaging.

'I got you some already.' Ekua reaches down to her handbag and pulls out a white rectangular box that reads: *Filetes de cavaka em azeite virgem e piri-piri biológico*. Spiced mackerel fillets in organic virgin olive oil. Blue mackerel swim across the box under a striking typeface.

'You got me some!' I smile at her. 'This is why I love you the most. You buy me boneless fish gifts.' I tilt back in my seat. 'No one sees me like you do.'

Ekua and I aren't from the same background, but similar – the sort that leaves you short of a Latin education, a basic understanding of art history and a comfortable knowledge of Europe before the age of eighteen. We understand one another, and often meet eyes over an uncomfortable conversation with a shared understanding, a secret unknowing: No, I don't know what that's like. Our situations are not identical but there's a bridge between us that Georgia and Ivy can't even see, let alone cross.

'I know how much you love mackerel, and I wasn't sure how the tarot would go down. It was a sweetener.'

'A fishner.'

'Precisely. So, you're excited, then? For the reading?'

'I mean, yeah. I am. It's very kind of you. Thank you. I know I haven't been an easy person to be around since I moved in.'

'That's the strange thing, though. Even when you're totally awful to be around you're still one of my favourite people. It's just even better when you're happy.'

I feel bad: bad that my pain is impacting on her; bad that I'm not the best version of myself; guilty that Georgia carried the burden of my cuts to the office that morning. I haven't just hurt myself, I'm hurting those I care for most. I need to solve it, to source its roots and rip it out of me. Unable to pinpoint it. Failing at placing it. That was the storyline I told you – and myself – but the truth of it is fading on the pages.

Shelta

After lunch, Ekua and I wander along the canal together. She fills me in on her new show and how it's going. Tells me more about some of the silent dates she went on, and I listen, intrigued, fitting in my questions when she pauses. I look at the rows of beautiful canal boats and how each reveals small secrets about its captain. A clover green boat has *PEGGY'S* written across it in yellow paint, and all around the bow small wooden crates are planted with lavender and basil, giving off the most incredible scent. The next one reads FISH & CHICKS and three women with long, skinny, tanned legs are fussing about, speaking Portuguese. They look like they spend all their money on rollies, bottled beer and expensive blue cheese. I smile and one says hi. We walk a little further and come across *NAUTI-BUOY*.

'The home of someone who deserves a gentle punch in the face,' says Ekua.

I laugh.

'Right, here we are, then.'

I look to the next boat and see we've already reached our destination: *MIRIAM*. The painted tarot-reading sign is still on the side of the boat.

'That was fast.'

'Yeah, we're on time. It's three on the dot.'

I look again at *Miriam*. It reminds me of the boat from the kids' show *Rosie and Jim*. It is the most traditional boat on the canal bank and is painted red, the shade of green that grass turns when it gets wet and a pale yellow. It has circular windows with shutters decorated in a bright candy-cane pattern. A very large wooden Buddha is smiling into the boat's entrance, and in front of this is an even bigger jagged rose quartz crystal.

'That's a lotta love,' says Ekua, eyeing it up.

'What's this woman's name?'

'Shelta,' she replies.

I look down into the bow and a face on a stool stares back at me. Her eyes have bushy lashes and dark defined eyebrows that clash with her bald white head and faded sugar-pink lips. I step back and stare at the mannequin. She stares back.

'What's the barge-boat etiquette?' I say, not taking my eyes off the mannequin's.

'Don't look at me.' She shrugs. 'I don't know.'

'Well, do we just step onto her boat and knock on the front door?'

'That feels a little invasive,' she responds. 'Perhaps just tap on a side window or summit. I'm not sure.'

I grab the rope and lower myself onto the bow assertively. I knock on the door and a loud bark erupts from behind it. It shocks me and I stumble towards Ekua, who places her hands over her mouth as the boat violently bobs.

The door flies open and a pale face with a head full of raggedy grey hair throws itself out horizontally.

'I'll be with you in *two* minutes, just give me *two* minutes.' The door slams behind her.

'That's fine. Great. Thank you! Take your time, please!' My voice rises an octave with each generic phrase that follows.

'I'm going,' Ekua says.

'What? No, you're not! Stay right where you are.'

'I'm not coming in with ya.'

'What do you mean? Why not?' I pull my sleeves down over my wrists.

'Because it's private. Personal. I'm gonna go for a walk down the canal and make a few calls. I'll come back in half an hour and meet you here. We can talk about it after.'

The door flies open again, and I look down into the cavern of the boat at a deranged smile.

'Do you like dogs?' says the woman through her teeth, her lips not moving.

'Uh, yes. Sure. Why not?'

The head disappears again, and the door slams behind it. The mannequin's expression has changed – she's finding this all too amusing.

'Are we sure this is a good idea, Ekua?'

'You'll be fine. I'll be just down the canal. Call me if you need anything.' She offers a reassuring look, like she's dropping her child off at school for the first time.

It starts raining and Ekua pulls up the hood on her yellow

raincoat and neatly tucks her Afro inside. I open the umbrella, gripping the chicken to hold it over us as we stand still in the rain, listening to the moans of the dog.

'This is a mistake,' I whisper.

'Don't be so ungrateful. Here.' She tucks some cash into my coat pocket.

'*Nooo*, I'll pay for it,' I stress.

'No, I want to. It's a gift from me.'

The shutters on one of the middle windows further down the boat whip open. My shoulders jump up – I'm startled – and Ekua leaps back. The woman's head appears again.

'I'll be *one* minute, just give me *two* seconds!'

This time I catch her worn face before the candy-stripe shutters slam. She's a living, breathing Jack-in-the-box. She seems to be running up and down the boat, but I can't see what she's doing. A couple of men on bikes cycle by and a woman with a sweatband on her head jogs past us, pushing the rain out of her eyes. Is it too late to make a run for it and leave Ekua here? I'm sure her spirit guides aren't that busy.

'Okay, come in! You must be my three o'clock.' She appears standing at the front of the boat, hands clenched and resting on her hips. She disappears back inside.

'Here,' I say, handing Ekua the umbrella. 'Take this.'

'Good luck!' she says, and I watch her walk down the canal into the rain.

I take a deep breath and lower myself onto the barge.

When I step inside the heat hits my face. There's a small coal burner to my right and the floor is badly scuffed. Opposite the heater there is a very faded candy-stripe upholstered seating area. It looks dirty.

'WOOF!'

My assessment is interrupted by a deep, hearty bark. I jump, instinctively backing out of the door. In front of me, the woman is wrestling with a worn piece of rope that's wrapped around the neck of the biggest French Mastiff I've ever seen. The thing pulls towards me barking more aggressively, and Shelta laughs, using her full bodyweight to wrestle the monster back.

'He's harmless, really, just a puppy! He'll do you no harm.'

I keep backing towards the door, smiling and nodding unconvincingly.

'No, honestly. Sit down. Come in, sit down.' She ties the tan-brown beast to something in the kitchen that's out of view and it continues to bark unfavourably at me.

'Thank you.' I turn my head to assess my exit route and I can see straight down the gently winding canal.

'Close the door now. Close those doors.' She gestures at me until I do what she says.

I sit on the edge of a seat as far away from the dog as possible. The upholstery is stained.

'Oh, look at the mess! He's such a mucky pup.' She starts slapping the seat next to me, both hands flailing in a circular repetitive movement, attempting to hit away the dried-in mud that's clearly been there for weeks. Dog hair lifts like mist, and surrounds her in the glow of sunlight that's coming through the window behind her. The dog growls at me and I give it an evil look, then remember the brute could leap at my jugular at any moment. For the first time ever, I miss Jeremy. I look at the floor, in a bid to call a truce, and it shows willing by settling down with a high-pitched whine.

It's stopped raining. The boat is shorter than it looks from the outside, the section we're sitting in no more than a few metres long. On her wooden dining table an even darker wooden hand is making an indecipherable gesture. There's an empty wine glass next to it (the type that has a measurement listed on the side and looks like it's been pinched from a pub), a clear crystal ball (because stereotypes), and a yellow tin where I can only assume she keeps her amphetamines. Beads and crystals hang above each window, and a thick but not overpowering smell of patchouli reminds me of Ekua. Behind her is the kitchen. There are more empty wine glasses, but the way they're placed – with no hint of guests and intimate late-night conversations – suggests they were used singly. I can see some Nescafé coffee granules with a £2.99 yellow label wrapped around the jar and there's a quarter-pint of milk, with a blue, full-fat lid, that's turned sour. Her head appears, blocking my view of the kitchen.

'Shall we get started then?' She rubs her hands through her short untamed hair in a circular movement, while smiling at me. 'We've got no water here at the moment so I'm a bit smeggy. Sorry about that.' She uses both hands to whip any debris on her rectangular wooden table onto the floor. She then pulls up a dark-green stool that's decorated with canal folk art; I note the familiarity of the red and pink painted roses.

'I'll only charge you if we connect. I'll start the reading and after ten minutes or so if you don't feel like we've connected you can go, and you don't need to pay me anything.'

'Oh, okay,' I say, a little surprised.

'There's no point in you paying for something you don't feel is relevant to you. Nothing worse than sitting through a reading that's not for you.'

I'm grateful for this get-out-of-jail-free card. Do not pass go. Try not to get violently maimed by the dog on your way out.

You always did love psychic readings, mediums and such things. I remember a woman knocking on the door, dressed in olive crushed velvet. She spoke in a whisper that further embellished her mystery. You'd invite her in and shut me out. She came a few times after that, this lady with hair black as night. You'd talk in hushed whispers as you ushered her into our living room where the colourful picture cards were splayed out on the coffee-table. That weird expression on your face.

'Are you ready then, lovely?' She smiles at me more gently now.

'Yes, thank you.' I'm nervous and she can tell. I notice this is the first time Shelta has kept still and the atmosphere on the boat has calmed with her. The dog is laid out on the floor, asleep, and there's a faint breeze coming through the window above the table we're sitting at.

'Are you warm enough?'

'Yes.' I smile back at her.

'It's important you're comfortable. Uncross your legs and put your feet flat on the floor.'

She starts shuffling the cards, looking down at the table in concentration, and I gaze past the kitchen to where a mattress and piles of worn bedding spill out over the floor.

'I won't make a lot of eye contact during the process because I don't want to be led by your response to things. It's better if I focus on what they're trying to tell me and what they want you to know.'

'All right.' Who's they?

'Now, shuffle the cards and once you're done divide them into three piles.'

I do as she says but I haven't shuffled cards since 1996 and I feel like a bit of a twat. I clumsily place them in three piles but misjudge how many cards there are, so the final pile is much fatter than the rest.

'That's okay,' she says, at my worried face. 'Now place a pile on top of another pile.' She senses my hesitation. 'Go on, any pile.'

I do as she says. She collects the cards and pulls three from the pack, placing them on the table. One has a tower on it.

'You've been having a bit of a hard time, haven't you? But it's okay to be sad. We can't all be running around happy all of the time.'

It's a fair assumption that the majority of people coming to her for a tarot reading probably aren't jumping for joy.

She pulls four more cards that are noticeably all shades of yellow.

'Ah, career. Things look good here. You've been in a steady job, you've been working in the same place for quite a long time, but you're happy and settled there.' She stops abruptly.

Well, that's not right.

She pulls more cards and places them on the table. I notice one has a man craning over, trying to hold a load of sticks as some fall to the ground.

'Gosh, you must be exhausted,' she says. 'There's a lot going on. You're working really hard to get on with things in your life. There's a door, a door you need to see but you're not looking at it.'

Doesn't every woman everywhere feel like she's exhausted and working too hard?

'And there is a young woman, a very powerful woman in your life. Is she someone you're trying to connect with?'

She carries on and it all feels quite generic, none of it necessarily applying directly to me. My body tenses as I mentally prepare myself to tell her we've not 'connected' when she glances up at me and shakes her head, seeing I'm not into it. 'No, that's not right. Put your feet on the floor,' she says directly, closing her eyes and tilting her head back slightly.

I do as she says and uncross my legs again. She pulls two more cards: one is the devil, a beastly figure with horns, and the one that follows this is death.

She sits staring into the cards for few minutes and I bite my bottom lip as I look around the boat, unsure of what to do with myself.

'Okay. That's much better.' She repositions herself in her chair as if to start again. 'You're in a time of solace and being on your own.' She looks at me with sympathetic eyes. 'You are past the worst of it and now you're in a time of sorrow, but sorrow is a calm and healing place. It can be a comfortable place – a place of acceptance.'

I look at Shelta, but her gaze is focused on the cards in front of her.

'There is a violent, aggressive man around you – a self-destructive energy that's causing sadness. Perhaps there's another man too. I can see a traumatic sudden ending leading to sadness and acceptance. Does this make sense?'

'Yes,' I say. She still doesn't look up, mesmerised by stories playing out on the table in front of her.

'This pain was imposed on you. It wasn't your fault.' She looks at me to convey this message. 'They want you to know that it wasn't your fault. You haven't done anything wrong. These things were imposed on you, but you need to stop looking for affirmation in others and find it in yourself.'

She pauses. 'I'm going to ask you now if you feel we've connected and if we have I'll ask you to shuffle the cards again and we'll continue with the reading.'

I'm not really sure what to say at this point. Ekua will be pissed off if I leave now . . . Maybe she was beginning to touch on something. I give Shelta a polite nod. She gives me the cards and asks me to repeat the process of shuffling and dividing them into piles with my left hand, except this time she asks me to think about why I've come here today as I do it. I shuffle the cards and lay them out again. I take the pile closest to me and hand it to her. She places a card on the table facing her and puts another on top of it sideways. The card is a knight and it has the illustration of a man riding a white horse.

'There's a man but he hurt you. He doesn't want you, does he? It's caused you great pain.'

Oh, come on, Mathilda. Don't cry at a tarot reading. But the words are brutal: two tears run down my face.

'I'm sorry. I don't want to upset you.'

'No, it's fine,' I say. 'I'm okay, really.'

She pulls three more cards and places them in a vertical row to her right-hand side and scratches her head, placing her finger on one that has the image of another knight on a horse, but this one is surrounded by green ivy.

'There's another man here. One who keeps coming in and out of your life. But he'll never commit to you,' she says, as a matter of fact. 'He is not good for you. You need to enjoy being on your own. It won't be for much longer, but this is an important time for you. You've been watching someone, someone with ivy around their door – does that make sense? But you don't know if you want that or not. That doesn't matter. Now is a wonderful and healing time to be alone. But you don't really know what that is or what it looks like yet. It's like searching for an emerald on a beach when no one has ever told you that an emerald is green and shiny. You could be picking up any old pebble! You need to learn and teach yourself what that means for you. You need to stop walking against the wind and walk with it. Everything will be a lot simpler for you. Don't look at anything as being lost – change your perspective about this man who hurt you. You need to be able to look at that situation and think, thank goodness! You've been walking on rocky shores for some time now and all you'll do is keep creating rocky shores because that's how you cope. This is what you learnt in your childhood. You want love, but you can't have it yet. If you had it now, you'd make a mess of it.'

She looks at me as if it's all so obvious. As if I've been a silly little girl, loading herself up with pointless, useless pebbles instead of the blatant emeralds that are in abundance in the capital.

'We need to heal you and the effects of this. You see, people tend to go on to their next relationship to try to solve what happened in their last one, or what happened in their past. But you need something different now. You need to heal yourself, and if you do that, you're free.' She lets out a long and heavy sigh and looks happy with herself.

'This is dragging on and it's unhealthy. Don't look back, look forward. You have lovely things knocking on the door. You've got to look up and open that door. The happiness hasn't gone, it's waiting for you. But not with him. Remember to be angry. You are justified in feeling angry. The anger can come out and then it will be done with. This will all happen very quickly now. You need to sit with something first, you need to see something – however uncomfortable it will make you feel, it is needed. It's like a thunderstorm. There's a build-up of tension in the air and then the storm will come and there's chaos, but it quickly passes. After it you'll be really powerful.' Her happy expression is interrupted by a frown that comes creeping slowly onto her face.

'There is another man here. He's cutting through you with aggression and it's bleeding into your relationships, affecting them. It's all very messy, like a washing-machine. It's all mixed up. Urgh!' She makes a noise and dramatically screws up her face as she acts out her disgust as what she's seeing. 'Yuck,' she says and shakes her head.

She pulls two cards, the devil and the death card again. She places her hands on them, making a light circular movement before pushing them apart slightly. 'There is a spirit that's recently passed over. I think this is the violent man. It's very close to you. Has someone close to you recently passed?'

'My dad.'

'Right.' Her eyes widen. 'Did he hurt you?' she asks gently, looking into my eyes.

I don't answer.

'You need to relate back to your core. It's okay to be aggressive. He's stopping you moving forward. He doesn't want you to. This isn't your fault. They want you to know that you didn't bring this on. Your dad is with you and there are things that need to be said between you two. I'm not going to do it, though. I don't practise mediumship on this boat.' She looks up at me accusingly.

'Uh, no. No, that's cool, I didn't want—'

'It's too much.' She cuts me off. 'It's all too close. Whatever you needed to say to your dad, it's stuck inside you. There's this psychic constipation. You need to let it out. I can see this is affecting your relationships now – the problems there are stopping you getting what you want. But there are easier ways of going about it than this.' She lets out another dramatically loud sigh and sits back in her chair, frustrated. Her elbows resting on the arms of the chair, she frowns more deeply into the cards.

'Are you haunted by him?' she says then, looking up at me and pulling her long cardigan around her.

I don't answer that either.

'He's so close. It's all a bit black, isn't it?' She says this so tenderly. There's silence for a while. I can't seem to coerce any words into my mouth. I'm thankful for the breeze that's gently running over my face. I look out of the window and hear men's voices as a narrowboat passes the window.

'You need to cut him. You need to physically cut him.' She looks deep into my eyes. 'It works. You need to cut him before anything can be done. There needs to be no emotion between the two of you. When you leave here go and buy some ribbon for your dad, get red, black and green. Hold them together and look at him, but don't let him in. Think of him for the last time, visualise his face and then cut him. Do it in a café and leave him there: visualise, cut and leave. Do you understand?' She then says, ever so casually, 'You can also leave some of this energy here if you'd like. I don't mind, I'll get rid of it,' as if offering to put my chocolate wrapper into the bin.

'I'll do that as soon as I leave,' I say thoughtfully.

The atmosphere in the room is heavy and it seems darker inside the boat now despite the rain stopping and the sun shining brightly outside. She puts her head into her hands and her scruffy grey hair covers her features. She looks up at me then, her face resting on her hands. 'They want me to tell you that you're very brave. They want you to know that you're doing really well – and that you're very gentle.'

I nod again and close my eyes. A few more tears escape down my cheeks.

'There is a man coming. But he'll be a friend first. This next love will not be chaotic and intoxicating like the others you've had, but it will be really lovely. It's a balanced, equal love, born out of friendship. It's happy and childlike. But they want you to lighten up. Don't look at relationships as heavy and think of settling down. Lighten up, they're saying!' She smiles into the cards again, pushing her hands against the wooden table.

'There's going to be real change. Change is coming but it's good change.' She stops then. 'Is that all right?' she asks, looking up at me.

I realise that the reading has come to an end. 'Yes, that's great. Thank you so much.'

'Those are the things I see. I don't want to tell you any more because you'll forget it anyway. But you must go now and do the cut. Go and get the ribbons, do it in a café and leave them there.'

'Okay, I will. I'll do that now.'

'Was it helpful?' she asks, with an air of genuine concern.

I reach into my jacket pocket and pull out the notes. 'Yes, it was.'

She thanks me for the money and the dog starts to stir so I say thank you another four to six times before pulling myself off the boat, levering myself with the rope. The door closes behind me.

Ekua is sitting on a bench just up from Shelta's boat. I see her right away in her sunshine-yellow raincoat.

'How'd it go?' she shouts to me, as I wander over.

'Yeah, it was pretty amazing.'

She nods knowingly.

'I need to go and buy some ribbon. Red, black and green ribbon.'

'Okay,' she says, unquestioningly.

I need to cut you out.

'She said I need to do a sort of spiritual cutting, to create some distance.'

You are too close.

'Okay,' she says. 'I know somewhere nearby, this stationery shop on Lower Clapton Road. They'll have ribbon.'

It's all a bit black.

We wander down the canal and back onto the main road and I tell her some of the things that Shelta said, reliving the experience, taking it in more clearly as I recite her words to Ekua, who nods at the ground expressively. As if it all makes sense, as if none of the information is new to her. We walk down Lower

Clapton Road for some time and then she stops outside a cute little stationery shop.

'Here it is.'

When we open the door, the bell attached lets out a jolly ring. Inside a man with a long beard is waiting for us. He's wearing a white shirt with high-waisted trousers that are held up by dark-red braces.

'Good day to you!' He chuckles in time with his bell.

'Hello, I'd like to buy some ribbon, please.'

'Ah, yes, of course. What type of ribbon?' He smiles with all of his teeth.

'Red, black and green.'

'Well, let's see . . .' He gets up and walks to the back of the shop where an entire wall is dressed in every colour of ribbon you can imagine. 'Any particular shade of red you were after?'

He talks us through the various widths and helps us select a pair of scissors, packaging everything in a blue-and-white-striped paper bag. When we leave, I go into the Sainsbury's a few doors down and buy a packet of cigarettes. Ekua and I smoke one in perfect silence together. We wander to a nearby café and I try to soak up everything Shelta said. I've never been here before and I'll never want to come again. We go in and I order us two sparkling waters. Ekua helps me cut each colour ribbon and then we wrap the three around one another. She holds one end and I hold the other, so that they're taut and there's no slack.

'Now close your eyes,' she says.

I do so. I think of you. I visualise you. You try, but I don't let you come in. You try again, and I thrust you out with a fibre-optic anger that's powering through me. I can see you standing outside me and I look at your face one last time, then feel for the ribbon with the scissors. I cut. I watch you disappear. We leave the coloured strips and the scissors on the table and walk out of the café back into the wet streets, leaving you behind.

Coconut

Hello there. I'm sending you this voice note from the bath because I know how much you enjoy those. *There's a gentle splash in the background* That was just a bit of splashing to prove to you that I am where I say I am. I've had a good day. I'm definitely getting into my stride managing all those fucking bitches in court. Why are men so needy? I just want to get on with my job without being doubted and judged because I have a clitoris. *She sighs gently, her bum squeaking against the bottom of the tub* I'm going to stop saying clitoris while I'm in the bath because it's weird. I'm currently drinking from a coconut Alex just gave me, which I mocked her for at first but it's delicious. *She sucks from a straw* How are you feeling after the banishing bathing last week? Still clearer and lighter? Have you had any more urges to burn your belongings or will his book suffice? Curious, isn't it? . . . I've been thinking about it a lot. How people mindlessly carry around belongings; stuff comes with us in our lives and we don't really think about what it means, do we? Like I still have the tickets from the first gig Alex and I went to – in fact, I still have the underwear I wore the first night we slept together. Too much? Fair enough . . . You've certainly inspired me, though. I went through some of my shit this weekend and threw out the bad juju I've been lugging around various continents. And guess what I found when I was going through it all? Go, on guess! Okay, you're not answering right now so I'll just tell you. I found some old notes we wrote each other back at school in a French class – do you

*remember Madame Dubois? What an absolute cunt case she was!
God, she hated me. She hated you even more. There was no coming
back from it after that day you 'accidentally' killed her fish. You sicko.
Anyway, I digress. In the notes we're talking about Adam Butler.
Now, I know you remember him. He fingered you at my house party,
the first man to have done the honours if memory serves me right –
which it does because I'm a shit-hot advocate with a photographic
memory. And that's one image I will never get out of my head.
★There's a long pause and some more light splashing in the
background★ Do you think fingering is underrated? Because I really
do. I think maybe it needs a comeback, eh? It seems to me that
people are overly eager to get their heads stuck in, but it's like, wait a
minute. There's a lot that can be achieved with a finger or two.
Think about it. When do you ever see women getting fingered in
mainstream films? Everyone is getting head, sure, but fingering? It
never gets a look-in. ★She pauses★ Anyway, in the notes I'm
pretending I fancy Adam and you're pretending you don't. I think I
might have fancied Madame Dubois, come to think of it – I always
did have a thing for women who were horrible to me. But it seems
we came to the same conclusion in the end, eh – who needs boys?
Who needs their emotionally charged baggage? That book was
probably one of the most romantic gifts a man has ever given you,
and you burned it. ★She laughs★ You literally cast it into the fire.
You continue to amaze me. . . I suppose the things we own, carry
around with us, do hold emotional weight. They hold these feelings
for us when we can no longer commit to holding them for ourselves.
Like maybe a lot of our emotional luggage is held online now, but
that's not a physical object, so there's a protective barrier, right? He
wouldn't have engraved a first-edition book if you met him today.
Oh, no! He'd probably just send you a gif or something. But a
physical thing – that's different. That holds energy, memory. It's like*

stone tape theory, isn't it? You know! How stone can record impressions of trauma, like image on film. That book held all the shit that went down between you and him and now it's gone – into the flames. *She pauses and sighs gently* Anyway, I think this coconut is going to my head. I'm shattered. Au revoir, mon petit choufleur. Remember I love you.
3.58mins

I listen to Eden's voice note through headphones while stretching. I've just run along the canal to Constance's, through the oaky smell of the wood burners and the serene composure of the boaters waiting patiently in the locks. I love the idea of living like that, self-sustainably. There's power in being able to fend for yourself, in being off the grid and not needing anything from another person. I looked for Shelta's boat, which had been in the same spot for the past few weeks, but it wasn't there any more. She must have moved on. She didn't strike me as the type of woman who stayed in one place for too long.

I had kept some things from ex-boyfriends, and to me they weren't negative reminders. Quite the opposite. When I was studying for my finals, I had mice in my flat, not just one or two but an entire army. I'd spend twelve hours a day revising at the British Library before coming home to an infestation that eventually led me to have an emotional breakdown. I'd wake Tom, my boyfriend, first thing in the morning and ask him to go and empty the traps in the kitchen. I remember one evening crying hysterically into my Texas BBQ chicken pizza with extra jalapeños – we exclusively ate takeout, refusing to cook in the kitchen-cum-rodent-basecamp – and telling him that I couldn't live like this any more, that I was considering moving into Eden's to finish my finals. I could no longer share a home with those furry cretins. The following day he came over with a pink Emma Bridgewater bowl, lined with clothed dancing mice. 'See?' he said. 'Mice are cute and fun, and they wear little waistcoats. How can you be scared of something that wears a waistcoat? You love waistcoats.' It was true, I did. I managed to stay until my exams were over, without the distraction of an upheaval. That bowl was a kindness that shouldn't be lightly disposed of.

After my tarot reading, I took down the photograph of you and put it away somewhere where I wouldn't have to look at it. I've stopped hearing the shaking in the night. It's also fair to say I feel a lot calmer after my banishing baths. None of them was as intense as the first, but there was definitely something freeing about meditating dark matter away. I felt lighter each time, each soak unloading. Who wouldn't feel calmer after taking an hour-long bath every night, seven days in a row? Or perhaps I really had meditatively connected with my ancestor. Ekua and Georgia say my face looks different and even got up my Instagram to evidence their point: 'Look, here's you cursed, and here's you not cursed. Cursed, not cursed. See! Can you not see the difference? It's amazing!' I'm not sure I can, although I do acknowledge sadness in my eyes in photos where I'm pink-cheeked and smiling under sunsets or baking in a floral bikini alongside an azure-blue pool. But many of us play that game. I became the master of painting gold foil over the cracks after you left. Happiness can be something we construct online; it doesn't need to be real there.

I call Eden but there's no answer, so I push the microphone icon down on my phone instead:

Hello, coconut. WHERE ARE YOU FOR ME? Answer. Answer the phone to me nooooooooow. Nope. Okay, fine. You're not answering. It sounds like you had a hard day and you deserve your rest. But of course I remember Madame Dubois, and it was quite obvious to me – and to Madame DB for that matter – that you fancied her. I'm still feeling calmer after the baths, thanks. Like I say, it could be psychosomatic. Who knows? I haven't burned any other belongings, much to Georgia's relief. Honestly, Eden, that dog. She's obsessed with him. He goes everywhere with her. I've found myself warming to the little guy . . . I must confess the idea of burning more items that remind me of him is invigorating but you made me throw everything out, remember? All traces of him must go! That's what you said. A more optimistic person might subscribe to the idea that throwing away a person and all semblance of them is something you'd regret – once the awful pain of the break-up eases. For example, the little fucker convinced me to spend three hundred pounds on a toothbrush. A TOOTHBRUSH! And you're the one person I can admit that to. 'You'll use it every day,' he said. Can't put a price on healthy gums. They used to sit there next to one another, our Sonicare Diamond Cleans, and I couldn't look at the thing on the basin all sad and alone after he moved out. That's when I missed him the most, you know? In those pointless hours of the day. It wasn't at weddings, or at the funeral, or even on days when I got some good news – those days were tough, sure. I'd go to call him and then remember I couldn't . . . Anyway, the bad news is I threw it out and now I wish I hadn't. The good news is that this realisation has given me a new business idea, and we know how much you enjoy those! It's called EX-PACK and it's a storage unit that specialises in holding the belongings and objects you associate with your ex until you recover from the break-up, and a toothbrush is just a fucking toothbrush. Why should you be punished for investing hundreds of pounds in good oral hygiene? Put it in

storage and you can dig it out when you're over him and need diamond-clean teeth for a special occasion. EX-PACK could store your favourite sweatshirt, which happened to belong to him first but is now the most comfortable thing you own, or the necklace with your name that he got you for your birthday. After all, it's your name . . . Things like that. And what a glorious day it would be strolling back on down EX-PACK lane – keys swinging in hand, ready to collect all your things. And in doing so the rest of the world would know you're well and truly over it. I'd like to give you the first opportunity to invest. Speak to Alex about it, let's throw some numbers around. Some good branding and the sell-in of a happy single person on our billboards and we could be rolling in it. It's the simple ideas that take off – you always say that. Right I gotta go, I'm just popping in to see Constance. Give me a call later. Je t'aime noix de coco.
4.16mins

Voice of the Universe

When I knock, Constance answers the door right away.

'Oh, I'd almost given up on you entirely,' she says.

'I'm only ten minutes late!' I say, surprised, checking the time on my phone before wrapping my headphones around it.

'Rightio. Water and a biscuit, then?'

She goes into the kitchen and I wipe the sweat from my face and push it back into my hair, which is tied up in a high ponytail.

'I used to go running,' she says, walking back from the kitchen with a glass of lukewarm tap water and packet of shortbread biscuits in hand.

I gulp down the water and walk across to the far wall to look at a new painting she's put up. 'Constance, if you don't mind me asking, what did you do with all of your husband's things after he passed away?'

'I don't mind you asking that at all. Why should I?' She throws her hands into the air.

'Did you just keep the things of sentimental value and give away the rest?'

'It's hard to decipher what has sentimental value and what doesn't after spending that much of your life with someone. At first, everything is a piece of them – there isn't a pair of trousers that doesn't remind you of a trip you took together or of a silly thing they did. But that fades, I suppose, and you realise they're just things, things that couldn't begin to capture the magnitude of that person and all you loved about them.' Her smile is etched with melancholy.

'That makes sense.'

'I got rid of most of Cliff's things about a year after he died. I have them with me here, though.' She wraps a wrinkled palm around a fist and holds it to her chest. 'They're in my spirit and in my drawings.' She gestures at the walls adorned with her art.

I look at one of Cliff bent down on one knee, as if he's fixing something. There's another sketch of her daughter – she has a thick, heavy fringe and a mischievous look in her eye.

'Your daughter was very beautiful, Constance.'

'Thank you,' she whispers, looking at the portrait mounted in a black frame on the wall.

'I went to see a tarot reader.'

'Oh, yes, and how did that go?' she asks.

'It was good. I was surprised. I thought she was very insightful.'

Constance doesn't say anything for a moment. She nods, then reaches for a cup of tea on the table next to her. 'Are you looking for something?'

'Like what – an emerald?' I laugh.

'An emerald?' she says curiously.

'It doesn't matter. Why'd you ask?'

'Why do I ask what, dear?' She stands up from the sofa, using both hands to push her weight off.

'Why do you ask if I'm looking for something?'

'Well, that's normally when people turn to psychics and that sort of thing, isn't it? When they're looking for something.'

'I suppose I am, then, yes.'

'I hope it's not a man, dear.'

'Oh, no, it's definitely not a man.' I guffaw. 'It's quite the opposite, in fact.'

'Finding a man cannot be the aim. If it is, you're going to be incredibly disappointed with life. Whether you find him or not. They're often not what they're cracked up to be, and they also die, dear.'

'That's not the aim, Constance. It just can't be.'

'Good.'

'I think I mentioned to you when we first met that I was going through a break-up.'

'You've really been mourning that relationship, haven't you? Along with your father.'

'I suppose so,' I say, pushing my ponytail behind my shoulders.

'Sometimes the only way to stop missing someone is to miss them wholly,' she says, walking across the room.

The only way to stop wanting him was to let myself want him so badly that it almost annihilated me.

'Gulp down that pride and have the strength to love the ones you love – even if you wanted them to be not who they were so much that it destroys you.' She looks at me with her wise eyes.

'I think maybe what I'm looking for is inside me. I'm just trying to figure out how to get to it.'

She starts to bob up and down in front of me.

'What are you doing Constance?'

'You've inspired me to exercise,' she says, up and down she goes, up and down.

She's holding on to the two handles of her walker and is lightly squatting, up and down, up and down.

'Well, be careful. Don't hurt yourself.'

'Oh, I'm fine. Don't be ridiculous.' Her short white bob blows back off her face as she thrusts herself up again. 'I need to move about a bit to keep the joints in shape. So how do you intend to find this thing inside you, then?' Down she goes. 'Binoculars? Microscope? You can always borrow my magnifying glass, if you like,' she says, cackling, using the long handles to edge her frail body down to the floor. She lies back on the carpet and starts cycling her legs in the air.

'Ah, I see, exercise makes you hilarious. Good to know.' I stand up and walk into the kitchen to pour myself another glass of water.

'We come out of the womb the same way we leave this world, my girl – battered, bloodied and bruised.'

'Cheerful!' I walk back in, emptying the glass as I watch her legs rotating in circular motion.

'I don't know where your generation find the time,' she says breathlessly, 'for these personal pursuits.'

'Can you stop, please? You're going to give yourself a heart attack and you're making me dizzy.'

She drops her legs to the floor and tries to catch her breath. 'That's the problem with your generation. You don't realise that sometimes the things you have are the things you forgot you asked for.'

'That makes no sense.' I roll my eyes.

'Of course it does!' She's still on her back, gesturing with one pointed finger in the air. 'We whisper them to ourselves at night, only to wake the next day from our happy, content slumber, having forgotten. We are only brave enough to ask for it when we are at our most feral. Think now, back to your wildest moments when you were chaotic and breaking free. What did you ask for, dear? What did you whisper to the universe when no one was listening?'

'I don't know,' I say, disappointed.

'We're often not brave enough to remember the very thing we willed. But the universe, my dear, is loyal. She is unrelenting! She will forge the path we requested and drag us down it, kicking and screaming. The universe will roll her eyes in disbelief as we make a commotion. *But you asked me for this*, she'll say.' Constance's throat crackles as she impersonates the universe in a deep, low bellow. 'She'll say, *Why do you deny and writhe against the pain? A pain that will turn you into the person you begged for, a person you convinced me you wanted to be.*'

I look down at Constance, who is smiling up at me. 'You actually do a really great impression of the universe.'

'I know.' Her smile turns into something more earnest. 'Now don't just stand there, help me up!'

I reach for her arms, lifting her gently and leading her back to the sofa.

'There's an exhibition next week at the Whitechapel Gallery

that I'd like to see.' She composes herself once more. 'Would you like to come with me?'

'Yes.'

'Excellent. I feel a little tired now, dear. I think I might have a lie-down.' She slides back on the sofa and I take her slippers off. I sit on the chair opposite her until she falls asleep, then lay a blanket over her. I unravel my headphones and pop them back into my ears, getting ready for the run home. As I walk down the corridor towards the front door, she groans sleepily.

'What's that, Constance?' I return to her.

'Being the voice of the universe.'

'Being the voice of the universe . . .' I whisper back at her.

'That's my real-life superpower.' She smiles, her eyes still closed as she drifts off.

Phone Voice

I run back from Constance's to the house and I'm dripping with sweat. I go into the bathroom and turn on the shower, pulling off the wet Lycra that's sticking to my hot body. I put on some Billie Holiday. Georgia is having a date night with Henry this evening, so I offered to babysit the bag of bones. I'm going to take him for a walk around Victoria Park, then a movie at home. Maybe a cuddle if he's lucky.

I step into the hot water and feel my muscles relax. I pick up a bar of soap and start vigorously washing my body, enjoying the feeling of being clean. Then my bloody phone starts ringing. I pull the pink shower curtain back and reach for it on the basin. I don't recognise the number. It could be any number of menaces: Eddie from Hatch, an old landlord asking where the yellow teapot listed on the inventory is or, worse, a peripheral friend inviting me out for a drink before I have time to make up an excuse. Nobody calls anyone any more, except energy suppliers, credit-card loaners, oh, and mothers . . .

'Hello?' I say tentatively into the screen.

'How the damn are you?'

I recognise the voice but I can't place it. 'Um, I don't think that's the expression.'

'What do you mean?' the voice asks curiously.

'It's how the devil are you.'

'Why are you always so obtuse?'

It's Ivy.

'Whose phone are you calling me from?'

'A friend's. I lost mine at a party last night.'

Typical. That unnerving feeling starts festering in the pit of my tummy.

'You sound different on the phone. Even more terse than you are in real life. Is this your phone voice?' I ask mockingly.

'No, this isn't my phone voice,' she replies drily. 'This is just my voice.'

'It sounds like a phone voice to me.'

'I hear you've becoming quite the arsonist.' Her tone stays flat.

'Yep, well. I knew the girls wouldn't keep *that one* a secret.' I reach for a towel.

'We sort of pushed past the pain barrier of secrets in that weird women's circle, didn't we?' There's not a hint of intonation in her voice.

I sit down on the toilet seat, wondering why she's calling.

'Have you ever heard of ayahuasca?' she asks.

171

'You know I have. We've talked about it.' I eye-roll down the phone at her.

'Do you still think it's something you might want to do?'

'I haven't really thought about it for a while, if I'm honest. It's a pretty big deal.'

'Well, I'm doing it. And not "one day". Next Friday, to be specific.'

'Really? Next Friday?'

'Yes.'

'Where?'

'In Italy. Some friends of mine have a place there and a group of us are going. It's been planned for ages. A couple of them met the shaman on an ayahuasca retreat in Peru and have done multiple ceremonies with him. We've all clubbed together to fly him over to do a couple of ceremonies for the group.'

'Wow. Flying in the shaman, eh? Casual.'

'Do you want in?'

'Seriously?'

'One of my mates just got booked for a big campaign. It's insane money and he needs the work. He's got to fly out to Cape Town for the shoot and he's not going to make it back in time. There's a free space and they asked if I knew anyone.'

My heart races in my chest and I offer the receiver nothing but my silence.

'Mathilda? Are you there?'

'Yep, she's still here.'

'So, do you want in?'

'Yeah.'

'Yeah?' She sounds pleased.

'I mean, definitely! Of course I do.'

'Cool.'

'Can I ask if I'll be the only person there who isn't a model?'

'No,' she tuts, 'no one else is a model. These are my old school friends, so they have normal jobs, whatever that means. Look, I know you're struggling at the moment, so I just thought . . .' She tails off.

'I just, I don't know, Ivy. I had this tarot reading the other day and it could all be codswallop, but this woman was convince-*ing*. This doesn't feel like it's just about the break-up any more.'

Something unsaid hangs in the air between us.

'So, I'm going to add you to the email chain that has all the details. You need to book your flights and you need to stop eating meat and chilli and a whole load of other things – there's a list on the thread.'

My mind heads to my accounts. I got my first instalment from Hatch this week, which I was planning on saving for a deposit on a rented flat. Then again, it's not like I've gone anywhere or spent any money recently.

'Oh, and no sex,' she adds.

'That won't be difficult.'

'And no masturbating either.'

'That might be more challenging.'

'Yeah, it sucks. But don't fuck with the rules. This isn't just some hallucinogenic trip. You need to prepare yourself.'

'Okay.'

'You were the first person I thought of. I think this could be good for you.'

'That might be the nicest thing you've ever said to me.'

'My heart bleeds.'

I picture her playing with her fringe. 'See? You definitely said that in your phone voice. It's sort of muskier, a little more upmarket . . .'

She sighs. 'Just read the email carefully and post on the thread if you have any questions. I'll send you my flight details and we can travel together. The others are going down on the Thursday, but I have a shoot the next day and my agent will kill me if I miss it. In truth I need to take the work where I can get it at the moment.'

'Sounds good.'

'Okay, I have to go. Just read the email and let me know once you've booked your flights.'

The line goes dead, and I stand in the bathroom dripping, trying to remember whether or not I washed my hair.

The Caravan

The sounds of sleeping-bag zips and the gentle click of the cupboards summon you. Some of the most vivid memories I have are when we were in our small caravan near the coast. A caravan that slept five and had indented corduroy sofa covers with large round buttons that you could wedge your fingers under. A caravan surrounded by donkeys we'd hear braying in the night. You'd call me in from playing in the park at dusk when the sky was still pink, and by the time I'd changed into my pyjamas it would be dark as I walked through the long grass with a small, green plastic torch in one hand and a lilac tooth-brush and children's toothpaste in the other. Darkness was all around but for the warm yellow-orange glow of the toilets. Inside daddy-long-legs were scattered across the walls and stretching their spindly limbs across the tubular lights on the ceiling. I'd set the torch and the toothbrush on the communal basins gently and creep over to a willowy daddy-long-legs. Their wings reminded me of church windows: faint lines demarcating different-shaped sections as if they were ready to be coloured in, like the raised-velvet felt on the colouring posters I had of tigers and tropical flowers back at the caravan. I'd sit and colour them in all day when the rain came down heavily, an echoing cacophony all around us and the bitter smell of your sticky tipple in green cans. I'd surreptitiously grab a daddy-long-legs by its wing and slowly start pulling its legs off, one by one. I didn't have an ounce of remorse for the helpless creature, or for the one I'd siloed the next night, or for the one I'd willingly amputate the night after that. It was a cheap power play, a shot at playing God. You had told me that daddy-long-legs were one of the most poisonous spiders on earth, but with fangs too small and weak to take a bite out of me. So there, in the warm glow of the campsite toilets, I played with something dangerous, knowing it couldn't bite back.

Some of our happiest memories were in that musty-smelling caravan near the coast. Feeding gingernut biscuits to the donkeys, going down a high wire with a round rubber Frisbee for a seat, made only more entertaining when watching you fly down it – I don't think it was for daddies and their long legs but that didn't stop you. You were playful and fun when you wanted to be. Childlike, in a way. One day it was hot and I was sweaty, wearing pink shorts that were a little too tight on my skinny, girlish legs, which were red from the day's sun. You were shouting. I'd done something wrong and you were angry. I was rushing, eager to appease you. And then I fell, slipping on the sharp grids of the caravan steps, cutting my knee open, the skin, fatty and textured, flesh spurting blood, a jolly tomato red. I yelped, screaming uncontrollably. Your face held horror and something else – something I'd not seen play out on it before. Fear? Fear turned to panic. You flounced clumsily around the caravan looking for tissues or some antiseptic cream. I continued to scream, and you grabbed my hand and led me through that long grass up to the communal toilets. I was embarrassed by my flushed cheeks matching my shorts and by the vigour with which you pulled my hand up in the air to meet yours as we strode past my friends, still jumping on the campsite trampoline. I was ashamed of how you were stumbling about. You used toilet roll and water from the tap. I screamed harder in pain as you dragged the coarse cheap paper across the deep cuts, trying to pull any dirt out with your fingernails. I remember being annoyed that you made no effort to be gentle as you slurred at me to hold still. All beer-stained breath. But then I watched the features in your face jive and jerk, performing these new movements I'd not witnessed before. I saw your fear, my childlike anguish too much for a drunk man to bear, and just like that your struggle overtook mine. Your pain would take priority in this new cycle where you became child and I the parent. Absorbing my fear to assist in absolving you of your own.

'It's okay, Dad,' I said, wiping the tears from my hot cheeks. 'It doesn't hurt any more.'

TAH DAH

The following evening the temperature really drops. I pull my beanie hat down further over my ears and my North Face jacket tighter around my body. Damn, it's freezing. I'm excited to get to the restaurant, to tell Ekua about ayahuasca. Georgia sounded reticent when I told her, but that's classic worry-wart Bailey. I'm also excited to show the girls my new dress, and that I'm not wearing any form of dungarees. What a triumph. They'll be excited about my trip too, impressed that I'm being proactive about things again instead of moping around the house. We're meeting at one of my favourite restaurants, a quaint wine bar with a bakery attached called Jolene. As I walk across Newington Green, the candle-lit glass-fronted restaurant glows, bewitching with its seductive warmth. I pull open the tall, heavy door and in front of me is a long bar with a brushed-cement top. It's lined with diners on stools, drinking red wine out of glass tumblers, picking at small plates. Ahead, a large blackboard lists the menu in white chalk: 'buttered beans', 'sea bream' and 'fennel sausage' catch my eye. I look to the tables on the left stacked together intimately; the decor is industrial and stripped back. The elegant ceramic water jugs sit alongside cloth napkins with red hand-stitching. Nothing fights for your attention: lavender hangs upside down on pegs and branches lined with red berries are placed in vases, offering a harmonic feast, delicate on the eye's palate. I spot the girls at a table at the back.

'Sorry I'm late, peaches.' I take off my beanie hat, barely making eye contact, 'but I have exciting news for you – TAH DAH!' I rip open my coat to showcase a long black dress with large white spots on it that ties neatly at my waist and offers a split up the side of my leg. Georgia and Ekua stare up at me, blankly. Nothing. NAH DAH.

'I'm not wearing dungarees!' I say, wrestling my puffer coat onto the back of my seat. 'Honestly, there's no pleasing you pair sometimes.' I look up and make eye contact with Ekua. Her eyes are even larger than normal, bloodshot, swollen and sore. 'Oh, my God. Are you okay? What's wrong?' I reach my hand across the table and tightly cover hers, a vain attempt to shield her from whatever she's upset about. Ekua snivels, wiping her other hand under her nose. I look at Georgia, who looks back to Ekua.

'Are you going to tell me what's going on, love?' I say, dipping my chin towards the table to try to catch her eye again.

Ekua's breathing is fast and heavy. She's trying to compose herself.

'Can I get you something to drink?' a lady in an apron asks, arriving at the side of me.

'Yes, a large glass of Pinot Noir,' I say, flashing my eyes to her, then turn my attention straight back to Ekua. I tighten my grip on her hand.

'No,' says Georgia.

I look at her.

'No, you're right! Make that a bottle, please!'

'No, Mathilda.' She sighs, sitting back in her chair.

'No?' I say, side-glancing her. 'Vodka shots?' I try again.

'No. Your new special "diet",' she says, making quotation marks with her fingers at me. 'Remember . . .'

The penny drops. 'Oh, fuck.'

The waitress flinches.

'You're right. Why are you always so right? It's irritating.'

Ekua laughs through wet brown eyes.

'Okay. In that case, I'll have a soda water with ice and a slice of lime, please. Try and make it look as alcoholic as you can – but with no alcohol.' I look pleadingly at the waitress, who nods with a confused expression and trundles off.

'What's gone on, Eks? Come on . . .'

'It's Lucia,' she whimpers.

'Oh. Okay. Did you finally speak? Was her voice awful?' I say, trying to make her smile. 'I warned you of that. Didn't I warn her?' I look to Georgia for back-up. 'Does she sound like Dobby from *Harry Potter*? Like a croaky choirboy going through the change. Is that it, Eks? Hey?' I move closer to her.

'No,' she cries. Tears compress in the corners of her eyes until they overfill and start to spool out. 'She's . . . she's not well.'

I take this information and hold it in the front of my brain for a few moments, trying to place it in the right part of my prefrontal lobe. 'She's not well,' I repeat.

'She's sick, like really sick. That's why she agreed to my dating project. She said she wanted to experience something new, something different.'

'I don't understand,' I say. 'What do you mean by she's not well?'

'She has a degenerative disease,' says Georgia, calmly. 'And she's deteriorating. It's a rare condition but it's hereditary so she's known about it for most of her life. She told Ekua that her doctors don't think it'll be long until she'll need, well, more support and care.'

'What?' I say, confused.

'We started talking. We broke the language barrier when I told her I loved her.'

I raise my eyebrows and push my head into my neck. It's unusual for Ekua to fall this fast.

'She wants to stay in London because this is where her life is, and this is where she wants to be while she's . . . I don't know, healthy!' I see a flash of hot anger and note her lips are missing their usual pop of colour. 'But when she eventually gets really poorly, she's going back to Pisa where her family can look after her.'

'Pisa? Oh, my love, I'm sorry.'

Ekua starts to cry, and I feel overcome with emotion. I want to crawl across the table and suck the pain out of her scrunched-up face.

'She said she never meant for it to get this serious. The opposite, in fact. She thought dating without speaking would be weird so we wouldn't get attached. She wasn't planning on meeting anyone. She was on Tinder for sex.'

'The irony, eh? Go on Tinder for sex and you'll find love. Go on Tinder for love and you'll find sex.' I smile and squeeze her hand.

'Well, the opposite happened and she's, well . . . *we*'ve fallen in love.' She gazes at me, and the lavender hanging behind her curly black hair looks sickly and disturbing.

Bird Library

I'm waiting on the porch of the Whitechapel Gallery, umbrella in hand. It's not like Constance to be late. I dig out my phone from my bag to find Ivy's email again with the long list of things I can't have: no fried or spicy foods, no alcohol or recreational drugs, no sexual contact, no caffeine, dairy products, pork or red meat, no refined sugar, avoid salt and steer clear of fermented foods. The list goes on. I sigh and my tummy grumbles back at me in agreement. I look round at the gallery. It's my favourite in London. Small and inalterable, it's premiered exhibitions for David Hockney, Jackson Pollock and Frida Kahlo. When I first moved to London, I came here on the days I felt homesick. It was a space that felt controlled and it contained me in a vast, momentous city. London was a gaping wound that I could bleed out in. The Whitechapel Gallery offered something of a relief, with its considered book collection, modest gift shop and seemingly small rooms and narrow staircases that bandaged the wound and led to more predictably large spaces secured with high walls. It was my safe place.

Constance is a member and gets invited to the gallery's private views. Tonight we're going to see 'Theatre of the Natural World', which, from what she's told me, is a natural-histories exhibition by the American explorer and collector Mark Dion. It's warm inside the bookshop as I wander around, soggy umbrella in hand. I'm growing to tolerate the red chicken. The shop's offerings stem from enough philosophy and psychoanalytic theory to invoke an existential crisis, to large photography books that are too cumbersome to thumb through. I don't think you liked galleries. You never took me to one, not that I can remember. Art wasn't really your thing. You were more in tune with the cruel realities of this world rather than the artistic statements being made about them. Were you a bad man? Or were you a good man?

Trick question! A person is neither good nor bad, rather an amalgam of both. But it's difficult to accept those two opposing concepts at once, to let them sit together in unnerving proximity. But in fact there are many small, intimate details that make up a person: you always ate really quickly as if someone might take your plate away at any moment; you had an archipelago of light birthmarks on your forearm; you went through a weird religious phase at a church where people sang with tambourines; you were acutely suspicious of cats and crossed the road if you saw one; you drank milk out of the carton from the fridge and whisky from a bottle when you thought no one was looking; the hazy drunken slurs, fists and tears and screaming replay in my mind when I'm still for long enough, or drunk enough to let them swim to the surface; oh, and you loved me, in an unsatisfactory and disappointing way but that doesn't change the fact that you did. Good and bad.

I thumb through the books on the table at the gallery and it takes me back to a time when we were in a bookshop together. You waited outside while I bought a couple of things, a magazine, I think, and a debut novel, which had a self-satisfied cover that said: I'm clever and brilliant. I couldn't find you after I'd paid for my books and wandered outside the shop to see if you were there.

'He's just gone inside to look for you, I think,' said the shop assistant, smoking a cigarette.

I walked back into the shop and wondered where you would think to look for me. The non-fiction section, maybe. Or perhaps you'd go upstairs to poetry. You may have thought I'd gone to look at the art books or even that I was thumbing through the political zines. I felt exhilarated in that moment, wandering around hardcovers, arching my head around tall bookcases and jostling down the stairs to see if you were searching for me in the self-help aisle. What would I learn from knowing where you'd expect to find me? Perhaps you thought me obvious and you were lingering front of store near the bestseller charts. Or maybe you thought me romantic and sentimental and were looking for me near the repackaged classics. Or, you may have thought me fickle and were seeking me out near the tables sporting satirical joke and gift books with neon covers. I couldn't find you anywhere and it dawned on me that you might be in historical fiction or crime. I sincerely hoped not. One wouldn't wander aimlessly if they were trying to find someone they know in a bookshop: a bookshop has detailed signage, extensive categorisation, and you were a man of detail.

Eventually I stumbled across you on a sofa allocated for readers. You didn't have a book in hand. You were sitting back, stroking your hair across your face and looking into the middle distance calmly. You hadn't gone to look for me at all. You were habitually – and as you had always been – waiting for me to discover you. Isn't that the role of a parent, to learn and study their child? Isn't there an obligation for you to understand who they are? If I ever have a child, I will gobble up their every idiosyncrasy. I will be doctorate-educated on the subject of who they are and what makes them tick, judicious about exactly what they are not. I will trace the intricate pattern of their scars from memory. Why were you so reluctant to get to know me? I will think about this throughout Mark Dion's show and let the anger burn inside me.

'Hello,' Constance appears from behind a bookcase. 'Here you are, I've been looking for you. I'm sorry I'm late. I'm getting a bit slow in my old age, dear.'

'It's fine. I was enjoying perusing the books.'

'Yes, I thought I'd find you in here.'

There's heat in my heart.

'Shall we go in and see the show?' she asks.

I follow her out of the shop and into the main gallery. 'How have you been? You were a little worn out the last time I saw you.'

'Fine. A little bit slow this morning but I'll perk up.'

We leave the niceties at that. I don't feel much like talking and it seems Constance doesn't either. We both find comfort in silence. We wander around the show together quietly until we decide to wait in line for a large cage that has a real tree and birds flying around its enclosure. The branches of the dead apple tree have been used as bookshelves, and all around the bottom of the trunk there are piles and piles of books. It's odd to hear the live flock of zebra finches fluttering around in the gallery.

'The piece is called *The Library for the Birds of London*,' Constance says. 'Isn't that lovely?'

'It's interesting,' I nod, 'the paper we've created from trees being stuck to and gathered around it, a bit like a self-integrated shrine.'

'Yes. Dion is setting out to explore how we exploit the natural world.' Constance's tired eyes follow one of the little finches. 'Edna loved birds. She had a little canary called Ralph that her daughter asked me to take on when she died.'

Edna was one of Constance's closest friends but she didn't often talk of her.

'I didn't like the thought of it, though, the little thing cooped up inside a cage. Edna loved it, but it seemed unnatural to me. Cruel, even.'

'I understand. I feel the same about goldfish.'

'Goldfish. Really, dear?'

'Yeah, their long drooping faces swimming around a tiny bowl, all melancholy.' I impersonate a sad fish to make her laugh. 'They give me this claustrophobic feeling. When you think about them swimming around the same bowl for the entirety of their lives, never getting anywhere, never progressing . . . It's morbid.

I stole a teacher's fish when I was in school, actually, set it free in the school pond only to find it floating on the surface that same day.'

'That's silly, dear. Fish don't have the capacity for such self-awareness.'

'Well, I'd think it unlikely that canaries do. Ralph was probably happy as a pig in muck in his cage.'

'So, what we're doing is projecting our own emotions and fears onto them.'

'Perhaps.' I consider this. 'Yes.'

'I wonder what happened to Ralph in the end. Edna's daughter has two incredibly unpleasant children. I hope he wasn't subjected to a life of being terrorised by Tweedledee and Tweedledo.'

'I don't think there was a Tweedledo.'

'What's that, dear?'

'It doesn't matter.'

'We'd had a falling-out, Edna and I.'

'Really? You never said anything. You two always got on so well – you were so close.' I knew Edna had died since I'd been visiting Constance, but I had been careful not to pry. We had a mutual respect for not overstepping on one another's grief.

She smiles. 'Well, we had an argument. I was annoyed with her for cancelling on me all the time. It felt like she'd just resigned herself to death. I'd go over and visit, take tea and cake, but nothing I could do would persuade her to leave the house. It was like she'd given up. I suppose I took that a little personally. I think she must have been depressed really. I stopped visiting her. I told her that if she wanted to see me, she had to meet me outside in the real world.'

'And did she?'

'She said she was too tired to battle with me. I was so fed up with her negativity and all this feeling sorry for herself . . .' she pauses ever so slightly '. . . so I didn't call her. Not for weeks. And then her daughter found her in bed. She'd been there for five days before anyone realised.' Constance looks mortified.

Before I can say anything, the gallery assistant waves at us. It's our turn to step into the large bird cage. I follow Constance.

'I'm so sorry that happened,' I say, closing the first cage door before reaching to open the second, a system to prevent the finches from escaping. 'I had no idea. When you said she'd died in her sleep I thought that had to be the best way to go. The most peaceful way.'

'But she was all alone,' her voice is filled with sadness, 'and I just can't bear the thought of it.'

'Oh, Constance . . .'

'I can't bear the thought of how we left things. My best friend, I left her to die alone.'

I look at her and she's standing with both hands in the pockets of her long beige coat. Her silvery bob is imperfect: strands rebel and splay out of place. She looks frail and old. I have nothing to say that would make her feel better. I remain silent as the finches chatter and chirp, flying above our heads. I turn to look at the picture of Alfred Hitchcock, stuck to the trunk of the tree. Give me some words, I say to him with a menacing gaze. Then finally some come.

'I left my dad alone too. In the end, I just couldn't face going to see him any more. I couldn't deal with the guilt and the shame I felt every time I left him. It was monstrous, the whole thing . . . He started to disintegrate on every level. His hands started to fold into themselves, like claws, and the muscles deteriorated in every part of his body. His skin was sallow and sticky, and his cheekbones looked as though they'd started to invert. He'd sit staring at me, and I'd desperately try to fathom whether he hated me, or whether he was asking himself who the hell this woman sitting at the end of his bed was.'

Constance doesn't pretend to look at anything inside the enclosure in that moment. Instead she stands there with her hands still tucked into her pockets, looking at me. Here was a mother who'd watched her own daughter's life slip through her fingers, a once-grieving widow, a sister-less sibling, and now she was being forced to grieve the loss of her best friend. Each time loaded with a new grief, a new mangled nest of pain.

'How can you stand it?' I ask. 'How can you bear it? Losing all those people you've loved. I don't understand how a person could cope.'

She smiles gently, raising an eyebrow ever so slightly. I wait for an answer, watching her remove her hands from her coat and hold them together in front of her.

'Let's give someone else a turn inside the bird library now, shall we, dear?'

We wander around for another twenty minutes or so and then I notice that she's tiring.

'I'm going to sit in the café,' she says. 'Why don't you meet me there when you've finished having a look around?'

'No, I'm done. I'll come with you.'

We take a seat inside the wooden-panelled café and I go up to the counter and order her a glass of Merlot and a soda water for myself. When I sit, I ask her a mundane question about what she's got on this week.

'It doesn't get easier, if that's the answer you're looking for.'

Her response is uncharacteristically blunt, calling me out on the triviality of my small-talk.

'Just as you said, each time death brings with it an entirely fresh bundle of grief. And working through it never gets any easier, or less painful for that matter. It does feel different each time. It's like each bereavement adds to this hand-woven blanket. Each piece of fabric is unique, impossible to recreate exactly. Grief is very much like that.'

'Well, that's something to look forward to,' I say drily. 'A patchwork quilt of grief stitched together by how much we love each person we lose – something to wrap around us in the lonely nights.'

'But I think I've found some comfort in that.' She stirs in her chair. 'No one else will ever have the same special relationship that Cliff and I had, or even me and Edna. It's special to us only.'

I take a sip of my drink, wishing it were wine. 'Is that a comfort, though? It sounds alienating, that no one can ever understand those finite layers. No one can ever share in them with you because what you had with that person is something only you can know.'

'I think other people can share in parts of your grief, but it's not possible for them to experience it exactly as you do. It is uniquely painful every time we lose someone because our grief for them is something unto itself. It's not a replica of sadness, rather it's a sadness designed out of how you felt about that person.'

'And with that, death bulldozes through our fallible human hearts all over again.' I swing my head theatrically to lighten the moment.

'It doesn't get easier, my dear, but the tools you're learning to use, to overcome the stifling loss of your father, will be more readily available to you next time. You will know how to pick them up, and you will understand how they work. At the moment grieving is entirely new to you, but you will unearth a better understanding of yourself through this process. That I guarantee.'

'There isn't a tool for everything, Constance. Some things are just broken.'

'Rubbish! Grief forces you to face yourself, and if you cannot do it, a part of you will be rendered unavailable to you. This is the worst possible outcome, my girl. You must battle to keep that part of yourself, even if it feels worthless or even contemptible in the roaring high seas of loss. You must still fight to keep it.'

I sense her desperation, the importance she feels in relaying this message. 'I'm sorry about Edna,' I say.

'Thank you. I'm sorry about your father.'

I raise my eyebrows and smile at her at the same time, making a facial expression that belongs to you. Looking out through the window into the streets of the city, I wonder at the uniqueness of you and me.

Bikini Wax

After I've walked Constance home, I wait for the 67 bus back to the house. It's stopped raining, but everything is still wet and I stand at the stop listening to the quick lashings of water hit the pavement as cars drive past. The bus doesn't take long. I find a seat on the bottom deck and then feel my phone vibrating in my pocket. It's Ekua.

'Petrichor.'

'What?' She says.

'I was trying to remember the word. The word for that delicious smell once it's stopped raining.'

'Oh.'

'Petrichor.'

'"Hello" is what most people go for, but sure.'

'What's happened?' I ask.

'What do you mean what's happened?'

'You only ever call me when there's something wrong. Ivy called me the other day as well. Why are people calling each other all of a sudden? It's weird.'

'Well, I were just calling to ask if you could help me out of a solution-less problem. The odds are low, but I felt I should give you the opportunity.' Her northern inflections are even thicker down the line.

'It sounds like an exciting and fruitful challenge,' I say.

'Yes. It is. I know how much you enjoy those.'

'Hit me.'

'It's lady-garden related.'

'Come again?'

'I'm seeing Lucia tomorrow and, well, I think it might be *the night*.'

'The night?' I ponder.

'Yes, you know. The night. As in the night we do it.'

'Ooh . . . *the night*.'

Have they still not slept together?

'But I'm still between waxes and the hair isn't long enough to go and get a wax. But if I shave, I'll be stuck in a cactus cycle and will have to wait ages for it to grow back. And it hurts more then – makes the hair coarser.'

'Wow. This is real insight into your mind.'

'Shut up. I do realise I'm asking for grooming advice from someone who has worn the same three outfits on rotation for months.'

'Do you really need to—'

'I don't really want to introduce her looking as she does.'

'This is a terrible conversation for a feminist to be having. Also, can we rewind to the part where you said "lady-garden" because that might just be the most offensive thing that's ever happened? She's a girl! She'll understand. She's got one. Does it really matter?'

'I think that's the most heteronormative thing you've ever said.'

'Okay,' I say, with total sincerity, 'before we go any further, I need to ask you a question.'

'Shoot.'

'Are you concerned with how she looks for yourself or are you worried about what Lucia will think of you? Because, honestly, the latter doesn't matter. If she is given the opportunity to sleep with you, she will be completely ecstatic and delighted – the hair on your vulva will be the last thing on her mind.'

'Okay.' There's a pause on the line. 'What was the question again?'

'I appreciate it's impossible to duck and dive the patriarchal notions fed to you in everyday life, so put more plainly: are you doing this for her or for you?'

'Umm . . . both, I think. Definitely both.'

'Well, that's not the right answer, Ekua!'

'Ah come on, it's not about the wax, I'm just freaking out about sleeping with her. Just help me regain some control will you?'

'Okay. What about home waxing? Give it a go yourself. You literally only have four hairs down there anyway.'

'I physically couldn't do it. It's too painful. And, as I say, it's not long enough. That's why we're in this right mess.'

'Okay, what about hair-removal cream? The stuff you put on there and the hairs just fall out.'

'Yeah . . . Georgia said that.'

'You put it on your lovely *Dame Garten*, the hairs fall out and you just brush them away. I've done it before. It works.'

'I mean, if it works then why are women still paying extortionate amounts of money for strangers to pour hot wax onto their genitals?'

'I feel it's not as mainstream yet.'

'Being a woman is such a fucking joke.'

'Yeah, but if we both got there – Georgia and me – it's clearly the correct solution, isn't it?'

'Okaaaay,' Ekua's voice glints.

The man sitting next to me on the bus fidgets slightly.

'In your hour of need, I'm leaning in for you.'

'So you've tried and tested it? The hair-removal cream. On your bits, I mean?'

'No, I tried it on my armpits.'

'Oh, great. It's not tried and tested, then. Pubic hair has a completely different consistency.'

'Yes, that is true.' I nod into my handset.

'Right. I'd better get myself to the big Tesco and get on with it.'

'Probably go for a fancy brand, though, babe.'

'Well, I wa'n't planning on going for a supermarket-own brand for a cream that burns through hair on my lady-garden,' she says, agitated.

'Stop calling it that.' I laugh. 'Say it with me: vul-va.' The man turns and looks at me with a curious frown. 'Vulva,' I say again.

'Vulva,' she repeats.

'I'm just saying if there is an organic option at a higher mark-up, this isn't the time for penny pinching.'

'Yeah, okay, ta.'

'Also, maybe do a test patch. Worst case, the armpit becomes swollen and inflamed and we can just keep that arm down when having sex.'

'Ha! Okay, cheers. Are you on your way home?'

'Yeah, I'll see you shortly and we can have a more detailed conversation about your guilty feminist ways.'

'Okay, bye then.'

'Eks . . .'

'Yeah?'

'Are you sure about this?'

'About the Veet?'

'No, about Lucia. Are you sure about getting more, you know, involved and . . . well, physical?

She doesn't respond.

'Is it the right thing . . . for you both?' I ask more gently.

'I don't know what you're trying to say.' Her voice hardens.

'I just don't want to see you get hurt.'

'Well, that's what life is, Mathilda. Albeit intermixed with some lovelier moments. And you've got to take those moments where you can.'

'I know but—'

'I'll see you later.'

'Okay.'

The line goes dead, and I turn to meet the gaze of the man beside me who is almost definitely thinking about my vulva.

When I arrive home, Ekua is in the kitchen unpacking her groceries and cooking something on the stove that smells coconutty. Georgia is reading the instructions on the hair removal cream, leaning back on two legs of the chair, one hand twirling her earring. Jeremy is on her lap, looking gormless as the day he was born.

'Yo,' says Ekua.

'How was Constance?' asks Georgia.

'Yeah, all good. We had a nice time.'

'Did you tell her about your ayahuasca trip?' asks Georgia.

'Why would she tell Constance that?'

'I was going to tell her actually. She'd probably already know about it. Knowing Constance, she's probably read a book about it. I think she'd understand.'

'Well, that's nice for her because I don't.' Ekua frowns. 'Do you care to explain to me? White girl in trouble drinks foreign hallucinogenic to heal herself. It's a bit—'

'Eye-roll?' Georgia interrupts.

'Yes, it's a bit eye-roll,' Ekua agrees. 'Can't you just work your problems out here?'

'That feels a bit judgemental.'

'I don't mean to be judgemental, but it's an ancient practice that doesn't belong to you.' Ekua's direct.

'Wow, Eks. I don't really see it that way.'

'How do you see it, then?' Georgia asks, genuinely curious.

'It's a natural medicine, one from the earth. We all have a right to heal from the earth, don't we? And the people whose culture this does belong to, they want to share it. They want to help Westerners with the toxic lifestyle they've created for them-selves. The mess we've got ourselves into.'

'Yes, but are they not just being exploited with money? Money they otherwise wouldn't have access to?'

'Ekua, I'm not popping to a countryside estate in Surrey to

do it with some trustafarian shaman who's only spent a summer tripping off the stuff. We are paying to fly a shaman over from Peru, someone who belongs to a family that has been practising these sorts of ceremonies for generations.'

'So you're paying him and, more than that, you're flying him over at your own convenience?'

'Absolutely, we're paying for his time. It would be an insult not to. And he's flying to Europe to see family and suggested he could come via Italy to perform the ceremony. What's wrong with that? A couple of Ivy's friends have been to his retreats in Peru. Besides,' I add quickly, for extra points, 'it's better for the environment than a big group of us all trekking out there, isn't it?'

'We just thought you were done with your druggy phase.' Georgia laughs, trying to stifle the tension. 'I mean we don't want *that* Mathilda back.'

'I didn't have a druggy phase.' I protest, scowling.

'Yeah, ya did,' Ekua says plainly.

'A few lines of coke at uni and the odd pill does not constitute a druggy phase, Ekua. And it's not a recreational amphetamine, I'm hardly going off to Italy for a wild weekend.' I roll my eyes dramatically.

'Well, those are usually the sort of weekends Ivy has in Italy, let's be honest.' Ekua flares her nostrils at me. 'Right, hang on. I'm pulling it up on Google.' She puts her Tesco bag down and pulls Georgia's MacBook towards her, typing in the password. 'It says ayahuasca translates from the South American Queca . . . no, *Quechua* language as "soul vine" or "vine of the dead".' She sighs loudly. 'The ceremony in which it's drunk has been practised for thousands of years by indigenous people who treasure the plant. It is led by a shaman who acts as a spiritual guide and protector throughout what is sometimes an eight-hour-long trip – Jesus! Eight hours?' She looks up and I nod casually, like it's no big deal.

Fuck. That is a long time.

'The potent, psychoactive, plant-based brew has healing powers and spirit-enlivening effects . . . sounds creepy.'

'It's not creepy,' I say this defensively.

'It's like DMT, right? You're going to reach the sublime and be in total ecstasy with God?' Georgia grins at me, amused.

'Don't be sardonic. It's ugly on you.'

'Sorry.' She shrugs, stroking Jeremy's head before placing him on the floor. 'It just seems like quite an extreme thing to do, that's all.'

'Look, I'm not going there to find myself or anything cringe like that. But, this curse—'

'I thought you got rid of it?' Ekua exclaims.

'I don't know, this thing . . . I just feel like I need to face something. And I've tried, I've really tried. I just want to take this opportunity that's being offered to me.'

'This is so typical of Ivy!' Georgia gets cross. 'So reckless and spur-of-the-moment. She shouldn't have asked you.'

'I don't think it cures anything, or anyone,' I say. 'I think it just makes you understand yourself better and forces you to face your shit. Maybe. I don't know! But I've always wanted to do it. And you know I've always wanted to do it, G,' I look at her pleadingly, 'and Ivy had a spot and she invited me, so why not? It basically came to me.'

'Why not indeed?' Georgia says grudgingly.

'Just be careful, I think is what she's trying to say.' Ekua is back at the computer screen. 'It says that ayahuasca is the most potent and strong hallucinogenic in the world. Have you done many hallucinogens before?' She looks up at me, one brow raised.

'No, she hasn't,' Georgia answers for me.

'You don't know,' I say, walking over to the stove to forensically inspect the delicious curry. I go to dip my finger but Ekua bats me away.

'It's tofu satay curry,' she chimes, 'no turmeric or spice, so the drinker of the world's most mind-altering brew can eat it too. It probably tastes *usgusting.*'

'You're a star,' I say, and kiss her cheek.

'Yes, I am a star. Now can we turn our attention to a real problem? My pubic hair.' She points downstairs with the spoon.

Georgia and I make eye contact and she looks away as if to say: leave it.

'You didn't respond well to our conversation on the phone earlier,' I try gently.

'What do you mean?' Her voice changes again into something cold and stony.

'Lucia's not well, Ekua. And she's not going to get better. I just don't want to see you hurt.'

'Well, it's a little late for that now. I've already fallen for her.'

'I know, but—'

'But what?' She interrupts abruptly.

'Mathilda, leave it,' says Georgia.

'No, go on,' Ekua provokes, with a long nod.

'You have a choice, that's all.' My torso is clenched and leaning as I point my palms at her in a prayer pose. 'You're pretending you don't, but you do. You have a choice here. You know the outcome. You know what's going to happen. You don't have to put yourself through that.'

'Mathilda, please,' says Georgia. But I can't bear the thought of Ekua getting hurt. Of her being abandoned all over again.

'I do not have a choice, Mathilda. I have fallen in love with her. What about that don't you understand?'

'But you're only making it worse for yourself. Why would you willingly subject yourself to that kind of loss?'

'You know what,' Ekua looks seething, 'you wander around here behind your curtain of grief, miserable and sulking around.'

I furrow my brows in feigned, comical confusion.

'Like a break-up is the worst goddamn thing that's ever happened to you.' Her eyebrows pull down together.

'Can we not do this?' Georgia stands up between us.

'Yes – you're miserable, we get it, Tilda. You've had a really horrible time of things lately . . .'

'If you've got something to say, say it.'

'Well, did it ever strike you that loving someone that much – feeling so deeply for someone – is a good thing? No. A *great* thing. That that's the whole fucking point. And although you think this fog of sadness, or whatever it is you're going through, is the worst thing in the world, perhaps it isn't. Perhaps it's a fucking brilliant thing that you loved him so much. Perhaps your capacity to love – how deeply you love, Mathilda – is a rare and wonderful thing.'

'It's not that straightforward for me, Eks.'

'WHY NOT?' she shouts. 'Why isn't it that straightforward for you? How can we help you if you won't tell us what's going on?'

I look down at the floor.

'Let's stop this,' Georgia raises her voice. 'We're stopping this, right now.'

I feel you and the anger stirs, but I don't want to lose it. Not with Ekua. Not like this. 'You know, it's probably a bit easier for you because you have a living and doting daddy who adores you. You have the capacity to love that much too.' My voice rises. 'So why not try loving someone who can love you back for a change?'

'Why won't you tell us, Mathilda? Why do you need to take ayahuasca?' Her voice is calmer now, which allows me to talk over her questions.

'You seek out people you know are incapable of loving you. Some re-enactment! You're recreating the trauma of your mum leaving, over and over again. Instead of just fucking dealing with it.'

'Try, Mathilda. Try and tell me what is happening to you.' Ekua doesn't rise to my vitriol.

'Ekua, stop it!' says Georgia.

I grab the spoon out of Ekua's hand and throw it across the floor. We all gasp and curry specks smear across the tiles.

'How about you reserve some judgement until you've figured your own shit out, eh?'

Ekua turns off the hob, snatches the Veet from the kitchen table and marches past me out of the kitchen. Georgia gives me that look, as if I know what she's thinking. But for what feels like the first time ever, I don't.

Unfollow

The week leading up to my trip to Italy there is a strange atmosphere in the house. Ekua and I avoid each other. Georgia seems a little distant, spending more time at Henry's than normal. I throw myself into the pitch and work all the hours God sends. I barely leave the house. I enjoy being consumed by this sense of purpose. I work so much I forget to go outside, but try not to miss a meal as I want to feel healthy going into ayahuasca.

I'm up working late again this evening and my eyes are aching from the glare of my computer screen. I push my glasses over my head and rub both sore sockets. I reach for my phone, no new messages. I find myself on Instagram and then on Oliva Wool's profile. I scroll through her most recent posts. One's of an impressive refugee campaign she's just worked on and there's a photo of her holding a huge bouquet of peonies, eucalyptus and daises to celebrate her first Mother's Day – every strand of her glossy long bob in place to frame a stretching smile. She's sitting on her stoop, all that ivy dressing the front door. I think of what Shelta said and wonder why I'm still watching. What's driving my morbid curiosity for this life I don't think I even want any more?

I flick onto her stories and there's a mirror selfie, her husband wrapping himself behind her. They're all dressed up like they're going somewhere nice. A cerise-pink type reads *Mummy and Daddy are going out, out!* I click on the next frame and they're at a restaurant with friends. The tables have flowers on them and there's a video of someone I vaguely recognise blowing out candles on a birthday cake. The next few frames take us to one of their friends' large living rooms for dancing and there are shots in the kitchen, and then there he is. Moving around in the background making cocktails in the way he does. I rewind the frame and hold it down when the camera points in his direction and Olivia asks him to talk us through what he's making. He looks doughy-eyed and tipsy. I lift my thumb and his movements resume, soft and puppyish after one too many drinks. He's talking through my phone and it seems as if all that separates us now is just a thin piece of glass that I could break with my fist if I wanted to. He needs a haircut – nothing new there. But he's wearing a smart navy workman's jacket I don't recognise. New clothes. New home. New point of view. It's hard to decipher all the things that might be new about him now, this man, this person, smiling hazily through a glass window at me. I click on Olivia's name in the top left-hand corner of the screen and go through to her profile, where my finger lingers for a moment before I press the unfollow button. That's enough Olivia Wool.

Rocket-shaped

We landed in Bolzano at 8 p.m. and have been in the car for almost an hour, so I know we must be close to the house now. In the end, Ekua gave me a big hug before I set off, and I apologised. She stood at the door, sceptical and wary, with Jeremy and Georgia, who waved us off excitedly. Ivy and I sit in silence as the taxi drives along the winding country lanes surrounded by tall mountains. It's dark, but I can see the fields with the odd outline of a large country house in the distance. These large white outlines, surrounded by vast amounts of green empty space, seem to me imaginary houses, built so far away from the world I exist in that it's difficult to imagine anyone living in them at all. There is a slow and ominous throb in the air, the sort that comes from a new and unknown place.

'The turning is coming up. It's just along here on the left,' says Ivy to the driver, who responds by flicking on her indicator.

I notice a clock that flashes 10:17 in red on the dashboard. We turn down a narrow country path with high bushes either side of the track and, for a moment, I can see nothing but darkness in front of us. Then the road starts to widen, and in the distance, I make out the house. Ivy rubs her skinny hands together in anticipation.

'Nervous?' I ask.

'No, excited.' She smiles, her teeth glowing white in the surrounding blackness.

When we pull up outside a large, rustic house built from stone, a bright light switches on above, revealing an immense, towering wooden front door. Ivy had mentioned it was a big house, but this really is something. The glow of the light glints on blue shutters, which frame dark windows. Each of the three front sections of the house have large triangular roofs and it reminds me of a much smaller version of Daphne du Maurier's Manderley, with mounds of overgrown ivy engulfing its eaves. As I open the car door, I gulp the countryside air. The driver gets our suitcases out of the boot and the giant wooden door opens to reveal two men. They whisper excited hellos and one gives Ivy an enthusiastic hug, lifting her slightly in the air. She crunches gently down onto the gravel path. The other man pays the taxi driver and I stand back, tentatively, watching her get back into her car and slowly drive away.

'This is Steve and Archie,' Ivy directs with one hand, 'and this is Mathilda,' she gestures with the other.

'Hi.' I smile, still standing completely still, clutching the long handle coming off my suitcase with both hands, unsure of what else to do with them.

'Hi, welcome to my gaff! Well, my parents' gaff.' Steve winks. 'It's nice to meet you. Ivy's told us a lot about you.'

Well, that can't be a good thing, Steve, given that since I met Ivy I've been a total mess.

'It's good to finally meet you,' chimes Archie. Until now, he was just a name on an email chain. He reaches for my suitcase. The intrusive white light beaming from behind him shows up three small moles running diagonally across the side of his face. There's something beautiful about the order of them, how they sit across his cheekbone, consecutive and established. I wonder if he was born with them, if these small circles constructed their place inside the womb, or if they appeared, faded at first, one sticky, humid afternoon after too much time in the sun.

'Let me take that for you,' he says, moving towards my case.

'No, it's fine, I can manage,' I say, wrestling with it.

'Packing light is not her strong suit,' Ivy says frankly. 'She had to check that thing in.' Her black wispy hair flicks in the corner of my eye as she dashes inside with Steve.

'You don't look like you're managing too well.' Archie laughs at me. 'That thing looks heavy.'

'Honestly, I can manage,' I say, veins protruding from my neck as I try to lift my case.

'Well, we must agree to disagree,' and with that he takes the case out of my hands with a playful tussle before walking into the house. I reposition my handbag on my shoulder and pat down my hair, tucking it behind my ears. I'm apprehensive about meeting the rest of Ivy's friends, unsure of what to expect.

I follow Archie into the large, high-ceilinged porch, which is edged with coat pegs and long wooden shoe racks filled with trainers, wellies and all manner of shoes in every shape and size. This brings you to mind, and your own personal collection. I note a small pink coat with a cartoon embroidered on the back and some pastel-coloured jelly shoes on the floor beneath belonging to a child. That this is a family home sets me at ease. I make my way down a couple of steps and into a vast open kitchen. I'm surprised by how modern the interiors are in contrast to the old stone exterior. Everything about the house seems unnecessarily oversized, a new and unknown wonderland too incongruous for me. There's a marble island that stands proudly in the centre with nothing but a teaspoon on it; seemingly thicker and larger than your average teaspoon. There are several people around the island, some sitting on metal stools. They smile and wave at me as Ivy introduces each person quickly and excitably. I don't catch any of the names because my mind has gone into overdrive at being the only person in a group who doesn't know everyone else intimately. A woman with blonde hair in neat, tight plaits and piercing green eyes holds my gaze after the introductions are over. She smiles at me purposefully.

Archie appears at my side. 'Would you like me to show you where you're sleeping?'

'Yes. Let's go up and get changed. We need to put lots of layers on. Your body temperature will really drop later,' says Ivy.

I follow them out through a side door attached to the kitchen, which leads to a wide wooden staircase that's been painted in a dark teal. The house is very still. We go up two, maybe three floors before reaching a double bedroom with a spaceship duvet and the planet Saturn painted on a wall that's chaotically peppered with plastic glow-in-the-dark stars.

'There are twelve bedrooms in this place, and we get little Frank's?' Ivy whinges.

'Last to arrive . . .' Archie says, smirking at her.

'It's fine,' I say, pulling my case towards me from where he's set it down. 'Cosy.'

I've not stayed in a house with twelve bedrooms before, so this one will do nicely.

'It's not fine,' Ivy exclaims, throwing her wheelie onto the bed and unzipping it. 'Where's Kate sleeping?'

Archie lifts his eyes and his head to the ceiling, shaking it at her affectionately, but it's for me to see. I smile, then stand in a way that signals I'm waiting for him to leave. He dawdles. Wedged between the door and its frame, his hand around a rocket-shaped handle, he leans his heavy body. As he looks at me with his blue eyes, it strikes me that he's handsome. He pulls his beanie off and ruffles a mound of soft, wavy brown hair, then pulls his hand over his face.

'Okay, I'll see you downstairs shortly, then.'

'Wait, Arch!' Ivy says, in a loud whisper. 'What time will the ceremony start?'

'As soon as you're both ready, so I'll leave you to it.' He closes the door gently.

When I turn around Ivy is completely naked but for her black cotton pants. I trace the outline of her ribs, which are pressing against her skin. Her thin black hair dangles limply.

'Get changed, Mathilda. You heard the man. They're waiting for us.'

I'm hungry. I've been hungry all week from fasting in preparation: no alcohol, vinegar, pork or beef, no dairy, nothing spicy, absolutely no lemon and, of course, no sex. We've been told not to eat after midday on the day of the ceremony and should even avoid drinking too much water, so my mouth is dry and powdery. This dietary cleanse is meant to maximise the ayahuasca experience and I don't hear anyone complain about it. I'm wearing soft, comfortable clothes, grey tracksuit bottoms, a grey tank covered with a long-sleeved black top and my favourite grey cashmere jumper, which I treated myself to after landing my first freelance job. Anticipation rises in my chest, like a shoal of fish. Everyone here seems friendly and welcoming, unlike some of Ivy's other friends. The connection between them feels rooted and genuine, it makes the house swollen with warm energy.

I look around the room and count: thirteen of us are partaking in the ceremony, as well as the shaman, Álvaro, and his assistant, Nuño. Álvaro is sitting with his short stubby legs crossed, and the expression on his large rounded face is accentuated by his triangular-shaped eyebrows, which are black and bushy. He looks Buddha-like in this position, his small body folded together. He is wearing a faded red jumper and equally worn-looking navy trousers. His hair is short and black; he has a wide-set nose, and large puffy cheeks extend off his face, kindness emanating from him. Nuño is a lot younger, probably in his early thirties, and he also has dark hair, but with stubble that forms the makings of a beard and moustache. He's handsome in a traditional sense, chiselled, with straight white teeth, large brown eyes and two large tunnels in each of his ears. He's dressed in a tank top, which shows off muscular brown arms, and he sits in a cross-legged position alongside his shaman. The atmosphere is surprisingly comfortable. When I am introduced the shaman smiles and nods at me. He doesn't speak much English but Nuño tells me they believe they've been practising ayahuasca ceremonies together for thousands of years, over the course of many lifetimes. I resist the urge to ask one of them for a hamburger.

Behind the kitchen is a huge open space, one that I assume would usually be the living room; all of the furniture has been removed for the ceremony. It, too, has a high ceiling, but with large arching wooden beams. There is no art on the walls, no photographs or mirrors and, I notice, no clocks. I imagine in my head what it looks like when it's lived in: toys spilt across the floor, with wide sofas still warm from the imprint of a visitor. The only decorative thing in the room now are these huge pieces of woven fabric running sporadically across each of the four walls; most are in deep reds and burgundies with circular mazes that are intertwined with snakes. Others are paler, with the traditional *shipibo* pattern woven in bright yellow, cerise and teal – these remind me of a more intricate Pac-Man maze. On the floor, we each have a soft, grey mattress, pushed against the walls to form a rough circle. Each mattress has its own pillow, a fleece-like blanket, a bucket for us to purge in and ten small cigarettes. I pick one up and finger it gently.

'It's *mapacho*.' A voice comes from behind me. I turn and it's the woman with plaits from the kitchen earlier. 'Álvaro can channel energy through the tobacco, so you should smoke them if you're having a particularly difficult time. It will help you with realignment.'

'Oh, right. Good.' I nod at her. 'Sorry, what was your name again?' I try my best to sound friendly. 'I'm terrible with names.' I signal the incompetence of my brain with a hand gesture.

'Florence.'

'Nice to meet you, Florence. I'm—'

'Mathilda. I know.'

Florence presents as a woman who knows a lot about a lot.

'We all have trauma.' This statement comes out of nowhere. She smiles, looking through and then into me. 'Don't run from it,' she warns sagely. 'You will never outrun Mother Ayahuasca, and any feeble attempt to do so would be foolish. It only exacerbates pain. That is the best advice I can give.'

I gulp. 'I won't run,' I say, folding my lips and shaking my head earnestly.

'What's that?' She points at my hand.

'Oh, it's toilet roll. I read the book and I'm quite concerned about the loss of control of bodily functions. Wasn't looking to shit myself in front of a room full of strangers, ideally.'

She laughs at this, then unexpectedly wraps her arms around me in a hug. I hold my hands out behind her, white cigarette in one, bog roll in the other.

'Good luck,' she says, and walks to the far end to settle down on a mattress.

I swing my hands back and forth, aware that I'm awkwardly standing in the middle of the room and don't really know where to sit or where I'm meant to go.

'You're over here,' a voice echoes. I swing around and Archie is readjusting his beanie as Ivy pats an empty mattress between them. The room would be in total darkness were it not for the several candles placed around its edges. I put the *mapacho* cigarette back in the pot I took it from and sit next to them. I watch as Álvaro and Nuño walk around the room blowing smoke to ensure the space is protected and everyone else settles onto their mattresses too. The two men start to make their way around the circle, one by one. They take out a tubular wooden object in the shape of a bow compass. With one side of the tube in Álvaro's mouth, he places the other up each of our noses and asks us to hold down our other nostril while he blows cleanly. When it's my turn, the rapé tobacco shoots a burning sensation through my tubes, clearing my sinuses. My eyes stream with tears. The space is engorged and womb-like. The candle-lit glare coming off the dark-red walls ensconces me. There is wavering fear below.

Ayahuasca

I first heard about ayahuasca when I was a student. It came up in conversation at a party and I was morbidly fascinated by the gruesomeness of it all. A friend described their experience to me, of a ceremony held at night in an altered state of consciousness, of a trip lasting seven or eight hours led by a shaman who sang songs in the darkness that sent them on a spiral of visual and auditory hallucinations that she could only describe as simultaneously past and future. Everything about it felt too extreme to be real. The handbook described it as 'a longing, part remembrance of something enduring and part intuition of future revelation'. Why would someone be willing to take something that would make their body violently convulse, vomit and shit? I went through a phase of reading about ayahuasca trips and I struggled to let the conversation lie if ever I met anyone who'd tried it. It's hard to say why. People who drank it spoke of long-term positive change in their lives, of healing and of purging something trapped inside them. Maybe I knew I had something I needed to remove, to force out. Something about this situation seemed inevitable for me. And so here I was, about to drink the most powerful hallucinogenic brew the world has to offer.

Álvaro offers each of us in turn a small shot of ayahuasca from – I'm amused to see – a red-capped Coca-Cola bottle. When it's my turn, I walk slowly to where he is sitting, Nuño slightly behind and to the left of him on a small cushion. They smile at me reassuringly and with a sense of pride in the medicine they are about to administer. The taste of the brown, bitter liquid is potent and distinctive, a sludgy dark cough medicine that's thick, earthy and slightly sour. I return to my mattress trying not to regurgitate it.

I sit for a while and nothing happens. I sit a little longer and still nothing happens. I hear dispersed coughing and readjustment from the people around me and it seems like nothing is happening to them either. The handbook said that it's important to come to ayahuasca with intention – think. Don't get distracted, Mathilda. Why are you here? You need to be clear. *You're here to face the overwhelming feeling of being stuck. You are here to unearth. You are here to endure those fears that disable you when you're alone and implore you to pull the covers over your head at night.*

How is it possible to be so afraid of something and yet not to know what you're afraid of? How can you explain the threatening fanged beast that sleeps under your bed at night and sits next to you when certain scenes flash up in movies – a knowingness that tangles itself around your gut and clenches? A squalid remembrance of something shameful and unforgiving that beds itself in familiar floral wallpaper and the tiny coats and miniature trousers belonging to Sylvanian Families? The wounds you have given me are permanent. There is no cure. They can be septic and oozing, or they can be scabbed and healed, but they are always here. Triggered and unpicked by your behaviours. I am here to face those parts of myself.

I feel you now: your physical weight, your essence suffocating me. These toxic vines are wound around my ankles, tight, keeping me motionless. I am sitting on this mattress, asking ayahuasca to unload me of the grief you gave me. Help is my intention: I am caught and I need to learn to move again. And eventually, after a long wait, it comes.

At first, there's a synaesthetic spiral of colour and energy, a new universe of otherworldly beings powered by hues and feelings and thoughts that previously seemed beyond my imag-ination. I sit for a while and try to slow myself in this world, flitting out of it and into the ceremonial circle, then back into ayahuasca. I give in to the trip and there are voices with me – not in the room itself but nearby. There are three speaking Spanish, which is an odd thing for me to imagine because I don't speak any Spanish. One voice is female and the other two are male. She sounds playful and seductive, but I sense she won't be kind if she discovers me. The male voices laugh, cajoling her. I realise I'm hiding. I can't tell if they're aware of my pres-ence, but my instinct is for them not to find me. The Spanish drifts away and my mind falls back into the room. I can hear people vomiting – a deep sickening feeling overcomes me. I start to feel balls of energy, like wool tangled in the back of my throat, making their way to the surface, and my skin tingles everywhere. I start to vomit, and time gets lost.

I am on my knees craning over a bucket, rocking my body back and forth as I retch, hitting the plastic bottom with brown, watery bile. More and more coarse balls of wool make their way up my oesophagus as I convulse and spit and heave. It comes and it comes. The sensation is relieving. The purge feels good, filling me with a sense of purpose. I look down and my hands are the size of a baby's, chubby and curled, and when I look up I see that I'm tiny, sitting in a large cot. You're here too. There is anger and fear, which I absorb. This happens more than once. I look down at the hands of my childhood self and resume a memory from my past, consumed with the disap-pointment of you. I heave and quiver until I vomit again, dispelling the pain, then collapse lifeless onto the mattress until the next wave comes. This experience is relentless. It rolls over me again and again, another memory, another purge. I think this goes on for several hours. The next thing I know, I'm looking into the eyes of the shaman, who is kneeling in front of me, singing a haunting melody, which unearths a pain so deep it seems pointless to relay it in words. I cry uncontrollably and unashamedly, rocking in harmony with his melancholy song. There it is again: release. I roll as a weight pushes my head down into my pillow. I cannot move.

Like absinthe's green fairy, but more potent and unrelenting, ayahuasca guides the route. Resist her and I suffer more. Try to outsmart her, and I lose. I call to mind a person or a situation and, like an endless corridor, I go through doors and feel twinges of my past that run through my spine and parts of my mind to which I've never had access. I shudder at a colour, a beige sofa, an ex-lover in a park, a bath you drunkenly put me into that was too hot and burned my skin. There's a quake that takes me back to a memory that reveals the source of my pain. Some doors I go through by choice: I summon a thought and, in a chartreuse swoop, the fairy takes me to the time and place that was once forgotten and subjects me to a visceral re-experiencing of it. Other doors she forces me into, thoughts, memories, fragrances she feels I need to experience. There is nothing linear or chronological about her fractious gliding from one source of discomfort to the next. On one of the endless levels, down one of the continual corridors – embellished with neon greens and sparks of yellow flashes – there is a pull towards one heavy door ever-so-slightly ajar, just enough to show me what lies behind it. A thing too horrifying to name.

At first she takes me gently – psychedelic inkblots splatter on a page to tell a story belonging to me. It burns and pricks in every cell, deep in my throat and inside my earlobes. Blistering

and hot, a toxic casing that has been smothered all over me
with a pastry brush, no surface left uncovered before it dries
and seals the horror inside me.

I go in through the heavy door, slightly ajar. I don't want to
feel the motion of watery movement under us, or smell the blue
plastic, so I think of the apple tree in our garden instead. The
image dissipates, replaced by a drawer full of white underwear,
your underwear, so bleached and clean. I think of the times we
played in the garden instead but she takes that image from me
too, replacing it with your weeping and crying as you wrapped
me in your anguish. I push myself up through the heavy dark
water, desperate to get back to the surface. She pulls me back
to that black iron door. I run. She takes me back to your
bedroom. I resist. She drags me, nonchalant and calm, as I kick
and squeal and spit. Álvaro and Nuño are in front of me and
I'm calling for them, screaming their names.

Until I stop.

I give in.

I go to her.

No turning away this time.

I melt into the scene.

I lose myself in an insurmountable space of time, frolicking on
the brink of something I might never come back from. Álvaro
and Nuño belt out a haunting *icaro,* which induces high-pitched
tones from the women in the room as they vomit in unison.
The men sit still and tall. My ego shed, any understanding of
self is pulled down around my ankles.

I move on to another door, this one slim and brown. Behind
it, for the first time, there's an opportunity to disentangle him
from my dad; to separate 'him' from 'you'. I step inside. Looking

around I see for the first time why he left me: it was impossible for him to stay.

Wilfully, I give myself to a sadness with depths unknown, and let us drown there, before I come up for air, calm and alone. On the bank, I scrabble around on my hands and knees, searching for the piece of me he'd taken when he left. And then the realisation hits: like watching a sunset, the subtle shifts in light bring new and undiscovered hues. Until, as swiftly as the sun disappears behind the skyline, all that is left is one solid block of colour: the truth. He had never taken it. He had simply exposed it as missing. I see this gaping hole in myself. A lack leading to an abyss, to a place where my construction of self through touch, tone, language and thought has to be discarded. It's here, on this ledge, that I forgive him and ask that he forgive me.

Some time passes, I can't say how long, until I am gently cradled back into the high-ceilinged room where the rest of the group are waiting. It takes some time for me to open my eyes, but when I do, I see Ivy. She is tucked up in the foetal position, resting her head on her small hands. She smiles as I turn to face her.

'You shat yourself,' I say earnestly.

'No, I didn't.' She laughs, pressing her face into her pillow.

'Yeah, you did. It was horrible. Nuño had to clean it up.'

She laughs again.

'Nah, just kidding.'

And we lie together like that until more light chatter starts around us.

God

I sleep solidly for four or five hours, but when I wake up Ivy isn't in the bed next to me. I feel uneasy being alone, dread firing through my body at the thought of having to do another ceremony this evening. I get up straight away and go downstairs in yesterday's clothes, the same ones I've slept in. I walk into the kitchen and find Archie by the island, writing something in a notepad. He pauses and closes it when he sees me.

'Good morning,' he says, and it's as if a window has been opened between us. 'How are you feeling?'

'I'm okay, thanks.' I smile, suddenly aware of how challenging it is to stay on the right side of his boundless corneas. These new urges for him are strangely familiar and I quite like the feeling.

'Would you like a cup of tea? You should try to eat something now as well, before the fast begins again,' he says, walking over to a modern-looking Aga and lifting the kettle off its stove.

'Tea would be lovely, thank you.'

'How was last night?' he asks tentatively, turning his back to fill the kettle.

Water gushes from the tap. I use this interruption to gather some thoughts, searching for words to give them meaning. He takes a long, bright blue lighter and clicks it to set the stove alight before placing the kettle down. It clangs. He walks back to the island where I'm now sitting, watching him.

'You don't have to talk about it, not if you don't want to.'

'No, it was amazing. I mean, it's hard to find the right words to describe it. I don't think words really can. It was terrifying and brilliant all at once. I've never experienced anything like last night.'

215

He smiles at me and says nothing.

'How was it for you?' I say.

'It's hard to put into words, as you say, but I'm trying.' Archie looks down at his notepad, then up at me again. 'Were you okay? You seemed to freak out a little at one point.' The wave that comes with his look crashes over me. I am sunk. I blush, not strong enough to withstand my own hypnosis the way everyone else had.

'Yeah, I'm sorry about that. I hope I didn't disturb everyone. It was just getting a little much. There was a moment when I felt I'd gone too far, like if I'd gone any further, I would never have been able to get back.'

'You don't have anything to apologise for,' he says then, leaning against the island on two large hands. 'And, yes, I know that feeling – like you're on the brink of irreparable insanity. But it looked like they got you under control.'

'I don't know if I want to do it again. I mean I know I have to, but I really don't want to.'

'It's different for everyone, I guess. Álvaro explained that was a cleansing ceremony and he has opened us up. Tonight will be a closing ceremony. It won't be as rough, I don't think, but he needs to close you.'

He makes the tea, then takes a bowl from the fridge, pulls off clingfilm and puts it into the microwave.

I'm distracted by those moles on his cheek and he smiles at me. He pushes the tea across the counter. I pick it up and sip, wrapping both hands around the mug for comfort.

'It was a fantasy, a disorienting dream where an internal magic show played out inside me. Some parts were awe-inspiring and beautiful, as though I had an unlimited under-standing of myself.'

'Yes, that's exactly how it feels. You should write that down.' The microwave pings but he doesn't move or respond to it.

I look at the microwave, then back at him.

'Some of it was terrifying, though. In fact, most of it was. It was black and dark: the most disgusting, vile and shameful parts of myself layered over and over one another, unpicked, pulled back and shown to me. And I sort of understood why I am the way I am. It was as if I relearnt what has happened to me in my life.'

His eyes change their expression now and he looks sad. 'You cried a lot when Álvaro sang your *icaro*.'

'Yes.'

'There's a lot of sadness in you.'

'Yes.' I don't flinch. It seems there is nothing to hide from now. He turns and goes towards the microwave. Opening its door, he puts his hand inside and draws it back sharply as he burns himself. He wrestles the hot bowl out with a thin tea towel, spooning the spaghetti and its tomato lava sauce into a new bowl. He pulls back a drawer in the island to reveal a large silver fork, placing it in the spaghetti before gliding the bowl across the counter towards me.

'Thank you,' I murmur.

'You're very welcome, Mathilda.'

I'm confronted by the overwhelming sensation of not wanting to leave his side. But I make myself go before I get pulled out by the current of his gaze. I go because it's the right thing to do. Outside people are sitting at the poolside. A man with blond hair is on on a sunbed facing Florence and they're laughing together. He has a coarse blanket wrapped around him, beige with cream stripes, and he's wearing sheepskin slippers. It's not quite spring, but it's showing signs. The scene is faded sepia; everything is pared back and beige. I sit for a while and look at the surrounding grass, which is covered with armies of dande-lions, some perfectly intact and others missing half of the seeds from their bulbous heads, like they've had a bad haircut. The only thing bringing colour is the light-pastel turquoise of the pool. I look down into my half-eaten bowl of pasta. Is it a good thing that he knows I'm sad?

Once I've finished eating I walk around the pool to the front of the house, where I find the gravel path we drove up last night. It feels like so long ago, a world away. Am I different now? Or perhaps just awoken to the thing that had always made me different. I stop by some grass edging the path and tear up a single dandelion with a proud head of hair. I close my eyes and make a wish, blowing the fragile seedlings into the air.

When I open my eyes there's a deer in front of me, gracefully gliding across the pathway, elegant and gentle. She stops and looks. She's beautiful; her long snout is poised, her expression pensive. Tall ears extend above her narrow head, and her nose is black and wet. There are white speckled blemishes on her fur. We look at one another. Serenity, nothing fleeting, nothing missing. I smell the fleshy-green stem of the dandelion squashing in my clasped hand. Iphigenia, sacrificed by her father. Everything is still.

The Cycle

Back inside the house, Ivy and I go upstairs together. I take out some clean underwear and fresh clothes. Ivy does the same, then leads the way to the bathroom. Something has shifted in Ivy since we got to Italy. In this new context, she's more tactile and a little protective of me. We go up several wooden staircases that seem to get narrower as we ascend, and I duck occasionally to avoid hitting my head on the beams that arch across the low ceilings. We arrive in a bathroom at the very top of the house. It's the attic and has a sloping roof, which forms a triangle. At the very back of the room there is a huge round window, wide enough that I could walk through it, were it not for the panes dividing the glass into segments. I squint out at the blue sky and green mountains. There is a gigantic bathtub in the middle of the room and a tall shelving unit, stacked with clean towels and wicker baskets. A bathmat is spread over the large grey marbled tiles, fluffy and long enough to lie out on. Ivy pulls out several of the baskets, riffling through them for toiletries. She walks over to the bath and turns on a long silver tap that emerges from the floor and curves over the free-standing tub. Water gushes out as she sets down the bottles.

'This is the biggest bathroom I've ever seen,' I say, trying to take it all in.

'I know. It's the best in the house. I live in it whenever I come here.' She pours some herbal-smelling bubble bath into the water and dips herself over the rim to swirl the mixture with her hand.

'Steve's family aren't short of a few bob, eh?'

'Mmm . . .' she mumbles, then says, 'Get undressed, then.'

I turn, and behind me I see a floor-to-ceiling gold Rococo mirror. I pull the bobble out of my hair first, then start to remove my clothing, placing my jumper on a tattered blue chair with a hand-carved wooden frame. On an antique dresser stand two matching vases, bright blue with gold baroque handles, and an eighteenth-century painting of women dancing in pink dresses. I slowly remove the rest of my clothes until I'm just in my knickers. I turn to face Ivy, my arms folded over my chest.

'Come on, get in.'

I pull my underwear down and kick it towards the chair before lifting my leg – almost over my head – to get into the giant bathtub. The water is already over my tummy and I lie back and stretch my legs out.

'Move over!' Ivy's skin is like sunshine set against the bright-white walls, and her long black hair hangs past her small breasts, revealing large, dark nipples. She hops over the side of the tub and settles herself opposite me, using her arms to push the water around. We lie back then, our legs stretching past the sides of one another's bodies. We lie in the quiet, enjoying the warmth as our breathing slows and our muscles start to soften.

'Now *that* was a hell of a night.'

'It certainly was. I don't want to do another ceremony, Ivy.'

'Really? Can you believe how toxic it is, though? The filth we were carrying around inside us.' She looks at me then, perhaps cautiously. 'We vomited so much.'

'It was a place where all of my fears were a kaleidoscope and I just had to sit.'

Ivy sits up a little, the tips of her black hair wet.

'But there was also something magnificent and illuminating about the whole thing too,' I continue, 'something I couldn't resist. The scenes and the memories were so much a part of me, so embedded in me, you know? What I learnt last night would probably have taken me years in therapy.'

'Oh yeah, that was a decade's worth of therapy.' She pushes the water up her body and over her shoulders.

'I saw myself in a way I haven't before: my innate fear of masculinity, the self-harm . . . And then the ayahuasca showed me all the reasons why I was like that, and when I felt I couldn't take any more, it just kept going.'

Ivy lies back in the bath and pushes her legs under the hot

220

water, running them back along the side of my body. Her tanned legs making mine look like extra long Mini Milks.

'When Álvaro was singing that *icaro* the sadness was rising off me. He was removing it. I've never felt anything like that. Those melodies were so primal, so haunting.'

'He was saying earlier that an ayahuasca shaman will diet on certain plants for years. As young children they're sent off into the rainforest where they live exclusively on plants to integrate fully with their qualities. That's where they learn their *icaros*. It's how they learn to understand the plant and how it works. They're sacred songs used to call on specific spirits or to accelerate the energy in a space. Did you feel that last night? The acceleration when they sang?'

'Hell, yeah, I felt it.' My voice leaps an octave. 'And did you notice at one point Álvaro and Nuño were singing but the only people purging were the women? All of the guys just sat there, completely unaffected, and we were all puking our guts up.'

'Yeah.' We looked at each other then, across the water and the flatness of our tummies and we speak, not for the first time that day, without language.

'You know, it's not just the women who have suffered. Most of the men in that room have in some way or another, or they've been born into this world from women who have. It's an endless cycle. Where some terrible trauma in our ancestry gets passed down and down . . .'

I turn my attention to the heat in my chest fusing, the shoal of fish re-emerging and darting across it.

'It's the story of our shadow, that part of ourselves we can't bear to see. We refract it onto every surface of culture and art so it's more manageable and bearable to observe. It's too painful to look at in ourselves.'

'Do you really believe that?'

'Of course I do.'

A few bubbles rise to the surface then.

'Ivy, did you just fluff?'

'No,' she protests, her mouth wide open with faux-outrage.

'You're disgusting!' I retreat, using my hand to splash water at her, and we both succumb to laughter.

Huayruro Beads

After we've cleaned up, Ivy and I head downstairs, where Álvaro wants to talk to the group. We each pull our mattresses to the front of the large living room and position them in front of him. He can't speak English so well, so Nuño – whose English is impeccable – translates for us.

'He says he hopes that you are all feeling well today and that last night was a beautiful ceremony,' says Nuño.

Álvaro continues to speak, looking around at us, smiling.

'He says you all did very well last night. He says his shamanism involves a three-way relationship between himself, the ayahuasca medicine and the plant spirits, and that it's his relationship with the plant spirits that enabled him to guide you.'

Álvaro stops talking then and looks around the room at us all, continuing to smile and nod. He goes on.

'He says that he used the *mapacho* as a cleansing agent to transmit the healing energies of the plants and to protect you against the negative energies, of which there were many in the room with us last night, as you are all aware.'

Álvaro speaks again.

'Tonight, we shall do a closing ceremony and your experiences will perhaps be quite different.' Nuño translates with a thick Spanish accent. 'I am here for the rest of the day if anyone would like to speak with me one-on-one about their experience. Or you can ask me questions now in our group discussion.'

Álvaro pauses, looking around at each of us.

'I'd like us to go around and for each of you to share something about your experience last night, for you to tell us a little about what happened or how you are feeling today,' says Nuño.

Álvaro smiles and nods in the direction of Steve, who is sitting on the far right of the group. We each take our turn to talk about the night and what we felt. People talk about psychedelic snakes, a fourth-dimension reality and a meeting either with God or their death. They try to put into words a complete breakdown of the ego, an overwhelming feeling of love they've never felt before, or the most terrifying reliving of the past. I keep swallowing hard on the saliva pouring into my mouth, the thought of sharing bringing on a sickness. This feels like a spiritual hospital and I can't quite compute how I ended up here, how I got my diagnosis. When it's Ivy's turn she cries and thanks them repeatedly for their help. Nuño translates that she's a beautiful person. It feels special to watch her hard edges blurring. When it's my turn I stumble over my words. I don't like having the eyes of all of these people on me and I feel more vulnerable, given I'm the only newcomer to the group.

'I don't want to do it again.' The words escape my mind and mouth at the same time. 'I'm afraid.'

Álvaro nods and looks down at the floor.

'When I freaked out, I thought I was losing my mind. It was too much for me.'

'He says you did have a very difficult experience last night, but it was not the worst he has seen. Many people in this room were struggling and having difficult battles.'

Great. Now I feel even more ridiculous.

'Tonight will be a different kind of ceremony. It will be a lot easier for you and Álvaro is saying he thinks you will have a different experience.'

'So it won't be as bad?' I ask, my voice cracking slightly.

Álvaro laughs once Nuño has translated this back to him.

'He says, no, it won't be bad. But he advises you to do the ceremony.' Álvaro nods at me and smiles, then averts his gaze to Kate, who is next to me.

'Thank you.' They look back at me. 'Thank you for what you did last night. I am deeply grateful to both of you.'

Nuño doesn't wait to translate what Álvaro says, he just smiles. 'You are welcome. We are very happy if we have helped you.'

They were right. The second time was different. That night, after drinking the thick brown liquid once more, I smiled at Álvaro, who beamed back at me. I retreated to my mattress and lay down with a blanket over my head, focusing my mind on the present, praying with all my might that I would resist its powers. It was very quiet for some time and I heard very few movements. There was just the deafening silence until Álvaro started singing. Then they came – colourful, snake-like entities emerging from the middle distance, pushing and trembling around my body. My heart pounded and thudded, but I let them come. I was lost then, to another eight-hour ride on a psychological rollercoaster I couldn't get off.

At first the snakes writhed through my body, slowly focusing on certain parts of me, massaging and wriggling firmly, up through my legs and into my jaw where they stayed for a lifetime writhing and healing, writhing and healing. Eating the decaying matter that resided in flesh and bone. I lie under the washing line in the garden of my childhood home where fresh cooking apples grow on a lush green tree. Colours I'd never seen before rained down on me and I was overcome with love and unbridled joy. A pre-symbolic experience of complete happiness and ecstasy, where I met with my own version of 'God' and visited the place I might go when I die.

The next day I feel calm. We thank Mother Ayahuasca together by planting an offering in the field behind the swimming-pool, and we each take our turn to thank Álvaro and Nuño. Nature is humming all around us as Ivy and I reluctantly go and pack our things. I'm overcome with respect and love for these people who move around me like the leaves outside, untethered but in a cluster together. I contemplate this after Ivy has left the bedroom, gliding with her small suitcase down the many stairs. I sit at the end of the bed, oddly at home in this spaceship-themed room. I don't want to leave but Steve has called a cab for us.

'Do you need a hand with your luggage?' I look up and Archie is in the doorway, leaning against the frame just like the first night. His chocolate hair falling around his face, his expression cheeky. There is an adorable boyishness to him and I feel drawn in. I want to get up and walk across the room. I want to take my forefinger and draw it along his wide mouth, tracing the edges of his lips.

'Are you okay?'

Oh, God, say something. I avert my hungry eyes.

'I'm fine. I can manage with my suitcase, thank you. I was just thinking . . . It's strange, part of me feels sad to leave.'

'I know. I think we all feel like that. Can I come in?'

'Yes, of course.' I shift instinctively to the side of the bed so that there's room for him next to me.

'Shall I sit?'

'Sure.' I smile at him.

He moves a closed fist over my hand, which I turn over in response and open. He places a bracelet inside it. It's made of bright red huayruro beads that have small black smudges on them and are tied together with string.

'Álvaro's wife makes them back in Peru. I thought you'd like one, something to keep.' He laughs awkwardly.

'That's really kind, Archie. Thank you,' I place it on top of my suitcase and turn back to face him.

'I was wondering if, when we're in London, you'd like to hang out?' he says. 'Maybe get some dinner, or go for a tonic water . . . at least until the diet lifts and then maybe we could get something a little stronger sometime.'

I go to respond.

'Sorry,' he laughs, 'I'm asking you on three dates there before you've even said yes to one.'

'Yes.' I smile confidently. 'I'd like that a lot.'

I give Archie my number. He taps it into his phone and saves it. He picks up my suitcase and carries it down the stairs for me. I follow with my handbag. Ivy and I say goodbye to the others – there's lots of hugging and embracing – and when I come to Florence she holds tightly, almost crushing me.

'You're not alone,' she says.

'I know.' I squeeze her back.

Archie and I share a hug that lingers a little too long and my heart sinks when he pulls away. Steve loads our bags into the boot of the taxi and I follow Ivy into the back seat and close the door behind me. She holds the button down on the electric window and stretches across me.

'GOODBYE, YOU BEAUTIFUL, GORGEOUS, FAN-TASTIC BASTARDS!' she shouts.

The car pulls off down the gravel path. The sadness subdues as I turn my mind to what's waiting for me back in London.

Ophelia

People do strange things when they're grieving. In *Hamlet*, after the death of her father, Ophelia adorns herself with flowers, sings maddening songs and drowns herself in a brook. Sylvia Plath followed in her footsteps singing her maddened poem to Daddy – four months later she sticks her head in an oven. You die and I cry dutifully at your bedside, etch the pain out on my arm with a razor and swallow a hallucinogenic vine.

I have these memories of you now. I suppose upon reflection they have always been there, lurking in the background. A passing shadow in front of a doorway, or in the corner of my eye – back, back, back in black corners of my mind. So deeply buried and repressed that when I start to recall a memory of you, I remember it in the wrong order. Like an intricate object buried under layers and layers of dry mud, I scoop back the dirt in small handfuls to reveal a corner, an edge, the gentle curvature of a moment – but the grainy soil slips back through my fingers, each time covering the glimpse I'd seen so that I couldn't make out what it was. These soft monochromatic flashes, delicately unearthed, are pieces of a story that had never consummated the narrative. My narrative.

The semblances of a story I haven't yet accepted as mine. Each flashback is a clue: the wooden wardrobe with a mirror on its front that was taller than the sky; soft sheets, the colour of which I can't say for sure; the smell, which I liked, of the plastic surface of a water bed that I remember was cornflower blue; white Y-fronts that smelt of fabric softener; a crying man who rocked and cradled himself; and burning shame – don't tell anyone.

I'd lifted my face to look directly at the sun and burned the image away, morphing light blots leading to those blind spots in my memory. For years I dismissed them, these fragments of memory. I strangled them with the bare hands of the men who loved me, wrapping them around my throat when the lights went out. I violently dismembered them in the back of my mouth with vodka that stung the edges of my lips. There are feelings we shun. They haunt us, reminding us of their existence with a resurfacing ache. So we create new pain for ourselves in our present, absolving us of the historical pain that we cannot cope with. This naive plan serves us for only so long: it gets shit all over in the men's underwear section at Marks & Spencer one sunny afternoon. Yes. White Y-fronts. My hands on your white Y-fronts. They were soft and fleece-like. Yours always looked so clean and brand new. You on top of me. I remember pulling open that wardrobe in your bedroom, then a drawer that was filled with white soft Y-fronts. Ordered and neat, so white. I sat there with them for a while, on the floor next to this drawer, and was overwhelmed by these pants. How many of them there were, and what they now meant. A little daughter in your bed, keeping you company when you cried yourself to sleep in your drunken states. A pain that is odious and sharp, a sourness pervading the mouth of a little girl who holds it in there, decaying. She releases it with her sweet, childlike breath. It's smelly, like a rotting kipper, salted in caramel.

This little girl sat with her knees pulled up against her chest in the corner of the room for years, in her nightie, her dark hair messy, tangled all around her face. I was too afraid to look at her. It took me two decades to see that she was more afraid of me than I was of her. And in your bed where we watched porn, and you were drunk, and she was scared and confused, the memory of me touching you ends eventually with your tears. You'd drunkenly stumble around the house, shouting and screaming. I'd have done anything to keep you from getting angry. I had loved you so innocently and purely until you had taken it away from me. I comforted you, my skinny girlish arms reaching around your tall high back as you cried and moaned into the night: *It's okay, Dad. Don't cry. It's going to be okay.* Now your shame bleeds into me as I turn away from the howling man who was meant to be my protector. You cry loudly and unashamedly, and I pull back the sheet a little, just enough to smell the cornflower blue plastic, which ripples as you heave and moan.

The new pain I sought was never separate from you; the two always mirrored each other. Inextricably linked by one long thread that grates as it's pulled through my body, my organs, my heart. A thing teased out by spiritual bathing rituals, a tarot reader, some healing plants, and now aloneness. It is a numbed expression of an unbearable friction that squalls and squeals and rages, so deep inside I thought I might never find it.

I'm sorry.

You have nothing to be sorry for, little one.

But didn't I do something wrong?

No, this is not your fault. You did nothing wrong. You're just a child.

I'm scared that he's angry with us.

He has no right to be. Only we deserve to be angry.

Please don't tell anyone.

Madeleines

When we arrive home, I'm thrilled to be greeted by Jeremy at the door. I lift up the skinny rat and bury my nose in his fluffy head, taking in his biscuity, warm, puppy scent.

'I told you you'd miss him,' Georgia calls from the kitchen. Ivy and I walk down the hall to find her and Ekua at the kitchen table, drinking tea. There's a formality to the occasion in the way they've placed themselves, marking out the two seats reserved for Ivy and me.

'So, did you lose your absolute mind?'

'Oh, we'd lost those way before we did ayahuasca. It was the nihilism and existential dread I was looking to shake off,' Ivy jests, only half of her face joining in.

'Yeah, well, we hoped you'd leave those in Italy n'all,' Ekua quips affectionately. 'Here,' she says, getting up, 'sit down both of you. I'll make you a brew.'

'How do you feel now?' Georgia asks.

'Erm . . . fine. A little spaced out, I guess, but other than that, pretty good.' I try to steady myself in the room. It all feels a little surreal here.

'A normal brew?' Ekua asks.

'A mint tea, please. No caffeine for us, sadly. We have to continue this diet for a little while longer.'

'Do you want to talk about it?' Georgia asks, smiling at me, wide-eyed and inquisitive.

'Nah, not really.'

'Okay.' She looks down at her tea, disappointed.

'Maybe tomorrow,' Ivy offers. 'We're tired. It's been quite a heavy weekend as you can imagine.'

'Yeah, of course we'll tell you all about it, but right now I'm knackered. It was incredible, though.'

'Well, that's good, then,' Georgia reassures herself.

'We missed ya,' Ekua says, putting a pot of mint tea on the table.

'Of course you did. We're the fun ones.' Ivy pours for us both. She pulls her jumper over her hands and wraps them around the hot cup.

'I'm sorry again about our row, Eks. It was stupid. And I shouldn't have—'

'It's all forgotten doll.' She squeezes my shoulder and leaves her hand there.

'What's this on your wrist?' Georgia says, fingering the to-mato-red huayruro beads.

'Oh, nothing. It's just a bracelet I got from the shaman.' I pull my hand back to pick up my mug.

'Well, you're both home in the nick of time. This one has called a family meeting.' Ekua throws her head towards Georgia.

'Sounds very formal,' I say.

'That's what I said.' Ekua pushes a punnet of green grapes towards Ivy, then helps herself to another Garibaldi. 'But there were snacks, so I agreed to show face.'

'I am not doing another of those ghastly women's circles,' Ivy broods.

'It's not another circle, don't panic.'

'How did the Veet go down?' I ask.

'Fine.' Ekua smiles gently.

'It went well, then?' I press a little further.

'It was lovely.' She says this shieldingly, the way people do when they fall for someone and become protective of something precious that wasn't there before.

'Good for you. I miss sex.'

'And masturbation,' Ivy adds painfully.

'And masturbation,' I chime in agreement.

'Mmm . . . Well . . . a little birdie told me you made a friend on your trip.' Georgia nudges me with her arm.

'A what?'

'A friend. Like a man friend.'

'I did not make a man friend,' I say defensively, caught off guard.

I look up at Ivy, who smiles behind her fringe and reaches for another grape.

'Most of the people partaking in the ceremony were men, so if you look at the data, statistically speaking it was more likely that I'd make friends with a man than a woman.' I pop a grape into my mouth and pout at her.

'Mm-hmm.' Ekua's unconvinced.

'It was nothing.'

'Do you like him?' asks Georgia.

'No.'

'Yes,' Ivy corrects.

'Handsome guy with piercing blue eyes and the emotional intelligence of Gandhi, is what the birdie told me.'

'Can we stop talking about Ivy as if she's not here, please?' I change the conversation. 'What's this meeting all about then, Bailey?'

'You don't have to marry him. But you could allow yourself

a little joy in your life . . .' Ivy leans back in her chair, cradling her shins.

'Yeah, nothing wrong with a bit of slap and tickle,' adds Ekua.

'I think it would be good for you,' Georgia says, as she fusses around, adding crisps and dip, some celery sticks, a bowl of raspberries and a plate of madeleines to the middle of the table.

'G, despite your unwavering confidence on the subject, you don't always know what's best for me.'

She stares at me then, offended. Her hands clutch the plate of madeleines, which she knows are my favourite and has bought for me especially.

'Georgia wants to go to the pub after,' Ekua adds.

Georgia lifts a madeleine to her lips and wraps her mouth around the entire thing.

I sip my tea.

'Mmm . . .' she moans in enjoyment.

'Yeah, it might be good to get out of the house for an hour. I feel a little strange.' Ivy places her chin on her knee.

'What's the family meeting all about then?' I ask.

'Georgia's pregnant,' Ivy states.

'It's chlamydia,' Ekua follows.

'You've finally decided to start bleaching your moustache?' I ask excitedly.

Georgia picks up a madeleine and throws it at my head. I shift just in time and it hits the wall behind me.

'No, the reason I've brought us together isn't to announce my contraction of a sexually transmitted disease. Nor am I pregnant. Thank God! I just thought it would be nice to spend some time together.'

'Thank God for that, too,' Ekua says. 'I thought you were

going to tell us you're kicking us out and have finally asked Henry to move in with you.'

The atmosphere changes and Georgia's fingers play with the corner of the table. She's looking uncomfortable.

'Oh, God,' says Ekua.

'That's great!' says Ivy.

'Henry's moving in?' I smile at her.

'Is that okay?'

'Of course it's okay. G, are you kidding? That's great news,' I say. 'I'm happy for you.'

And I really mean it.

'There's no rush for any of you to move out. You can stay for as long as you need. Until you find another place, or another set-up. I don't want any of you to feel rushed or put out.'

'Oh, Lord, no,' says Ekua, in her deep northern drawl. 'You two will be at it like rabbits. We don't wanna be subjected to that.'

'We haven't been at it like rabbits since 2013,' Georgia says unenthusiastically. 'I thought the expectation to have a buoyant and thriving sex life lifted after over a decade of being together. I'm not sure I want to go back to the days where we were at it five times a day.'

'No, it's very aggressive on the labia.' Ivy nods.

'Yes – it got so swollen once that I thought it might—'

'Okay – that's enough! Let's wrap it up, kids,' Ekua says, taking the tea I'm still drinking from my hands. 'I fancy a pint.'

We put our coats on and leave the snacks out for our return. It's a mild evening and the sun has just started to set. Georgia and I walk arm in arm behind Ekua and Ivy, who are talking about the future. Ivy mentions a friend who has just broken up with her fiancé and is looking for a flatmate to help cover her mortgage on a gorgeous flat in Notting Hill. Ekua talks about Lucia and the possibility of them getting a small place together.

'It's nice to have you back,' Georgia says, drawing closer to me so that our linked arms are knotted together. I feel the warmth of her down the side of my body.

We walk like that for a couple of minutes, pressed closely but with a space between us she's deliberately holding. And then I start to tell her about what happened at the weekend. Like a sponge being squeezed, it's fast and gushing at first, then more modest as I drip the rest of the information into her slowly, carefully. Afraid of the damage it might do. And when I tell her about my dad, she stops in the street and says, 'Oh, love, I'm so sorry. If I'm honest,' she pauses gently, 'I'm not surprised by that information. I sort of . . . well, I sort of always wondered if . . .' Tears start to form in the corners of her eyes.

Her words move in the breeze, echoing against themselves like a wind chime. *I'm not surprised by that information.* They pull on the string that grates through my body, my organs, my heart. The shame burns, but it's not my shame. It's his. So I give it back to him and she holds me under a streetlight tightly, burying her head in my shoulder.

'Come on, you pair!' Ekua shouts, from a distance.

'You are so brave,' she says, holding my face now, 'and I love you so much. There is so much love in your life. You know that, don't you, Mathilda? You are so loved.'

'I know.' I smile into her hands before she removes them to take my hand in hers and we run off down the street in the dusk, towards the others.

Gate Crasher

The next morning, I wake up to the sound of my phone ringing. What time is it? I open just one eye: it's 9.03 a.m. Not as early as it feels. I don't recognise the number, but it could be a client, so I answer.

'Hello!' I say, feigning perkiness.

'Oh, hello, there, am I speaking with Mathilda Mannings?'

'Yes, this is Mathilda.'

'This is Amika from Age UK calling.'

'Amika, hi. It's good to hear from you. Am I late on filling out my time slots with Constance again? I'm sorry! I do keep a note in my personal diary, but I forget sometimes.' The guilt drives on my babble. 'I know I haven't done it for a while, but I'll make sure I do it later today. I'm really sorry—'

'Actually, that's not why I'm calling.'

'Oh, right.' My mind busies itself.

'I'm afraid I have some bad news. Constance was found this morning by her neighbour. She . . . she's very sadly passed away. We think it happened a couple of days ago but I'm still waiting for the autopsy results to come back. It was most likely a heart attack. They don't think she suffered.'

'Oh.' I feel my own heart hard against my chest.

'The funeral will be next week at the Honor Oak crematorium in Peckham. It's on the third at two p.m. Do you have a pen to hand?'

'Honor Oak Crematorium, two p.m.,' I repeat. 'That's okay, I'll remember.'

Constance's death had been something I'd thought about, of course it had. It came to my mind when she didn't answer the door for a really long time, and to the pit of my stomach if her phone rang out for too long. But I had always imagined her funeral would be at the church near her house. It was where we'd gone to a carol service together at Christmas. She'd wandered around, drinking a glass of champagne, eating the snacks and charming everyone with her dirty giggle. The vicar had known her by name.

'Mathilda, are you still there?'

'Yes . . . sorry. I'm in shock.'

'I'm really sorry for your loss. I know you were close. She was such a character and she loved your time together very much. She always said such lovely things about you whenever we checked in with her. She was always concerned that we were going to pass you on to another service user. You brought a lot of joy to her life.'

'Thank you.' I swipe the tears from my eyes with the back of my arm. More come to replace them.

'Please don't feel obligated to attend the service,' says Amika. 'It's not a requirement for our volunteers.'

'No, I'll be there. Thank you for letting me know. I really appreciate it.'

'All right. Take care and we'll be in touch again soon.'

'Thank you.'

'Goodbye.'

She hangs up, and when I look down there's a text on my screen.

Hey, how are you getting on? It feels very strange to be back in London. A little overwhelming. I think everyone's feeling it. I'm in your neck of the woods today if you fancy a decaf? Archie xx

I turn my body back into itself and under the quilts, where I stay sobbing for most of the morning, until Ekua comes and finds me.

Later that day I pull myself together and get a bus to Shoreditch to meet Archie in a café on Club Row. I arrive ten minutes early, not expecting him to be there. I sense him before I see him. He's sitting at the front, waiting. Not on his phone, or jotting things in his leather notebook, no. He is simply, and ever-so-coolly, waiting.

'Hi.' I raise my hand and gesture a wave.

He stands up as I make my way across the wooden floor-boards, under the hanging light-bulbs of this modern east-London café. He's beside a high table that has two tall stools at either side of it, and when I get to him, we hug.

'How are you doing? I'm so sorry to hear about your friend.'

'Thanks.' I smile at him sadly.

'How long had you known each other?'

'Eight, nine months or so. I suppose it's not that long, really.'

'It's a long time when you were seeing her once or twice a week. Here, take a seat.' He gestures. 'From what you said on the phone, she sounded like a pretty extraordinary woman.'

'She made me look at things from a different perspective. When I was out with her in London, wandering around streets I know really well, she'd point things out, small details. A door and its funny gargoyle knocker, kids playing in the street or a cat peering through a window. When I was with Constance, I noticed the seasons . . . She was so focused on a sense of community – it was something she felt part of. And when we hung out, I guess I did too.'

'She must have loved having you around, though. It's a really good thing you did for her.'

'She was the good one. She was from a different time. We concern ourselves with our next Tinder date or the form of our Downward Dog, but her generation were in bomb hideouts wondering if they'd make it through the night.'

Archie nods. 'When's the funeral?'

'It's this week so . . .' I quiver. 'It always makes me feel weird how quickly it all happens once someone has died.'

He reaches across the table and puts his hand on mine. 'I could come with you, if you'd like. You shouldn't go alone.'

I withdraw my hand almost instinctively, a reflex that makes him look uncomfortable. 'No. Thank you, Archie. But I think I'd rather go by myself. Thanks for offering, that's kind of you. I appreciate it, really.' The hair on my arms stands on end.

'No problem. Well, if there's anything you need, I'm around, you can call me.'

I realise then that it was a mistake to have come. To have brought this new grief to a hipster café where I thought it might be absolved by a man, grated down by his affection.

'Shall I get us a drink? What would you like?'

We drink our boring herbal teas under the gorgeous stench of rich coffee and lament the masochism of meeting here. He talks about the others and what they've been up to, and how he feels about going back to work. He asks me lots of questions too and smiles shyly from under his beanie. He looks handsome in a white T-shirt and a navy canvas Carhartt jacket. His chinos are rolled up to reveal white socks in Vans. I still feel this urge to touch him, to be near to him. When the time comes it's hard to say goodbye: it feels unnatural, wrong almost. My body growls bad-temperedly at any suggestion of separation but my skin rejects the idea of his hands. This desperation to put part of myself inside him: it's a frenzied urge and it outlines to me something fundamentally wrong. I tell him I need to be getting on with work and that I'm late for a meeting at Hatch, which is true.

'Are you around this weekend? There's this exhibition on at the Barbican and—'

'Archie.'

'Yes?' He grins at me.

'I don't think you're the sort of person I could be with without falling entirely *into* you.'

He stares at me, seemingly taken aback by my honesty.

'And, instinctively, I know that's not what I need right now. In fact, it's probably the worst thing I could do. Does that make sense?'

'I think so.' His cheeks redden.

'I like you a lot. I mean, I *really* fancy you. But I don't want to get involved with anyone at the moment. And that's my bad, I shouldn't have come.'

A woman is never really satisfied by a man's love. I know this now. No matter how much he's willing to give, it's never enough to quench our thirst. I needed to figure out being on my own.

'Perhaps we could just be friends,' he asks soberly.

I think about Shelta's words on the boat that day: *There is a man coming. But you'll be friends first.*

'I'm not ready to be just friends yet, Archie.'

'I am.' He grins back boyishly, holding onto his elbows, leaning towards me.

'Well, then,' I smile at him as I reach for my coat, 'we must agree to disagree.'

He smiles thoughtfully, looks down at the floor and then nods, yielding. I comfort the groaning fear that fevers inside me: I'm here, I silently whisper. You're not alone, you have me. I leave Archie at the café, I want to look back at him through the glass windows that are lined with hanging plants, but I don't.

Funeral

*I just wanted to say good luck for today, Sharon. I know 'good luck'
probably isn't the right thing to say but I'm so proud of you for how
strong you're being about all this, but also, don't forget to let yourself
be sad. You are allowed. Grief is a good thing. It means that you
loved someone. It means that they mattered. I wish I could be there,
but I'll be back in just a couple of weeks. I can't wait to see you. I
have the longest day at court and then I plan to ricochet myself into
a mound of Thai noodles. What did you decide to wear again? The
trouser suit or the black dress? Either will be perfect. Anyway, that's
all I wanted to say really. Be brave. I love you. Did I say that
already? I'll call you when I get home.*
48 seconds

It's a crisp morning, the sun is shining through the train
window and the warmth hits the back of my neck, lighting me
up, like a Gothic angel. I take my headphones out and look down
at the black dress I'm wearing, which has wide, puffy sleeves.
It's long and oversized, finishing near my ankles. I'm wearing
the heeled black court shoes – that I only ever seem to retrieve
from a box under my bed for funerals – and my long coat. I
don't feel myself. I feel like someone who's dressed as a grown-up,
impersonating someone sensible. The Overground is quiet at
this time of the day and I'm distracted by a woman sitting
opposite me who is trying to convince a little girl to sit nicely
on her seat. The child refuses, jumping off and then clambering
back onto the orange fabric, full of too much life to sit *nicely*,
like a good little girl. Her long, brown hair falls to her waist, like
Georgia's, and she grins knowingly as her mother's patience

starts to wane. I wink and smile back. I get off at Honor Oak Park station and rush quickly through the park. It's 2.10 p.m. – I'm late. I hear Constance's voice, telling me *Oh, well, I assumed you weren't coming anyway. I thought you'd be too busy.* Before the crematorium big white pillars support the open gates, and through them I can see the large, grey building, which is square with a triangular slate roof and a tall, slim bell tower. I rush up the grey concrete steps and inside the building.

The first thing I spot when I'm inside is a rectangular-shaped platform that has the coffin slid inside under the altar. There are some white lilies on top, which annoys me because she hated lilies, for the smell and the malicious pollen that she never forgave for ruining her favourite trousers. I never made that mistake again. Tulips were her favourite. I'd always disliked them – they seemed to me uneventful, relishing their averageness. A bereaved man in a grey suit greets me.

'Thank you so much for coming,' he says, and hands me a white pamphlet. 'He'd be thrilled by today's turnout.' He must be a friend of Constance's husband.

There are two tall windows on either side of the high white walls that allow the sunlight ever-so-slightly to warm the cold and otherwise bare room. The first four or five rows are filled on each side, so I join an inconspicuous wooden pew near the back and sit next to an old man, who frowns and tuts at me. He doesn't appreciate my lateness any more than Constance would. I look to the front, where I think I spot the back of Claire's head – she owns one of the local art galleries. I don't recognise anyone else, but I'm pleased with the turnout, too. Despite Constance's many friends, there are a lot more people here than I was expecting. A man in a suit is at the front leading the service. It occurs to me that it's odd that it's a non-religious service, but his voice is so monotonous and the ceremony so impersonal that it's hard to concentrate on what he's saying. I don't think she would have liked this. My heart pounds in my chest from running through the park, signalling that I am very much alive.

'Jonathan's son will now read us the eulogy,' he says.

Jonathan? Who the fuck is Jonathan? I look around. Okay, that's not Clara. A tall man in his fifties with blond hair walks up to the stand at the front of the room and unfolds some paper. He's very smart, his hair combed neatly, and he smiles at a woman in the front row who is rocking her hips from side to side with a wriggling toddler in her arms. Constance didn't have any grandchildren.

'Dad would have taken great delight in having us all gathered here today.'

Dad?

'He loved a party. He was always the life and soul, even into his old age. If he were here now, he'd say, son—'

'Son?' I shoot up and the congregation turns to look at me. The blond son freezes.

'I'm ever so sorry. I am sorry. Excuse me. I'm so sorry.' An endless series of apologies leaks out of my mouth in my personal and unwelcome oration as I edge along the narrow pew to the aisle.

'I apologise. I thought this was, well, someone else's . . .' I say, backing out of the crematorium and tripping over myself. 'I am so sorry. Shit. Sorry. Good luck!'

Good luck? The self-loathing begins before those two words finish rolling carelessly off my tongue and into the primed ears of the grieving congregation. The man who was sitting next to me is red in the face, whether with anger or mortification on my behalf, I'm not sure. I turn and run out of the door, back down the concrete steps and towards the white pillars. I have picked up such a speed that by the time I reach them I almost crash into Georgia and Ekua.

'Oi!' Ekua grabs my arm as I go galloping past. 'What you doing?'

I swing around. 'It's the wrong funeral! It wasn't Constance's funeral,' I blurt out. 'It's the wrong fucking funeral!'

'What?' Georgia says, her face crumpling in disbelief.

'That is someone else's funeral in there?' Ivy asks, looking towards the crematorium.

'It's Jonathan's funeral,' I say breathlessly, handing her the white pamphlet.

'Who the fuck is Jonathan?' Ekua says loudly, her eyes widening.

'Well, precisely.'

At this, they each turn their heads to look at one another for permission, before erupting into laughter. I laugh too, gently at first, until my body eventually folds itself over, my long black dress dragging across the ground. We stand there, tears rolling down our faces, hands clutching arms, hair swaying, as we rock against one another and I give way to the hysterics that come fast and uncontrollably, hot in my belly.

'No, I understand that, Amika, but you definitely did say two p.m. at Honor Oak Crematorium to me on the phone.'

The girls are tittering in the background as we bunch together to fit on a wooden bench in the park.

'I am so sorry. I could have sworn I said twelve thirty. That was the time of Constance's funeral.'

'Well, I don't think you did, Amika, because if you had I would have been here for twelve thirty, prompt. But instead I made my way into Jonathan . . .' I search the pamphlet for a name '. . . Jonathan Knight's funeral and his family were unamused to say the least,' I say sadly.

The girls chortle again. I frown and shake my head.

'We've never had a situation like this before. I'm not quite sure what to say.'

'Is there a reception?' I plead hopefully.

'I think the church was planning on having a small get-together with some of the community-hall regulars, sandwiches and soft drinks, that sort of thing. I can pull up the address.'

That's the other side of London.

'No. That's okay,' I say briskly, knowing I won't make it in time. 'Were there many people there? At the ceremony?'

'I'm sorry, but I didn't make it myself.'

My heart sinks at the thought of sparse, empty pews.

'My sincerest apologies again.'

'Okay, thanks. Goodbye, then.' I disconnect the call. 'What the fuck is wrong with people?' I'm exasperated.

'How long have you got?' says Ekua, taking the lid off her coffee and handing it to Ivy so she can add some sugar.

'I think maybe it's a good thing you weren't there,' says Ivy.

'Yes, maybe Constance planned it on purpose,' says Georgia. 'She probably didn't want your last experience of her to be at a gloomy crematorium. They're so bleak and sterile. This way, you can remember her as she was.'

'When's the last time you saw her? It was at that exhibition, wasn't it?'

'Yes.'

'And what did you talk about?' asks Georgia, lighting her cigarette and sucking in the smoke.

'Grief.' I smile. 'She had a lot of opinions about that.'

'I like a woman with a lot of opinions,' says Ekua.

'Me too.' I take a cigarette from Georgia's packet. 'I can't believe you all came.'

They had all taken time off work. 'We know you said you wanted to go alone, but you didn't say anything about afterwards, so we thought you might like to go for a late lunch.' Georgia smiled.

'We didn't want you to be on your own,' says Ivy, almost reluctantly.

'That's sweet.' I feel a little overcome at the thoughtfulness of their gesture. 'I'm fine.'

'No one is ever fine,' Georgia says. 'That's just something people say. People are very rarely just *fine*, so stop saying that all the time.'

'Okay,' I say, breathing out and nodding. 'I'm not fine, but I haven't worn my dungarees in weeks. So that's something.'

Ivy laughs, scrunching her eyes.

'Hear hear!' says Ekua, raising her coffee to toast the park.

And we sit like that, together on the park bench. I lie back with my head on Georgia's lap, the sun on our faces, and share more stories with the girls about the wonder that was Constance, and her unique superpower as the voice of the universe.

Roots

A week later I'm hopping on one leg in the hallway, trying to pull my other trainer on, when Georgia appears in the living-room doorway, with Jeremy in her arms. Still in her pyjamas, which are white and silky with cherries on them. She squints at me contemplatively, her hair frizzed and messy. 'It's early. Are you going to get coffee? Can you get me one?'

'I'm not going to get coffee,' I say, bending over, flicking my long hair down over my head to gather it together.

'Are you going for a walk?'

'*Nein.*' I flip my head back up, tying the wavy ponytail in a tight bobble.

'Why don't you take Jeremy?' she prompts, with sleep still in her eyes.

'Because I'm not going for a walk, Georgia.'

'Well, where are you going?' she riles.

'Georgia?'

'Yes?' Her tone's impatient.

'What are you gonna do when I move out and you can't surveil my every move?'

'WhatsApp and call you incessantly.'

'Nooo . . .' I shake my head, signalling that's the wrong answer. 'You're going to stop thinking about my every move and focus your attention back on yourself.'

'Okay, fine. And I will do that, just as soon as you move out. But right now we do live together so just tell me where you're going, won't you?'

'I'm going to my Reiki appointment,' I say casually.

She scoffs at me and rolls her eyes. 'Are you going on a date? Is that why you don't want to tell me? You're off to meet Archie again . . .' Her shoulder lifts with excitement.

'No, babe. I'm going to my Reiki appointment,' I repeat.

'Mathilda Mannings does "Feiki"?' she says, putting Jeremy down and folding her arms across her chest, her expression sceptical.

'That she does.'

'Since when?' There's a hint of accusation.

'Since the last month or so, if you must know everything.'

'So you're just voluntarily going for Reiki of a Sunday morning at eight a.m.?' she says sceptically.

'Mummy's so cynical,' I tease, giving Jeremy a rumbunctious rub on the head. 'Want to meet me for pancakes after? The appointment's only an hour. It's on Broadway Market. We can meet there if you can be bothered to wash your face.'

'Yeah, okay. That'll be nice.' She smiles at me.

'Good. I want pancakes with maple syrup *and* bacon.' I kiss her cheek and pull the front door shut behind me.

It's my third appointment with 'Lucy Light' and despite the questionable – if not ridiculous – brand name, I like her. She has a large round bosom, a deep bellowing voice better suited to a London cabbie, and eyelashes that are caked in mascara. I lie on the bed with a mask over my eyes as she places crystals on my chakras and sprays me with things like frankincense. Her hands are always really warm, and I like the way it feels when she cups them around my head. After she's done working on each point of my body, she taps it lightly three times. I find the synergy and repetition reassuring. I don't know if my stomach really pulls and aches when she places her hands over it. I don't know if my throat really tingles or if the mystery pressure on my chest is even there. I don't know if it's quackery or if for one small hour I am able to just be inside my body shifting the difficult things that still reside there.

'You really need to work on your root chakra, darling,' Lucy booms. She puts one hand on the bed and one on her hip as I finish my breathing and pull myself up.

'Have you been doing the grounding meditation we talked about?' she asks, handing me a cup of cold water.

'Well . . . I've tried but—'

'I know it's hard. You're busy. But you must try. I tell my busy customers like you to do it when they're walking in nature. If you're in the park, close your eyes and imagine roots stretching from your root chakra,' her hands hover over my crotch, 'and down into the earth. You need more grounding, darling.'

'I know. I will try. Thanks again for the session though, I enjoyed it thoroughly.'

'Oh, good.' She seems genuinely thrilled at having helped in some way.

I receive my small lecture on the importance of meditation, which I know I'll never realistically do, and finish my water before saying goodbye to Lucy and making my way to the brunch spot. Georgia's texted me to say she's running ten minutes late, so I grab a takeaway coffee and wander down into London Fields, where I find myself in the long patches of grass. I stare down at my feet, imagining large, bulky brown roots. I close my eyes as I lift my legs up in the air and then bring them down, the weight of their gnarly bark covered with soil, crashing my feet onto the earth, wandering in a circle with knotted mud strings connecting me to something much bigger and more momentous than myself.

'Mathilda, what the fuck are you doing?' Georgia appears out of nowhere.

Her Lens

I still can't stop thinking about Constance and start my weeks planning which evening I'll go and visit her, only to tumble down into the reality that I can't. But it's such a different type of grieving from when I lost my dad. I can't stop buying tulips and pineapples from our local fruit and veg shop, which Ekua has started berating me for. She hit me on the bum last night with her wooden spoon, refusing to incorporate pineapple into yet another of her dishes as I sat pairing small yellow squares with blocks of Cheddar, spearing them with cocktail sticks, much to Georgia's horror. Ivy's cheeks were wide like a hamster's as she popped another into her mouth. But today I can't think about Constance. It's our big Fitness Now pitch and I need to focus. I keep my nerves fizzing quietly under the surface as I listen to Sylvia practise her opening one more time. Eddie thinks I'm presenting, which I will. But Sylvia has real talent and breathed life into this idea. She deserves the airtime.

'Are you ready?' I ask her.

'I'm ready,' she asserts, tugging at her dress.

Man-bun, or Carl, as I've taken to calling him – not least because he hasn't actually worn a bun in a while – takes a deep breath and pushes out the air through his lips.

'Don't be nervous.' I pat his shoulder reassuringly. 'We've practised this over and over. It's a solid idea and we've done the research to back it up.' I stand at the front of the line as we wait for Eddie to settle the Fitness Now team in the conference room, where I've removed every egg-shaped trope I could find.

'I know, I'm good,' Carl says smoothly, sharply pulling apart his ponytail to tighten it.

'New shoes?' Jessica asks then, pointing down at my black patent brogues. She's an experienced creative and is on her game this morning. I wink back.

'I'm not sure I can do it.' Sylvia looks up at me with pained eyes. I can see the tension writhing in her narrow shoulders.

'Yes, you can. Don't be ridiculous. You literally just did it for me and you were word perfect. Smile. Be yourself. Don't be afraid to crack a joke. If something goes wrong, laugh it off and bring their attention back to what you want them to focus on.'

Sylvia nods along to my every syllable. 'Aren't you nervous?' she asks, her voice strained and high-pitched.

'Nah. Why would I be? I'm prepared. *We're* prepared,' I shrug, 'and I'm proud of our idea.'

With that, I march down the side of the office towards the conference room, the team marching unanimously behind me, and pull the glass sliding door across with a wide smile and a look of total conviction.

After we've shaken hands and exchanged niceties about refreshments and respective journeys in, I give Sylvia the nod and she opens the pitch beautifully. Carl follows up with the reams of market research and competitor analyses, treading the careful line of flattering the client's business while not being afraid to pinpoint its shortcomings. I can see from their faces that they're impressed. The owner is wide-eyed as she listens to our solution, which Jessica and I run through smoothly.

'Your current advertising speaks on behalf of women. You hero the individual's perspective but always through the Fitness Now lens. You take authorship and ownership of women's stories by telling them how to embrace well-being in the Fitness Now way. You have become the gaze. You are the narrator. Women don't want to be spoken for. Speaking on behalf of them is the wrong way to drive new membership.' Carl lays out the close.

'Instead,' Jessica takes her cue, flicking her black plaits off her shoulders, 'Fitness Now will be using their power and resources to leverage a community of women who already identify with that experience. The campaign will platform the real people who are already inside your gyms. We'll send a diverse range of women these self-capture kits, which will allow them to tell their own fitness and health stories through still and moving images. Hatch will be there to support and offer them advice every step of the way. But they will paint the true picture of what fitness means to them, as individuals. You're handing the reins back to the modern woman.' Jessica looks across to me and smiles confidently.

'The Fitness Now experience,' I say, standing to walk over to the projector that Sylvia flicks to the last image, 'will be told through her lens. Her gaze. Her voice. Her perspective. She is the author and subject of her own story. She doesn't have to strive to be like anyone. Fitness Now offers the space for her to become who she wants to be. Thank you.' I nod graciously, then look up to the owner of Fitness Now, who is sitting with her arms folded, biting her bottom lip.

'I love it.'

Afterwards Eddie pops a bottle of champagne and Carl orders a new pair of trainers on the spot to celebrate. I sit with them all, enjoying watching Sylvia as she luxuriates in her new-found poise, bantering back and forth with the senior team. Eddie asks to see me in his office, where he thanks me profusely and runs a permanent contract under my nose with the highest salary I've ever been offered. I am momentarily filled with excitement, but then politely turn it down. Being held down or restricted in any way feels intrinsically wrong at the moment. I received an email this week about an exciting film project, which may mean some travel. Sometimes it's the things you say no to that define you.

'Are you coming for a pint then, Sabrina?' Carl shouts across the office at me.

'Oh, you must,' demands Sylvia, like she's the youngest sibling.

I ponder the invitation for a moment. *Go and have some fun, my dear.* I hear Constance's voice in my head and it crushes like ice on my chest.

'Good luck getting that redhead out,' Jessica grins, winking at me.

'Okay sure.' I beam at them. 'Are you going to Nix? You lot go ahead, and I'll meet you there.'

They nod and pile into the lift, cajoling one another into a boozy night ahead.

There's no one to rush home to and, for the first time in a long time, that feels emboldening. Part of the aloneness morphs into something more resembling freedom.

Glowing

I pack my things and walk down Liverpool Street on my way to Nix, gliding through the City in my new brogues, excited for that first margarita and the feel of salt between my lips, when I hear a voice.

'Mathilda. Is that you?'

I freeze.

'Oh, my goodness,' I manage. 'Hi. Wow. Umm . . . how are you?' I fold my arms into myself protectively.

The awkwardness hangs in the air between us and I let it because it's not of my making. But then I look again and see the worry gazing back at me.

'You look great. Wow. You're glowing.'

'Oh, thank you.' I push my wavy hair behind my ears. 'It's probably gloat more than glow, I just did this big pitch today.' I grin confidently.

'How'd it go?' The question is accompanied by a weak smile.

'It went great. We won it.' I raise my eyebrows and flash both palms, all jazz hands. Then quickly wish I hadn't.

Silence lingers between us again and I can't think of anything else to say other than 'Are you okay?'

Olivia Wool stands in front of me now, one leg crossed over the other, her small hands tucked into tight jeans pockets, real and fleshy instead of pixilated and smoothed over. There are large dark circles under her eyes and her skin has broken out with acne on her forehead that looks irritated and sore. Her brown bob is not its usual voluminous self. She hesitates, and then starts to tear up. 'I'm sorry,' she says, covering her nose with the flat tips of her fingers. 'How humiliating.'

'Oh, my God, not at all. Come here.' Instinctively I take her hand and pull her into the nearest open door. It happens to be a juice bar, quiet at this hour of the day, so I order us two pick-me-up shakes and sit her down in a low black leather chair. She reminds me of a small jellyfish floundering inside it, tears glinting in her eyes, still with the power to sting.

'What's going on?' I ask gently.

'Honestly,' she says, looking down at the branded napkin she's scrunching and unfolding in her lap, 'I don't even know how to answer that question any more.'

We start tentatively. I ask her how she's finding being a new

254

mum. She says all the things you'd expect a new mum to say about this new bright love and how much she adores her baby. But then she talks about depression, about a traumatic birth, and how hard it's been to claw back any semblance of herself. She talks about living between Cornwall and London because she needs support from her husband's family, but he needs to be in the City for work.

'It just feels like it's driving us apart. And I miss him, you know? God, I miss myself! I don't recognise this new life I'm in. It doesn't feel like I'm me.'

The waiter arrives and places the shakes in front of us. She tells me about her mum passing away very recently, and I tell her about my dad and how hard it's been to process. We bond over the complex grief that comes with having alcoholics for parents.

'I had no idea you went through that,' she says, shaking her head with real sympathy. 'Your life always looks so perfect on Instagram.' Her playful smirk shifts. 'I suppose that's a silly thing to say.'

I close my eyes and shake my head, taking in the acute, piercing irony. 'That's not a silly thing to admit. I always feel the same about you.'

'Is that why you unfollowed me?' she asks softly.

'No. I unfollowed you because I didn't want to see Grant.'

His name hangs in the air between us.

'That mound of brown hair bobbing in the background of your stories, quite frankly scaring the shit out of me.' I wiggle in my seat and throw my eyes to the ceiling to signal the silliness of it all.

'I'm sorry about what happened with you two—'

'Don't be,' I interrupt calmly. 'I'm not. Not any more, anyway.'

255

'Well, you look fantastic. As I said, you're glowing.'

Her smile turns into something else then, an expression I recognise but can't name. I watch the heaviness seep into her bones, the jelly-like movements stiffening, hardening into submission.

'I don't know what I'm going to do, Mathilda.' She bites the sleeve of her lilac angora cardigan.

I pause then and think really hard about what I'm going to say. About whether I should say it. About whether I'm the sort of person who would advise such things.

'Olivia, have you ever heard of a banishing bath?' I tilt my head and hold the straw between my forefinger and thumb, sucking my pick-me-up as I wait for her response.

'No . . .' She leans forward curiously, and I tell her all about it.

Epilogue

'It's just up here.'

I lead Georgia up the stairs and open the door – a new door, with a new set of keys. They are not misplaced this time but found. My very own set. The keys to a small and empty flat, on the top floor of a Georgian maisonette in Stoke Newington. My own place. I will be almost financially sunk by the rent, but it's all mine.

'Oh, wow! Look at that skylight! In fact, look at this light! It's so bright.' Georgia rotates around the empty space, chin reaching for the ceiling. 'Oh, it's charming.'

Her voice echoes into the bare living room. The floors are wooden with no rugs to absorb the sound yet. The ceilings are high, and the walls are white, a blank canvas for me to write another chapter on. It's a small flat. A tiny kitchen leads off the living room, which is large enough for a dining area as well as a sofa and a bookshelf, maybe. I walk over and pull back the glass doors that open out to a reasonably sized balcony with terracotta pots housing dead plants that didn't survive the winter. Two small black metal chairs and a matching round table have been left.

'Free garden furniture!' Georgia beams.

'It appears so.'

'Oh, yes. I can see us here. I can really see us here. Sitting outside in the summer, smoking and drinking rosé. This will do nicely.'

'Do you like it, then?'

'I love it. I think you'll make it beautiful.' Her sigh, induced by relief.

I show her the bathroom, which is plain and inoffensive, but most importantly has a tub. We go into the last room next to it, empty and blank, but big enough for a double bed and some wardrobes. I fold my arms and look around admiringly. 'It's not much, but it's what I'll call home.' I grin.

'It's just perfect. Jeremy will love that little balcony too.'

I walk back into the living room and lie down on the floor underneath the skylight so I can look up at the blue sky. Georgia comes and lies next to me. We watch as the clouds pass, absorbing the light. In this little flat, I shall line the back of the toilet seat and behind the washbasin with white-spined books. I shall hang plants in the kitchen and put fairy lights along the balcony. I shall stop asking other people questions, and instead find the courage to answer them for myself. In this home.

'There is shame in being alone.'

I'm not aware I've said this out loud until Georgia replies.

'What do you mean?' She turns her head to look at me.

'Well, we're taught that we're better with a man, aren't we? But I just don't buy it. Women are never encouraged to be alone and happy, are they? I mean, a woman drinking from a well of joy brought on by her own company. Can you imagine?'

'How dare she?' Georgia exclaims. She looks back up at the skylight. 'I think we get distracted from ourselves. I feel distracted.'

I want to ask her how it's going with Henry but now doesn't feel like the right time.

I interlock my hands and place them on my tummy and it's quiet between us until she says, ever so cautiously, 'Mathilda . . .'

'Hmm . . .'

'Do you think . . . well, do you think that . . . the curse . . . Has it gone now?'

'Mmm.' I muse on this. 'Well. No amount of spiritual practice, yoga or psychedelic potions can eradicate any part of myself I don't like. I know that much. But maybe they can help ease the burden sometimes.'

I can tell she's unsatisfied with my response. 'You don't need to worry about me any more,' I say, sitting up, resting back on my forearms.

'I know.' She breathes out heavily.

And I'm dissatisfied with hers.

'The curse was my unwillingness to face something from my past. Something that scared me. Facing up to it, that was what was important. It doesn't matter how I did it or how I got there, I suppose, just that I did.'

'I think so too.'

'I'm looking forward to some solitude here.' I sigh peacefully, placing my palms flat by my sides, grounding my body in the floor, imagining the muddy roots pulling me back down into the earth.

'Yes, but not too much solitude,' and she reaches once again for my hand.

What is your pain? From where does it come? After my trauma surfaced, I remembered it like it had happened yesterday. It was silly to conceive that I had ever not known it. I had tried to build houses with men from the concrete he used to lay the foundation of me – genuine love, and abuse. Good and bad. I take over those dark corners of myself, I lay claim to them and stop burning my corneas in the sun to avoid seeing. Traumas verbalised, or put down in ink, viewed through a new lens. Ceasing to be mine, suffering resigns itself to the patchwork quilt of other women's stories.

To love oneself is to seek out the worst and most terrible parts. A curse, lifted. My shame no longer sits cloyingly around me. It no longer leaks inside, seeping into my view of the world. What is your pain? From where does it come? I partake in their happiness, moving forward in the waves of jubilation that swell from their lives – a self-resuscitation. The rippling effect of their love pushes me through the smelly green swamp; my avowal prevents it from engulfing me as I rise to the surface and let out a final gasp for air.

Acknowledgments

My first thank you is to Romilly Morgan, for being the first person to read this book. Thank you for being the wise and safe space that I needed, for your softness and honesty, and for your faultless instincts, always. *What a Shame* would not exist without you, you are its biggest champion.

A huge thank you also to my agent, Kate Evans at PFD. Thank you for reading this novel so ferociously and for your true passion. Thank you for seeing past the most atrocious pen name ever – *Jessica Sharpe* is forever grateful. Your support and conviction have been unwavering since day one, you were the backbone this book needed to get out into the world.

Thank you to the entire team at Hodder. I know from experience how many people it takes to publish a book well, and I am so grateful to be working with you all. And to my lovely editor, Lily Cooper, you have maintained a steadfast and solid vision for this book, despite my flapping (and complex relationship with fonts!). You saw Mathilda's potential and connected instantly with what I wanted this book to be. Thank you for your edits, thank you for being patient with me and for offering endless support, even when limited to the feeble Zoom!

I want to say a humongous thank you to my Mum and Stepdaddy. Thank you for telling me I could be anything I wanted to be. Thank you for always making me believe I have something to offer the world. Thank you for being the first people in my life to tell me I have a talent for writing. You have championed me as a human every step of the way, through heartbreaks, failed attempts, disappointments and grief. You are the safe place we all circle back to in our time of need and the first home we want to be in to celebrate our successes.

This leads me nicely on to the witches. Thank you, Nicola Bergstrom and Amy Faulkner, because I literally have no idea who I would be without you. You formed the very morsel of my being. You're the first people to tell me when I'm being a dickhead and the last to stop calling when something goes awry in my life. You are my bedrocks, my muses and my deepest inspiration. Who knew it was possible for a heart to house so much love?

Thank you to Lydia Pang, soulmate, left leg and bud to my root. Thank you for the voice notes, the hours of reassurance, the endless years of love and care and holding. Thank you for the brutal truth, the soft vulnerability and the relentlessness of always – and I mean always – being there for me, no matter what, no matter when. I carry your heart with me, I carry it in my heart.

Thank you to 'The Super Chickens'! Amandine Neyses Van Schelven, Camilla Pang, Daisy Collins, Gavin Wilson, Karlie McCulloch, Kathryn Timmins, Pip Jolley and Richard Lee. Thanks for not reading that *terrible* first draft and telling me to give up the pen right there and then. You are beacons of love and joy, and I am deeply grateful to have each and every one of you in my life.

Thank you to my other early readers, Amy Powell Yeates, Cherry Swayne, Elinor Fewster and Nicola Ambler. Your thoughts and words of encouragement have made this a better book. Thank you to Mary Gayton, you're a needle in a haystack and I can't tell you how much our friendship truly means. Thank you to Anna Cope, our work together has been life-changing and I'm so glad it was you. Thank you for helping me untangle myself.

And last but certainly not least, thank you to Mark. It's possible that you've still not read this bloody book, but if you ever do, I hope you read these acknowledgements. You are an exceptional human. You are my person. I love you with every inch of my heart. Thank you for pushing me to be better and for inspiring me to build the life I want to lead. You and Luca are my happy place.